the Italian
Villa

DANIELA SACERDOTI

the Italian Villa

bookouture

Published by Bookouture in 2020

An imprint of Storyfire Ltd.
Carmelite House
50 Victoria Embankment
London EC4Y 0DZ

www.bookouture.com

ISBN: 978-1-83888-010-1
eBook ISBN: 978-1-83888-009-5

To you, who always rises when she falls,
And to your beautiful soul

PROLOGUE

Eyes of a Soldier

Montevino, April 12, 1945

I tossed and turned under the starlit sky, a cold, harsh moon watching us as we hid in the cabin in the High Woods. In the shadow of the mountain's gray granite boulders I prayed the soldiers would not come all the way up here, or that they'd march past, in too much of a rush to notice we were here. Maybe these soldiers had already fulfilled their tribute of blood. With my kin, my people.

Below us Montevino was on fire. Shots rang through the night — each bullet destined for a woman, a child, or a man too old or too sick to fight. They were all who remained now. All the young men had gone already.

I don't know how I fell asleep amid such horror, hugging the rifle I barely knew how to use, my cheek against the barrel's cold metal, but I did. It was a sick, feverish sleep that brought with it a sort of delirium. A memory from a time so close and yet so far, when Leo and I were together; a time when everything that happened after was just unthinkable.

In my dream-memory, Leo and I lay together in a field not far from my home, with the sky so blue, dotted with soft white clouds. Sunlight played in the leaves of the poplar trees, rippling all around us like bunting at a village fair, and his hand, rough and used to manual work, was holding mine. Was it always meant to be, between Leo and me? Or would we dance around each other for years, with him offering his love and me forever running, forever having other plans?

I'd known him since I was a child, this man with eyes so perfectly black they reflected my soul, the man with a passion for vineyards, the motherless boy who'd spent evenings at our home basking in the warmth of our family. He had a strong mind and a kind heart.

Leo Bordet was the man I was going to spend the rest of my life with, before the war came and tore everything apart.

He kissed me under the spring sky, and for a moment I couldn't breathe for happiness. In my dream, my family had gathered for us. I could hear them in the distance, not far away.

"Will you marry me?" he said, and his words echoed in my mind like I'd heard them a million times before. Like it was always meant to be, only it had taken me years of growing up before realizing it was so.

"Yes. Yes. Of course, I will. I will," I said, and let his eyes and mouth pull me to him.

My family's voices rose to the sky as they surrounded us, their hands full of daisies and poppies and buttercups, teasing us, calling for another kiss. In the glare of the sun I thought I could see Papa rising out of his chair and standing tall, and Mamma was young and beautiful again, like she was before childbirth, before years of hard work, before grief. My Zia Costanza was there, her dark hair beautifully curled, a sweet, somehow other-worldly smile on her lips, her beloved rosary wrapped around her wrist. And Pietro! My little brother Pietro was there as well, wearing his soldier's uniform. Oh, Pietro!

Tears began to fall down my cheeks. Why was I crying when everyone was with me again, alive and well, and I was surrounded by love?

Because a part of me, even while asleep, knew it wasn't real.

It was then that my family began to fade, starting with my little brother. He waved his hand and slowly disappeared.

"Don't go. Don't go!" I cried, as the light of the sunset in his eyes passed by and died. And then Leo, too, began to dissolve right in front of me.

"No! Don't go!"

He held me against him, one hand on the back of my head, the other around my waist, and whispered in my ear: "I'll never leave your side."

I screamed Leo's name as strong hands grabbed my arm and pulled me up, my rifle falling useless on the ground.

*

An eternity later, dawn found me alive, wide-eyed and shaking against the mossy stone wall of the cabin. I staggered through the High Woods in the light of dawn, towards the smoking remains of Montevino. My mind flew into action, as it had been trained to do. The dead needed to be buried – but not everyone was dead. As soon as I saw the wounded, all those familiar faces covered in blood and ashes, women and children calling for help, I remembered: I wasn't just a broken, bleeding woman. I was a doctor, and I was needed.

CHAPTER 1

San Antonio, Texas, 2019

With a sigh, I let myself fall into a chair, the din of the "Family Wednesday" crowd seeping through the door. Thank goodness my coffee break was finally here. Usually a ball of energy, the monotony of waiting tables was sapping the life out of me. I hadn't taken a day off in… I couldn't remember. And today, of all days, I felt it. It was my twenty-first birthday and I was on my third double shift in a week.

Rummaging in my rucksack, I took out some college brochures to cheer myself up. Not long now. A couple of years at the most and I'd have enough saved to quit and go to college. *Maybe I could be a teacher? Or a lawyer, a physiotherapist – better still, a librarian!* I have no idea. I was so jealous of people who felt a calling, but at least I was heading in the right direction.

The Windmill Café had been my lifeline when I'd come out of the care system. It'd given me structure, allowed me to rent a place of my own and make a little family of my co-workers. It wasn't all bad, I supposed, but it was so time to move on. As soon as I could afford it.

"Callie?"

I mustered a smile for my friend, Kirsten, as she entered the breakroom beaming. Her waist-length blonde hair and her braces made her look so much younger than her twenty years, those big blue eyes and bright smile distracting everyone from her sometimes bossy, stubborn streak until it was too late. Beside her, when we were both wearing the black, knee-length cotton uniform, I looked extra tall, dark, and serious.

Following Kirsten came Shanice, our manager, and then Latesha, one of the other servers. "Hey," I said, confused. Then I did a double take – Shanice was carrying a slice of cake decorated with a lit candle.

"You didn't really think we'd forget?" Kirsten said, and they broke into "Happy Birthday", making me smile properly for the first time that day.

"Guys, you shouldn't have!"

"What? It's your twenty-first birthday, of course we should have!" Shanice protested.

"Did you make a wish?" Kirsten asked.

I closed my eyes briefly and tried to wish for something practical – enough funds to go to university, a divine sign to show me which path to take – but something else entirely came out. *Not to be alone in the world.* My deepest desire bubbled up from the depths of me, an unwanted guest among the clapping and cheering of the makeshift party.

My parents had died when I was ten, in a house fire. Neither of them had had any surviving immediate relatives, so I was raised in foster care, and, in my heart, I was a family of one. As far as I knew, nobody else carried my blood in their veins. I made a point of not feeling sorry for myself, but... well, sometimes the loneliness was too much to take. And so, caught unawares and with enough time to feel, but not to think, I'd let my deepest wish come up for air.

"Okay, now go," Shanice said, with her hands on her hips.

I stilled, unsure of what she meant. "Go where?"

"You're taking the afternoon off. And I will not take no for an answer."

"I don't need an afternoon off, honestly—"

"Here she goes again!" Kirsten rolled her eyes.

"Well, you're getting it," muttered Shanice. She had the gentlest soul inside, but outside – well, you wouldn't want to cross her.

"I don't really need—"

"Yes, you do. You're going shopping. That's the plan. There." Shanice handed me a bright pink envelope. "From all of us."

"Oh, guys." I slipped out the card inside: *Auguri!* it said in Italian, my parents' native language. I brought a hand to my mouth, laughing in surprise and delight.

"I hope it's correct," Kirsten said. "I had to google that!"

"It's perfect." With the card there was a gift voucher for Francesca's, one of my favorite clothes stores.

For Callie, from everyone at the Windmill
Not to be used for anything practical
NOT TO BE USED ON YOUR COLLEGE FUND
Awesome new clothes and cocktails only!
(We'll check!)

"This is *awesome*." I was so touched; I didn't know what to say.

"We *will* check, Callie!" my boss repeated, a manicured finger tapping the card's last two words.

I placed my hand over my heart. "I solemnly swear your gift will be used for something completely unnecessary."

"Good girl. That's what we want to hear. Now, give me that apron and get out of here. Happy birthday, Callie," she said again, and hugged me before heading back into the café, followed by Latesha. Kirsten and I were left alone, and I began getting changed.

"I'll make you coffee. Have your cake," Kirsten offered with a smile.

I hadn't thought to organize anything for my birthday. Almost everyone in my little life worked here at the Windmill. So I don't know what made me say what I said next.

"Kirsten, I was wondering... Oh, never mind. Come, share my cake."

"Hey, silly, come on, tell me." She smiled and fished out a spoon from our cutlery drawer.

"Maybe tonight you'd like to do something? Go out for dinner, or..."

"Oh, Callie, I'm sorry, I can't! I'm going to my sister's for something. Her husband got a promotion, and we're all—"

"Of course. Of course."

Kirsten had a huge extended family, and they often got together.

"Remember you said you didn't want to celebrate, and—"

"I did. It's fine, honestly."

"Tomorrow? I'm so sorry, I just couldn't disappoint my sister."

"It's fine. Please don't worry." My cheeks were burning. I regretted asking her so badly, now. What had possessed me? I never asked anything of anyone. It always ended in tears.

Kirsten laid a hand on her chest. "I feel terrible now."

"Don't. I'm going to have a movie marathon."

"Well, you do love that kind of thing," Kirsten said.

That's so sad, she meant.

"I most definitely do," I said, finishing the last of my bit of cake. "Thank you so much for the card, and the present. You're the best." I grinned, then wrapped my arms around Kirsten, and she returned the hug.

"So are you! Now, go and enjoy shopping! Sorry I can't come with you. Shanice would be too short-staffed."

"It's okay. Don't worry." There was a weird lump in my throat.

"You *will* be buying a dress, won't you? I want to see you in pink!"

"You'll never see me in pink! But I might go for red. It goes with my coloring," I said, pretending to fluff my black hair. "Bye," I called, and opened the back door onto the warm spring day. I slipped on my sunglasses and stepped outside, then turned around to give Kirsten one last wave, but she was gone already.

The River Walk was buzzing with people, and the water shone under the Texas sun. Even though it was midweek, everyone seemed to have gathered here to shop and eat and chat. I stopped at a clothes-store window beside two women. "This will look lovely on you, darling," the older lady said to the younger one, pointing at a peach-colored, off-the-shoulder evening dress on one of the mannequins. I quickly turned away, almost tripping over a young man, crouching with his arms around a wayward toddler. He picked her up right before she toppled over. "Careful!" he said, and then placed a kiss on her chubby cheek. She seemed so small in the tall man's arms, so safe. I wondered where I would be now if my parents had been alive, what I would be doing. Losing them so young had changed everything for me.

I shook myself and walked on. *Callie, enough. It's your birthday. Enjoy the moment. You're safe. You have a roof over your head. You have a job. Everything is looking good. And if you keep saving there is a better future out there for you. There's no reason to be sad. No reason at all.*

But my mind was scattered, and my thoughts raced all over the place. I didn't want to acknowledge it, but there was this nagging feeling in the back of my mind that nothing would ever change for me. That I might make it to college, learn to open up, maybe even fall in love, but this deep black hole of loss in my heart would never be filled.

To distract myself, I stepped into Starbucks for my favorite, a mint latte, when my cell phone rang. A number I didn't recognize stretched across the screen.

"Hello?"

"Hello, Callie?"

A croaky, husky voice. A voice I instantly recognized. Hearing it again after all these years made my heart gallop.

*

Brenda was 'a good apple', as my mom would have said. She was a capable, dedicated social worker and a fierce advocate for the children in her care. Yes, she was all that, but she was also the living reminder of some of the worst times in my life, which was why I hadn't visited her since the day I'd left the system. But here I was, on my twenty-first birthday, taking a detour from Starbucks to Child Protective Services.

Stepping into the Starfish Outreach headquarters made me break into hives. Everything in that building made my stomach tie in a knot, from the automatic doors, to the elevator that always smelled of instant coffee and disinfectant, to the green-walled hallway that led me to Brenda's office. I should have asked to meet somewhere else.

How many times had I walked that hallway, each time a little older, each time a little closer to eighteen, the magical age when I could escape the system for good? How many times had I sat in that tiny waiting room, on those orange chairs among the worn-out plastic toys and sticky children's books, reading the posters on the walls for the hundredth time – *the dangers of smoking, coffee mornings for single moms, reach out to your elderly neighbor* – bracing myself for Brenda's most recent scolding?

I took my sunglasses off as I reached the door to Brenda's office. There was no reason to be anxious. I wasn't a little girl. I was an adult, and nothing she said would change things for me. They couldn't take me away from my own apartment or make me live with strangers. They held no power over me anymore.

No reason to be anxious at all.

And yet, I brought a hand onto my heart for a moment to steady it before knocking at the door. Somewhere inside me, the little girl I used to be trembled.

"Come in," a voice rasped, and my breath caught. Hearing Brenda's voice after so long was almost good. Almost. Had I missed her?

I opened the door just enough to slip in. "Brenda?"

There was stuff everywhere, as always – children's drawings tacked to the walls, framed motivational quotes, books, folders, tins of cookies, and half-empty bottles of hand lotion scattered over her desk. In the middle of all that sat a small, gray-haired woman of color, still wearing her trademark vibrant hues, just as I remembered. She'd always pushed the office dress code with a bright shirt or big earrings, or a tropical-colored scarf. When I was in care, she always got me a psychedelic T-shirt for Christmas. I never wore any of them, but I did keep them out of gratitude.

"Callie!" My heart did a somersault when she rose from her chair with difficulty and limped towards me. Her arthritis had just begun to take root when I was in care, but it must have grown worse. I instantly felt guilty for having put off visiting her for so long. "I can't believe you're twenty-one! You still have a baby face." She rested a fresh hand on my cheek, and my anxiety almost dissolved. "Like when you first came to us."

"Do I?"

"Yeah. The face of a porcelain doll."

I smiled. "The face of a doll and the temper of a devil!"

There it was, her laugh. That part of her, cheery and loud, hadn't changed at all. "Hardly. It was strength, that's what it was. You're gutsy. It was one of the things I loved the most about you."

I smiled and handed her the tin of peanut-butter cookies I'd grabbed on the way. "For you. You still love them?"

"Oh, I certainly do! Thank you! Let's open them together. Coffee?"

"Sure."

We sat in front of our mugs, the biscuit tin open, and, almost subconsciously, I prepared myself. I could feel she was going to tell me something – yes, there was a specific reason why she'd called me here. But what she did next was unexpected.

"I have something for you too," she said, and handed me a bright yellow gift bag.

"Oh, thank you… you shouldn't have."

That *was why she'd asked me to come over? To give me a birthday present?*

"And… this." She handed me a large white envelope.

"A card! Thank you again, Brenda. Really, thanks for remembering."

"You're welcome. But that," she said, pointing to the envelope, "is not a card. It's a letter for you. From a law firm."

I tilted my head to once side, staring at the piece of paper. "A… what?"

She shook her head. "I only got it this morning – FedEx, you know – and I called you at once. Let's just say, this is a first."

I examined the letter. In the corner of the envelope I read: *Baird and Associates, Law Offices.*

Brenda continued, "They sent me a note to go with the letter. It said they were entrusted to give this to you when you turned twenty-one."

"By my parents?" I looked down at the envelope, then back to Brenda.

It was impossible. Surely I would have got it long before today?

"I assume so." She shrugged her shoulders; she seemed as bewildered as I was. "Whatever it is, it's horrible that it's stirring up these memories for you. I promise you nobody told me about this. The firm had specific instructions to *only* give it to you when you turned twenty-one, which is why, I suppose, they had it FedExed today."

"Weird," I muttered. I didn't trust myself to say anything more. I was swallowing my feelings back, as I usually did, but I knew Brenda could see how spooked I was.

"I'm not happy at all with the way this has been handled, Callie." The look in her eyes made me think that she'd probably given the law firm a piece of her mind already, or if not, she would do so as soon as she got the chance.

"So… you really have no idea what the letter says?" I asked.

"No idea. And no clue it existed, I promise you, hon—" She stopped herself. She'd remembered that when I was in care I'd hated being called honey, or sweetheart, or any other pet names. Only my parents could call me that – and my parents were gone. For everyone else, it was Callie.

"Brenda, if you don't mind, I'd like to open this at home."

"Of course. Do drink your coffee. And let me share these cookies with you."

I nodded. I had a lump in my throat, but I forced myself to take a sip. I didn't want to disappoint Brenda or make her feel like I was trying to leave quickly.

"Open your present," she said, and I did. Inside the bag there was a multicolored, tie-dyed T-shirt. I had to smile. "D'you like it?"

"I love it. Thank you. Really, thank you."

She reached across the desk and put her small, rigid hands over mine. "You're welcome, hon— Callie."

"Honey is fine," I said, surprising myself. There was no reason to be wary, to be the abrasive, wounded child I'd been. "It's a nice thing to be called."

Back in my tiny studio apartment, my legs curled underneath me on my second-hand IKEA couch, I fiddled anxiously with the unopened letter in my hands. I couldn't wait to open it, and at the same time I dreaded it.

I went to open the window for some air, and a small, furry body made its way inside. "Hi, baby," I said as my white cat, all snow but for one black paw, jumped straight onto my lap, rubbed herself against me for a moment, then made a beeline to the corner where I kept her bowl. She didn't exactly belong to me; she lived in the small park beside my building and took food and shelter when and where she chose. She was an independent creature, and I loved her for that. I'd named her Misty, but I was pretty sure she had a few different names, depending on who she was with. I knew that the elderly lady next door called her Ribbon – because of the black stripe she had around one leg – and fed her freshly grilled fish and bowls of cream. Misty-Ribbon was one lucky cat.

I looked back to the letter, my hands resting on the cat's soft fur, and swallowed. "Here we go," I said to myself.

Carefully, making sure I would not tear anything that was inside, I opened the envelope. The paper I drew from inside was heavy and expensive-looking. I unfolded it and saw that and it was printed, not handwritten. On the upper left corner there was the name of the law firm again, and a flowery, elaborate logo. I imagined an office furnished in dark wood, with old-fashioned prints on the walls – a lawyer's office like you'd see in the movies.

My heart was jumping out of my chest; I began to read.

> *Dear Miss DiGiacomo,*
>
> *We are writing to you on behalf of Mr. Joseph DiGia-como and Mrs. Carol Elisabeth DiGiacomo. We are in possession of some documents Mr. and Mrs. DiGiacomo deposited with us, to be given to you on, and not before, May 24, 2019, your twenty-first birthday. Mrs. Brenda Thibodeaux, social worker for the state of Texas, was the only contact we could find for you. We were sorry to find out that your adoptive parents have passed away…*

I blinked. I must have read that wrong. I was probably tired, confused. I re-read the last line. *We were sorry to find out that your adoptive parents have passed away.*

There had to be a mistake. I'd never been adopted, only fostered. They must have got it wrong. Child Protective Services were flooded with work and chronically understaffed, so it was entirely possible. Of course, it was all a mistake.

Still, I kept going over that sentence, zooming in on that word "*adoptive*".

> *Had we known of their sudden demise, or had we been given specific instructions for such an eventuality, we would have contacted you earlier. However, no provision had been made for such circumstances.*

I stood, much to Misty's annoyance, and paced the room a few times. My parents had entrusted something to a law firm, to be given to me on my twenty-first birthday. They had died, and nobody had told the firm – so there had been no change to the plan, even if I was now an orphan. I forced myself to take a breath, sit back down, and finish the letter as calmly as I could.

> *We should be grateful if you would phone our offices to make an appointment with us; we'll be delighted to supply you with the documents in question and discuss any questions you may have. We imagine there will be many.*
>
> *Our sincere condolences for your loss and our very best regards. We remain at your disposal,*
> *Anthony Baird*
> *Baird and Associates*

For a moment, I was tempted to scrunch up the letter and forget all about it. Maybe it was some sort of scam.

But…

Doubt.

The niggling lie that I could be *adopted* also had to be squashed, as far-fetched as it was. Misty jumped on the couch, looking outraged at the lack of attention. I poured some more dry food into her bowl, and set out some milk for her, working on autopilot.

Climbing onto the kitchen counter, I read the letter all over again. It *had* to be some strange misunderstanding. "Garbage," I said aloud.

On impulse, I grabbed the phone and dialled Brenda's number.

"Brenda? It's Callie," I said, pacing the room as best I could. My apartment consisted of one room that served me as a kitchen, living room and bedroom, and a bathroom where I had to shower sideways.

"Hey, did you open the letter?"

"I did. There's a mistake. I don't think the letter is for me."

"Are you sure? Because they specifically said it was for Callie DiGiacomo, that the only contact they could find was me. Callie, I'm pretty sure there was no mistake."

I shrugged. "Then it's a joke."

"What did it say?"

"Are you sure you don't know? Because how can it be—" My voice was shaky.

"Callie, you're not under our care anymore. It would be illegal for me to open your mail. We have nothing to do with those lawyers or whatever is in that letter."

"It mentions my parents. But it calls them my *adoptive* parents." I hoped she couldn't tell that my voice was breaking a little, and tears were gathering in my eyes – but of course she could, she'd known me since I was a child.

There was a pause. "What?"

"I have never been adopted, as far as I know." It was more of a question than anything else.

"That's absurd! When you came to us we decided, together with you, that fostering would be a better option for—"

"I know. I know," I cut in. "Somebody messed up, that's all."

"Us? The lawyers?"

"Someone! I have *not* been adopted."

"Unless... unless this happened long before we came on the scene. Which is why we had no idea. Maybe..."

I closed my eyes. "Don't say it." I didn't want to hear.

"Maybe your parents kept it from you. Maybe they were planning to tell you, but then the fire happened."

"It can't be."

"It *could* be. It's unlikely, but it could be."

"No. No. It makes no sense. *You* would have known!"

"Not if the adoption happened somewhere else entirely, or if it was an informal arrangement. Sometimes there's no official record of an adoption, even birth certificates can be deliberately filled with wrong information. I'm not saying that's what your parents did, but it is possible."

I swallowed as Misty settled against me, purring softly, happy after her meal. From the road came the rattle of a bus stopping, then moving on – my hair quivered slightly in the breeze coming through the open window. Everything felt unreal.

"Let me help you." Brenda's voice came from the cell phone, as unreal as the rest. "Please, come to the office tomorrow, and—"

"I'll deal with it."

"We can look at it together, we can meet the lawyers together—"

"It's fine. Thank you though." I couldn't face another trip to Starfish Outreach.

"Okay. I'm here for you if you need me."

"Thanks. I'll let you know what happens."

"Call me as soon as you speak with the lawyers. Please."

"I will. Thank you, Brenda."

I put the phone down, took my face in my hands and, finally, allowed myself to cry.

CHAPTER 2

Baird and Associates made its home in a tall, steel-and-glass building in the heart of San Antonio. I'd passed it many times, not knowing, of course, that one day life would take me here in such an unexpected way. Bracing myself, I made my way into the immaculate reception. My hands were shaking, I'd been awake since dawn, and all the coffee I'd downed since then was churning in my stomach. Looking around at the marble lobby, the men and women in suits and heels, I regretted wearing jeans and trainers. I had to steady myself before I approached the receptionist's desk.

"Hi. My name is Callie DiGiacomo," I began, and leaned lightly on the cold marble counter. "Anthony Baird – his firm – I guess this place? – sent me a letter. He said to make an appointment, so I thought I'd come here in person."

The receptionist – a tiny face peeping out of hair extensions rigid with hairspray – looked up from her computer screen, offering only a sigh in response. She clicked away at the mouse, then slid her eyes to me. "The first available appointment is next week. Monday, three o'clock?"

"Monday? That's days away."

"I know. Are you going to take the appointment?"

"Well, I understand Mr. Baird is very busy, but it's quite urgent."

"Everything is urgent in this office."

I bit my lip. "Are you sure you don't have anything earlier?"

She didn't bother to look at her computer again. "I'm sure."

"But I—"

"Excuse me," a voice interrupted. "Did you say you were Callie DiGiacomo?" I turned around to see a man walking toward me. He was gray in every way – hair, suit, tie, eyes. On a foggy day, this man would disappear entirely.

"Yes."

"I see." He looked at me kindly, as if he knew who I was, more than just knowing my name. "I'm Anthony Baird. Come on up. And morning, Marissa."

"Good morning. Mr. Baird, it's appointments back to back this morning—"

"Just ask them to wait a little. This is important."

I stopped myself from giving the lovely Marissa a triumphant look as we walked towards the elevator. Mr. Baird was older than I'd first noticed, and I saw warmth in him. A touch of… *sympathy*, maybe? Not at all what I was expecting. He certainly didn't look like a con man. But then, con men *should* look trustworthy, shouldn't they? My mind was going in circles.

"Thank you," I managed, stepping in beside him, "for fitting me in. I appreciate it."

"It's no problem, Callie. Your situation is quite… unusual. And it must have caused you quite a lot of grief. I'm going to try and make it easier on you."

I swallowed.

His office was exactly how I'd imagined it: dark wood; old prints on the walls; papers strewn across the desk, some organized into piles while others fanned out in one long line.

Mr. Baird pointed to the chair on the opposite side of his desk. "Please, take a seat."

I lowered myself onto the leather-upholstered chair and took the letter out of my bag. "So. This."

"Yes." He sank into his chair behind the desk. 'First of all, my condolences on the deaths of Mr. and Mrs. DiGiacomo. I'm very sorry. We had no idea."

The force of their loss hit me all over again, so strong even after all this time. The concept of death connected to my parents still had the power to almost break me. I cleared my throat, and Mr. Baird waited patiently for me to be ready to speak. "Thank you. But I don't understand… how come you didn't know they're… gone? When did they give you these documents?"

"Your adoptive parents entrusted the papers to us when you were born, with a legally binding agreement they would only be given to you when you turned twenty-one. Had they survived, they might have decided to give them to you earlier, but sadly…"

Hearing him use that word "adoptive" was like a stab in my heart. "Mr. Baird, they were my mom and dad. My *biological* parents. I was never adopted."

"Miss DiGiacomo" – his voice was soft; he wanted to break it to me gently – "according to Mr. and Mrs. DiGiacomo, you were. They told me themselves, in this very office," he said. That look again: pity. I'd seen it so often in people's eyes, ever since I'd been orphaned. I loathed that look.

My fingers curled around the letter, crinkling it. It was a huge effort to keep myself calm. I looked for something to say, and couldn't find anything coherent, only a helpless, "It can't be true."

"Your parents said they didn't want you to know you'd been adopted until you were old enough to deal with it."

I closed my eyes for a moment. "They told you themselves?"

"Yes. I can't believe we are in this situation now."

"*We…?* I assume *you* know who your parents are," I snapped.

"*Were.* But yes, I do know, and I understand how distressed you must be. I'm so sorry. I don't think Mr. and Mrs. DiGiacomo dealt with this the best way, but here we are." In saying that, he bent down to take something out of his briefcase – a tiny key – and stood to open a dark wood filing cabinet. He searched for a moment, then produced a box from the cabinet's highest shelf. Attached to the box with a rubber band was a blue cardboard folder. Box and folder were placed in front of me, and sat there like living things, calling me and yet repulsing me.

"Yes. Here we are," I said, only just managing to speak.

Seamlessly, Mr. Baird opened a drawer in his desk and took out a packet of tissues, which he handed to me. I took one out of politeness, but I had no intention of sobbing. I tried to make a joke. "Do people often cry in this office?"

"Sometimes."

I smoothed down my hair and tried to compose myself. "So… inside that file are my real parents' names?"

He tapped the blue file. "I don't know. It's sealed."

Both of us looked down at the box and the cardboard folder: thin, a bit faded, secured with a rubber band; inside there was my history. The box gave out a strange energy, almost pulsing to the rhythm of my heart. In all my hardest times, I'd clung to the fact that I didn't have a terrible past, unlike so many other children in care. My parents had loved me, and the tragedy that had befallen us had been nobody's fault, just a terrible accident. I had a legacy of love to keep me strong. But whatever was in there might change that.

Mr. Baird cleared his throat and snapped me back to reality. "Maybe you will allow me to open it for you? I can read it and give you the gist? It might be easier for you."

"You're very busy. That... Marissa downstairs said. I should go." I extended my hands to take the box. I was trembling so much that it almost fell out of my hands.

"Callie, take your time. Stay for a moment," Mr. Baird said. I hesitated.

"When you know about your past, then you can look at the future, knowing the whole truth," he continued, and convinced me.

"Yes."

I placed the box on the desk again and removed the rubber band, my hands still trembling. Suddenly, I became hyper-aware of my surroundings: the smell of wax wafting off the furniture, voices outside the door, the light, rhythmic tap of Mr. Baird's foot under the desk. Little did I know that all those details would forever be burned in my memory.

With trembling hands, I opened the folder and took out the pages nestled inside. The first was a letter.

My dearest daughter,

I clasped my hand over my mouth.

I write this to you in English because you will grow up in America. I was called to be your mother.

I have no family anymore and your father is gone. But surely now you want to know my name. My dearest girl, my name is Malva Stella. Stella means "star" in Italian. I was born in a little village in Italy where the mountains are very high, they almost touch the sky. It's called Montevino. Not many people live there, and we all know each other. Up on the hill there is a castle and there are four churches at the four corners of the village, to protect it.

I cannot explain in English all the beauty of this place. I wish I can take you back there. I also wish I can go, but it is not possible. I love you very much, and I wanted to be with you forever, but I can't.

We are all on this earth, under the sky, and we must make the best of what we have. Sometimes families bring you love, sometimes pain, but most often they give you both. Now that you know that I am your mother, you must know that I kept a house for you, Casa delle Lucciole. Our family lived there for a long time, and now the house is yours. I hope you will love it as much as I do. I hope that one day you'll go home.

Ti voglio bene. *I love you.*
Your mother in heart,
Malva

I read the last word, and suddenly the tears I was holding back overwhelmed me, and I found myself sobbing. This couldn't be a joke. It felt too real. I cried because I was angry that my parents had kept this from me, and I cried for Malva and the years we didn't have together. What had happened to her?

I was barely aware of a hesitant hand on my shoulder, and of Mr. Baird's voice coming from far away. "Marissa? Tell Jack I'm very sorry, but he needs to wait a little more... Yes, I know. But they'll have to wait." A pause, and then: "Callie? Are you okay?"

"Yes. Yes. This is from my biological mom, apparently," I managed to say. I handed the letter over to him. The far-left corner was wet with tears.

"She sounds very loving," he said, after reading. "I'm so sorry."

"She doesn't say *why*? Why she had to leave me?"

"There's more," he said, and gestured to the open folder and the box. I dried my tears and looked at the other papers. They were all formal documents; I handed them to Mr. Baird. "Would you mind?"

"Not at all. Let me see. It's all copies of stuff – in Italian, with an English translation. This is... Oh. It's the deeds of a house. The house talked about in the letter, presumably."

I was too shocked by everything to register that. All I could think about was the woman who had written the letter... my birth mom.

"Here. It says you need to make everything official with a local lawyer's in your mother's... Oh." He looked up to me.

"It's okay. I suppose 'mother' is the only word I have to call her by, at the moment."

Mr. Baird nodded. "The lawyer's in... Montevino. Yes, that's the name of the place. The law firm is called Studio Tava. They've been entrusted with making it all legal. They'll probably have you sign some papers; feel free to call me before you sign anything, of course."

"Sign? Papers?" I said.

"Yes. That's what it says."

"But that means I'd be going there."

"Well... I suppose that was taken for granted. That you'd go to this... Montevino... place, and sort it all out."

Suddenly, I felt very hot. "I think I'm going to faint."

"No, no. None of that, please. Here, have some water." He handed me a glass from somewhere. "I'll open the window. Do you want me to call someone?" He seemed panic-stricken, and for some absurd reason, I found it funny.

"I have a few things to think about, I guess!" I sipped from the cup and almost spluttered as the water risked going down the wrong way.

"To say the least," Mr. Baird replied. "Are you okay?"

"I'm fine. Just lost it a bit."

"Please… drink some more." He let himself fall into his leather chair.

I obeyed, and then, a sudden thought hitting me, I looked up. "I might still have a family. I mean, I thought there was nobody left but me."

The wish I'd made earlier at the Windmill: *Not to be alone in the world*. Could it be…?

"Callie. As you can imagine, with the job I do, I've heard a few stories. And I just would like to give you a piece of advice, if I may?"

I waited.

Mr. Baird's eyes met mine, and for the first time I saw a hard expression on his face. It was the expression of a man who'd seen a lot, and lost quite a few illusions. "Don't have too many expectations. Circumstances might be different from what you imagine. I would say, if you can, don't have any expectations at all."

"I'll try."

Go tell that to my heart.

Malva Stella. Her name rang like a bell in my mind. A couple of times I even whispered it under my breath. *Malva*, my birth mom.

I was kneeling on the floor in my apartment, the noisy street buzzing outside, going through the documents again, trying to work out what they said, trying to digest everything that had happened.

I'd read the letter from my birth mom a million times now. It was the moment to open the box. Time stood still as I lifted the lid – its contents were covered in a linen cloth. An aroma of forgotten things – compact powder, mold and old books, together with a gossamer scent of dried flowers – filled my nostrils. It was the fragrance of memories. Lost voices whispered in my ear.

Reverently, I laid my hands on the heavy, hand-woven linen cloth that covered the box's contents. In the center were two initials, embroidered in burgundy thread: *ES*. I took it off slowly, gently, and folded it on my lap, my eyes drawn to the contents of the box: a notebook with a dove-gray leather cover, a tiny black ribbon peeping through the pages, to mark the place, and a pouch made from the same linen as the cloth. I lifted the notebook: it was heavy, and thick, and smelled of old paper. There was a beautiful inscription on the first page. Flowery, cursive letters: *Elisa*.

Elisa – maybe that was why there was an 'E' embroidered on the cloth? I thumbed through pages covered in the same neat, small script, and then the notebook fell open to an inserted photograph of a dark-haired young woman with glasses, and a man with his arm around her waist; they stood beside bicycles, leaning against a stone wall.

"Elisa," I whispered.

Inside the pouch was a set of keys – one big, one small, bound together by a metal ring. Attached to them was a label encased in plastic, written in old-fashioned sepia: *Casa delle Lucciole*... Firefly House. I translated it in my mind. Well, Fireflies' House, literally, but Firefly was a more accurate translation.

The keys to the house that my mother had left to me.

It was real.

I could feel it, it *was* real. I held the keys tight against my chest; maybe, if I tried hard enough, I would see the house in my mind's eye, I would see my mother waiting for me...

I jumped up and almost grabbed the framed photograph of my parents –the only people who had been loving parents to me – which I kept on a shelf by the couch so that I could see it at night in the light of passing cars.

Adoptive parents.

It was still so, so hard to believe.

Nearly all our belongings had been lost in the fire, but the photograph I had in my hands now had been protected from the flames by its silver frame. It was slightly browned on one corner, but otherwise intact. I'd carried it with me everywhere, pinned on the wall beside or behind my bed in the different homes I'd lived in, tucked under the pillow in strange beds I'd slept in as the nobody's child I'd been. That photo had been my anchor.

The three of us, my parents and I, were on a day out along the San Antonio River Walk; I must have been around three at the time. Little did I know I only had seven short years left with them. That was the time *before* – an impossible era of love, peace and calm, almost forgotten but not quite, floating on the horizon of all my memories.

On the left was my dad, holding me up. He was smiling at the camera, squinting into the sun. He wore a football jersey, and it was clear he was in the early stages of balding. On his shoulder, I clutched an ice-cream cone covered in sprinkles, most of which were around my mouth. My mom, on the right, was turned toward me, caught in the act of trying to clean my face. She was smiling too, a big straw hat dipped over her head. She had short, plump fingers, and I thought I remembered the feeling of them, soft on my skin – or maybe it was just my imagination. Whenever I saw her smile, her scent came back to me – a scent I couldn't quite identify, I couldn't describe with words. I closed my eyes briefly and ran my fingers over the photograph, as if I could touch them again that way.

I'd looked at the picture so many times, I knew all its intricacies. But this time it was different. Did it make sense to still think I looked like them? Everyone always said I had my father's tall frame, my mom's dark hair. Her smile… How could they believe that keeping the truth from me for so long was a good idea?

They didn't know they would die young, of course – a spark in a faulty plug, a tiny, unexpected event that had led us to disaster – but they'd left no official record of my adoption, no trail I could follow. How was the adoption done? An informal agreement? Maybe my parents and Malva had known each other before I was adopted. Maybe they were friends, and they had organized the whole thing between them, which was why there was no record of it. Had my biological mother not left that letter, I would never have known...

I placed the photograph back on the shelf.

It suddenly seemed inevitable that I should go to Montevino and find out the truth for myself. My heart told me there was no other way. I needed to discover who I really was; I needed to follow this strange thread, wherever it led me, otherwise, I would never know.

Happy birthday, Callie.

CHAPTER 3

"Would you like something to drink?" the flight attendant offered, waking me from a light, fitful sleep.

My eyes fluttered and it took me a moment to process what she'd asked, and where I was. "Oh. Yes, thanks. Coffee, please. Black."

I wrapped my fingers around the cup and looked out the plane window. The ocean below was impossibly far, the blue expanse broken by little white licks of waves. It seemed to go on forever.

It was my first time on a plane, my first time out of Texas. Just like the sea below, my time in the air seemed to go on forever too. I rested the hot cup on the tray, slipped my jacket on, and tucked one leg under me as comfortably as I could. Sip after sip, the caffeine jolted me out of sleep.

Everything was about to change. Soon I would have answers, at last. I would find people who could tell me who I was, where I came from. But I had to remember Mr. Baird's words of warning. If those people had given me up, they must have had a reason, I said to myself, and as soon as I'd formulated the thought, I was sorry I had. I could be so cruel with myself.

Nevertheless, even I, with all the layers of cynicism I'd wrapped around my heart, couldn't help but hope. Malva Stella and my father were out there somewhere. Maybe I had a sister, or a brother. Or both. Aunts and uncles. Cousins. Like those noisy Italian families that filled the Windmill Café when they came to celebrate birthdays and engagements and baptisms.

Lost in thought, I grabbed my backpack from underneath the seat, careful not to spill my coffee, and took hold of the notebook I'd found in the box. I hadn't had time to look at it properly, but now I opened it gently, taking care of the yellowed, dried-up pages, and began to read.

Montevino, June 12, 1939

Caro *Diario*,

I think this is how you are supposed to start diary entries, aren't you? So, caro *Diario, happy birthday to me! Because, yes, yesterday I turned eighteen! And you, little notebook of mine, are one of the presents I received. I adore you. How thoughtful of Zia Costanza to take in more laundry work so that she could buy me a birthday gift. I am beyond grateful. I got so many presents – two pairs of stockings and a handkerchief from my parents, and my little brother Pietro, bless, gave me a bouquet of wildflowers. And finally, I said goodbye to the convent and I'm back home in Montevino, with my family.*

We had a big party last night, with the tables outside and a big spread of biscuits, bread, cheese, peaches, grapes, cake, as much as my parents could afford, and lashings of wine, of course. My family knows how to celebrate! Our neighbors and friends came, and a couple of them brought a fisarmonica…

Fisarmonica? I had no idea what the word meant. I'd brought my small dictionary with me, thankfully. *Fisarmonica…* accordion.

...and a clarinet or two, and we danced until late. Mamma always says it's good my birthday falls in the summer, so we have more food and a long, warm night to celebrate. Even Pietro and his friends were allowed a drink! One of the fisarmonica boys kept his glass beside them as he played, but our old dog Nero helped himself, and then he was walking all wonky and made everybody laugh before falling asleep with his head on Zia Costanza's lap – you know Zia Costanza is not keen on dancing.

Father is in a wheelchair – oh, it'll take me ages to tell you all about the family! – because of an accident on his tractor, but he plays the clarinet, so he's kept busy during parties. He's not one to brood and curse fate, anyway; he has a cheerful nature and always sees the best in all situations. Mamma, instead, takes everything seriously. I can see why; her life hasn't been easy, and it still isn't.

Anyway, I must spare a word for the boys. Yes, the young men who came to my birthday. Carlo Caporale, of course, was there. He is from the wealthiest family around here, after the Conte's, obviously, and he's the only young man in the village to own a car. He smokes expensive cigarettes and he's always dressed like he is about to go for a stroll in Turin with the best in society. He's not a bad guy. Just really pretentious. And since he's the most eligible bachelor in Montevino and beyond, I really don't see why he's so stubborn where I am concerned. He'd come to see me when I was in Montevino for the weekend, much to my parents' hope, but no: he's simply not my type.

And Leo came.

My best friend since we were children. I know it's strange that a girl has a boy for her best friend, but that's how it is for us. I hadn't seen him for a while, and I was a bit taken aback, I must admit. I looked at this tall, strong man and I almost didn't recognize him. Only then I realized how many times I'd listened out for our signal – the three owl hoots he'd make with his cupped hands to call me out of the house to go and play – and missed it when the night was silent. Perhaps we were too old for all that now…

When we first met, he was a scrawny, filthy little boy – his mother unconcerned about him after his father left without looking back. He'd spend every evening at our house after a day of backbreaking work on his parents' farm, no time to go to school. It was my Zia Costanza who taught him to read and write, and I helped too. We had a few dances, but they don't really count because we're like brother and sister. So there. Nothing going on at all. Boys don't interest me anyway, I have other plans for my life and none of them include marriage.

I had the best party I could have wished for. The best dance I had was with my mamma. She whispered in my ear: "my clever, clever girl", and that brought tears to my eyes. Maybe my tears sent a message to the sky, because it started raining! We all ran inside and continued the party in the warm and dry of the cow shed, where we spend our winter nights. It hadn't rained for a while, and the women of the village had gathered around the sacred image of the Christ, the one painted in the Via Cavour. In that image, there are clouds around the cross; so we pray to it for rain. Rain is all important around here: if it's too dry, we starve. If there is hail, we starve. Life isn't easy. But it's my home. And never before did I feel so surrounded by love than last night with my family and my home all around me. I'm like the new walnut tree my little brother planted in our garden: small, but with its roots sunk deep, deep into our soil.

I looked up from the diary, dazed. The description of Elisa's birthday had floored me. How different it'd been from my slice of cake with a lonely candle on it. I pictured Elisa's family and friends gathered outside, the music playing, people dancing, and Elisa's mamma whispering words of love in her ear: *my clever, clever girl.*

I'd never felt like that, never. I was always cut off, moved around, unable to take root at all.

But who was this girl? Was she a Stella, maybe? Why did my biological mother give me her diary?

Staying at the convent was a necessary evil. It was the only way to keep studying after elementary school, and I was lucky that my parents agreed to it. Most young people here, both boys and girls, don't go further than a few years of school. Many don't know how to read or write. Girls get married straight away or go work in the rice fields down the plains, into service, or in a factory. I always wanted more. I always wanted to know more, do more, even if it meant leaving my family and friends behind and becoming an outsider. You see, the girls who go and stay at the convent are upper-class girls who are being groomed for marriage to men as wealthy as themselves. I was the only one who did it because I wanted to go to university.

Suor Fulvia, the Mother Superior, made it clear to me that my being there was only to keep a good relationship with the bishop, who had championed my cause to continue my studies. The bishop, in turn, had done it because of his long-standing friendship with our Montevino priest, Don Giuseppe. But Suor Fulvia didn't see the point of filling my head with knowledge I would have no chance to use, and with ambitions that would just work against me. It would be better for me to find a man from my village and settle down.

Had it not been for Mamma's letters from home, brief but full of love, my Zia Costanza's, so full of details that they made me feel like I was there, and Pietro's little notes, his childish handwriting getting better and better as years passed – I would have given up right at the beginning. I'm a little bit ashamed to say that, but it's true. I owe them so much. At home, I was beloved; but at the convent, I was the rebel.

Anyway, all of this is in the past now! I'm home and I'll enjoy this summer in Montevino. In the next few days, I'll go to Torino and apply for the university.

Yes, me, little Elisa from Montevino, at Torino University! Well, if I get in, of course. It seems impossible, yet it's been my dream since I was a little girl: I want to be a doctor.

Healing runs in my family. My great-grandmother and my grandmother were the village midwives. Mamma would have liked to study as a nurse but married Papa very young; she, too, is a midwife to the village women and has gained a reputation for being the one to call on when a baby is on the way. People come from miles away to see her, often shunning Dottor Quirico, our local physician, and she gives them herbs and teas and tinctures. I have learned so much from her, but I want to know more. My dream is to be like Dottor Quirico, to work here in Montevino and make people better.

So much stands between me and university: I need to pass an impossible exam, get through a rigorous interview, and then, if I'm accepted, find the funds to go. But I must believe it's going to happen. There's nothing else I'd rather do, nothing else I could do. I truly feel this is what I'm on this earth for...

I paused reading and wondered what it felt like to have a purpose in life. I, too, was working hard to save to go to college, but, unlike Elisa, what I wanted to become was still a dilemma. I looked outside the small window to a blanket of clouds set on fire by the sunset. I had lost all sense of time. I knew that something new would begin for me the moment I stepped off this plane. But, until then, I wanted to cram in as much as I could of this diary.

I slipped the photograph out from between the pages, and looked into the woman's deep, dark eyes behind the thin wire glasses. Her smile was like a sunny day. *Elisa...*

Montevino, July 25, 1939

Caro *Diario*,

At last, the exams results are out...

I've been accepted into the medicine course in Torino! And according to the lists pinned outside, I am the only woman among 112 new students.

Zia Costanza saw my name first, and she very nearly shrieked! Can you imagine, the calm, quiet Costanza shrieking? I must admit, I was so happy I nearly cried! But there was no way I would shed a tear in front of all my future fellow students. I must be tougher than they expect – and twice as tough as any man.

When we came home on the train and gave everyone the news, I could see that Mamma and Papa had mixed feelings. Their happiness was muted. And I know why. I am now faced with a challenge bigger than any entrance exam. I must find the funds to support me there. My family own almost nothing – the clothes on our backs, Papa's tools. We don't even own Firefly House and the small working farm that goes with it – we got it from the Conte of Montevino, who took pity on us when Papa had his accident. That's why we can't ask the Conte for another favor, we are too proud to beg. My parents work to eat and to keep us warm and clothed; there's nothing left over. I need to look at other ways, and I will. I know I'll find a way, no matter what.

I have already applied for the one and only scholarship available. Soon the applicants will receive a letter with the result of their application. I'm going to go to the post office every day in the morning, before helping on the farm, because I can't stand waiting until lunchtime, when our postman does the rounds. Zia Costanza went to church this morning to light a candle for me, and she, too, will do it every day until the letter arrives.

Yours,
Elisa

August 24, 1939

Caro *Diario*,

I didn't get the scholarship.
This diary is secret, so I can admit here that I cried.
But, I must keep going.
I'm looking for another solution. There must be one!

As soon as I got a hold of myself again, after reading that horrible letter, I went to Don Giuseppe. He promised he'd petition the bishop again, but the bishop already paid for me staying at the convent to get my diploma. I doubt his superiors will let him help me again. The only other person I can turn to is the Conte, but my parents are very much against the idea. Today I brought it up again, but Mamma said no.

My Zia Costanza was quiet, as she usually is, and my brother Pietro is too young to be listened to. And Papa?

He deferred to Mamma, on this one, something he almost never does.

I'm left with two choices: to become a mondina, *a rice girl, working in the rice fields away from home, ankle deep in water and bent in two all day, like so many girls my age; or get a job at Leone's, Montevino's candy factory. But neither position will allow me to save enough money to ever attend my medicine course, so I suppose that's the end of it.*

Yours, crushed,

Elisa

"You'll want to put a jacket on when we land."

One of the flight attendants, pretty in her uniform and perfect make-up, interrupted my reading. She'd spoken to me in Italian, the first time someone had done so since school, and then it was only in a lesson. Being spoken to was different from reading words in Italian; words laid out black on white, waiting patiently to be deciphered. All of a sudden, I was nervous, but tried to hide it and pretended to be confident.

"*Sì?*" I felt myself blushing intensely. I clutched the diary to me, as if it were a precious secret.

"Oh, *sì*. There's a storm preparing."

"*Ho solo questo* – I only have this," I said, tugging on my thin jacket. I was surprised to find the words rolled off my tongue after all these years.

"I'm sure the storm will pass soon," the flight attendant said smoothly.

The captain's voice came through the intercom: "This is your captain speaking, we'll be landing in Turin shortly, twenty minutes ahead of time." I put the diary away and began to prepare for landing. "I hope you had the chance to admire the mighty Alps from the air."

I had. In seeing the snow-capped peaks I'd been half awed, half freaked out. It really was another world, so far from Texas and everything I knew. I ignored the wave of fear that hit me as the plane lowered its wheels, ready to hit the runway. Where does fear end and excitement begin?

*

I had imagined being greeted by blue Italian seas and flowering pergolas, but, just like the flight assistant had predicted, I was surrounded by people wrapped in rain jackets, gray-blue mountain landscapes, and fresh, crisp air. I fiddled with the heating dials in the bright red FIAT 500 I'd just rented, my cross-body bag beside me on the passenger seat and my backpack and suitcase in the back. The evening shadows were beginning to fall, and on both sides of me were illuminated signs to industrial sites, malls and warehouses.

After not even twenty minutes of semi-urban landscape, I was already out of the highway and onto narrow country roads, farms and fields having taken the place of the brightly lit buildings in Turin. Even the GPS seemed confused, because it kept guiding me into tiny villages, where I would take turn after turn onto alleys and small, stone-paved roads. It seemed to me that Italians make great artists, poets and designers, not to mention their food – but one thing was sure: they were not great at putting together road signs.

Every place I passed – even in the rain – was ancient and beautiful. Spotlights illuminated the facades of lovely churches, and I passed cafés, ice-cream parlors and restaurants all lit up, as I drove along cobblestone roads. Often, built into the walls of houses and alleys, I saw tiny shrines with statuettes illuminated by electric candles. Some villages were nothing more than one road, a small cluster of houses and a church, mounted on the landscape like a gem on a ring. Where I came from, street lighting simply had a practical function; but here, it seemed to be used to accentuate the beautiful, ancient buildings, almost like stage lights in a theatre.

Over the fields and woods loomed a darkening sky, the moon and stars blocked out by a thick cloud cover. Ahead of me stretched the dark gray shape of the Alps, growing closer and closer until, suddenly, gone were the woods and fields on either side. In their place towered walls of gray stone; rock faces that seemed to become steeper and steeper as I drove. There were clusters of lights scattered here and there: small villages that appeared to cling to the mountain sides. At one point there was a castle on top of a craggy hill, illuminated in yellow and white. I almost gasped as I saw, passing on my left, what looked like a fortress, rising from the stone as if it was born of it.

"This is *amazing*," I said to myself, startling at the sound of my voice after so much silence.

And then the road began to rise again, at first gently, then scaling the mountain, the treacherous bends becoming tighter and tighter, the road narrower and narrower. And just as suddenly as I realized this, my little red car was swallowed by the darkness. No lights, other than the reflective lights at the edges of the road. Only a guardrail stood between me and the steep slope down the mountainside.

My clammy hands gripped the steering wheel. I was almost shaking. Up and up that stubborn mule of a car climbed, until finally the streetlights appeared again, and to my relief I saw that a softer valley had taken the place of the abyss. At that moment, just as I was murmuring words of thanks for having made it up the mountain before the storm, *and* in one piece – a white road sign appeared: *Montevino*.

I had arrived.

*

I drove along a long avenue that led up to the village. It was lined on both sides by tall trees, each one gleaming almost gold under the light of old-fashioned, wrought-iron lamp posts dotted along the way. Beckoning me was an ancient, red stone belfry with an old-fashioned bell on top. My heart began to beat faster as I passed tree after tree, all of them tall, gnarly and ancient. Then the road ended, and I came to a small, stone bridge running over a stream. The GPS told me to keep going, and I drove on through narrow streets, where small shrines were encased in the walls, with red candles inside them burning like St. Elmo's fires.

"You've reached your destination."

The robotic words of the GPS felt almost like a sign. I stopped the car by the side of the road, just across from what seemed to be the village square, then opened the door, stepped out onto the cobblestones and inhaled the thin fresh air, laden with the scent of burned wood and pine trees. Everything spoke of rain to come, and the wind was intensifying even as I stood there, slowly but surely. A thought hit me then. Elisa must have been here, in this same square. That church, with its red stone belfry, which I'd seen from a distance, was it there that Elisa had gone to ask Don Giuseppe for help with university funding? I laid a hand on my cross-body bag, where the diary lay, waiting to tell me more.

I turned around to take in the whole scene. At the four corners of the square were four ancient pines, tall and almost black in the night air, and in the center there was a monument. I walked closer and noticed that it was an angel cradling a soldier in her arms. A sign at her feet read "To the Fallen," followed by a list of names. At its base sat a laurel wreath with a red ribbon. Beyond the village, white and illuminated, was the castle Malva had written about, sitting on top of a dark hill. And beyond the castle were the mountains, etched against the night sky, encasing Montevino like a rocky nest.

There were alleys departing from the square, and I couldn't wait to see and explore more. I wondered where the painting Elisa had written about was – the Christ with the clouds around the cross, who they used to pray to when rain wasn't forthcoming – but my exploring would have to wait. I needed to find the B&B I'd booked, the Aquila Nera, confirm the room, and then look for Firefly House.

I walked past the row of small stores, all closed now, except for a well-lit window in which an old-fashioned painted sign told me that here was the place I was searching for; I stepped inside. It seemed to be both a café and a restaurant, but it was half empty. No wonder, if a storm was preparing.

"*Buonasera…* Callie?" A short, black-haired woman with a colorful apron tied over her woolen sweater, all red flowers and swirls, came to greet me. She pronounced my name "Call-ee", and it made it sound exotic. A few locals looked up, and a couple of them smiled. I supposed there wouldn't be many American girls turning up in the village, just like that.

"Yes, that's me. Callie DiGiacomo. I booked a room for tonight."

"Welcome, I'm Adriana. Nonna, she's here! The American girl!" the woman called.

An elderly lady with a wizened face – just the Italian *nonna* you would see in a film – sat in the corner behind the counter, also with a colorful apron over her clothes. "*Oh, la ragazza Americana…*! My goodness, what a night to arrive! Will you want to eat something after you settle in? You must be famished, after the long journey…"

I swallowed, lost for a moment in the stream of Italian words that followed. Nonna had a strange accent, different from the

Italian films I'd watched and the audio bits of the books I studied. It would take a while to get used to it.

"We are speaking too fast, Nonna Tina!" Adriana said kindly, laying a hand on my arm. The touching and the offering of food, now there were two very Italian things right in front of me! "*Scusa, cara.*" Sorry, dear. "We will speak more slowly." She nodded at the *nonna* as she spoke.

"No, no, it's fine! I need to practice," I said, smiling. "Just, I'm looking for a house... I'd like to see it before I settle in my room. Casa delle Lucciole?"

"*Oh, sì, sì,*" Adriana and Nonna both said, looking at one other. "It's really easy to find, right behind the castle," Adriana continued. "But are you sure you want to go out there again? There's a storm coming."

"I would just like to check it out, then I'll come back."

"And eat something," Nonna said slowly and deliberately, making me smile. Out of the corner of my eye I'd seen some pretty amazing-looking plates of pasta on the tables. "I make it all myself, you know?" she told me proudly, catching me looking at the food. "I make pasta almost every day, and I'm—"

"Eighty-two!" Nonna and Adriana said together, the younger woman smiling at me. "Enough about pasta, Nonna. Call-ee, you can't go wrong. There are only a few houses up there and Casa delle Lucciole is the biggest," Adriana said, showing me with her hands in a way that reminded me of my parents so much, it squeezed my heart.

"Nobody has lived in Casa delle Lucciole for years now," Nonna said. "People wonder why. There are many stories around the house and the Stella family, but who can tell what's true and what's hearsay?" She looked at me for a moment, as if to see if I had understood what she'd told me, but I wondered if she was really asking herself how much I knew.

So… Firefly House was empty? Of course, it made sense. I had the keys, the house had been left to me… I was desperate to ask them about Malva, but first I wanted to see what awaited me at the house, and then to take some time to process everything.

I left the warmth and light of the Aquila Nera to go out into the night again, just as the first few drops of rain hit my face and hands. Full-bellied clouds filled the sky now. I had to hurry.

I got back into the car and drove out of the village and up the hill, bend after bend, heading for the castle. At one point, two pairs of bright, frightened yellow eyes looked at me from the road, before jumping away into the undergrowth. I saw, in the headlights, that they belonged to deer. I drove the rest of the short distance slowly and carefully until I arrived on top.

Up close, the building looked more like a fortress than a castle, the inclement weather adding to the atmosphere. It was imposing, rising up stark and gray against the dark sky. I drove on, hoping to find a way round it, so I could get to Firefly House without having to get out of the car and wander about in the dark. A cobblestone road led me along one of the walls to a wide field bordered by dense, black woods, and on the edge of the woods – nearly invisible had it not been for the car headlights – was a small villa.

My heart began to beat faster. *Was that Firefly House…?* It had to be. I could see maybe two or three other cottages around, but this was the biggest one, just as Adriana had said.

The headlights illuminated a wrought-iron gate, a yard dotted with what seemed like centenary trees, a red-tiled roof, a small round tower, a terrace. The main door was framed by a porch with small, unadorned columns and stony steps.

It was perfect. Even lit by the simple beam of car lights and seen through rain-lashed windows.

This house is mine? Seriously?

I had to pinch myself. There had to be a mistake.

No, I would not believe it was mine until I heard it from the lawyers.

A sudden flash lit the sky and illuminated the castle, the house, and the mountains all around me. *Horizontal lightning*. It was time to be indoors, for sure.

I got out of the car, hunched against the wind, the downpour drenching me instantly, and fumbled among the keys I'd been given to find the right one for the gate. Finally inserting it and twisting it any which way, and rattling the lock until my hands were wet and frozen, at last the catch sprang open. I ran across the garden, trying not to slip on the wet earth, and stepped up to the elegant porch. Slipping the smaller key into the lock of the wooden front door, I stepped out of the rain and over the threshold.

My breath seemed to fill the whole house in an instant. Frozen on the doorstep, all I could hear was a strange *whooshing* sound in my ears and the beating of my heart. I cursed myself for not thinking to bring a flashlight, then I thought of the torch on my phone.

Praying I had enough battery, I took it out of my backpack, switched it on and scanned the walls beside the door, where I soon located a switch. If the electricity didn't work, which surely it didn't, there was no way I could explore the house with the weak light of my phone. Holding my breath, I flipped the light switch and, quite unexpectedly, an exquisite, small chandelier lit up a hallway leading away from the door, illuminating everything with a yellow glow. I exhaled, relieved, letting my guard down at just the moment that a clap of thunder, so deep and rumbling it felt like it was shaking the ground, made me jump out of my skin.

The blonde wood floor creaked as I walked along the hall, and a moth flew from somewhere and disappeared again behind the curtains. Although abandoned, the place felt strangely alive. Or maybe it was just my imagination, flaring up with the tiredness, the upheaval of the last few days. Through the rain-covered windows I could see dancing black branches and an inky sky, lit up by lightning in the distance. The room was strangely warm, not freezing as you would imagine a long-empty house to be. I noticed there were radiators underneath each window. The idea of central heating was strange, in such an old house – but I supposed they'd been installed before the place was deserted. I touched one; it was warm.

Was this house really abandoned? Had nobody lived here in years, like the *nonna* in the village said? Because not only was the place warm, but it appeared to be clean. As I entered what seemed to be a large drawing room, I stopped to flick a light switch by the door. Once the room was bathed in light, I was surprised by what I saw. There wasn't a speck of dust on the floor, on the windowsills, on the coffee table, on the lamps. A brightly colored rug covered part of the wooden floor, its colors vivid, not dimmed with dust or dirt. The air in the room smelled subtly of... vanilla... and cinnamon.

Anxiety fluttered inside me as I made my way deeper into the house, towards a rhythmic banging noise that appeared to be coming from the small round tower I'd seen from the road. My sneakers squelched on the floor as I walked, leaving a wet trail behind me. At the end of the hall, I plucked up my courage and opened the door in front of me, to reveal a study, complete with bookshelves floor to ceiling, and a wide, dark wooden desk. Beside the desk was a shuttered French window. The shutters were open and one hadn't been secured. It was banging against the wall with every gust of wind. Running over to the window, and with white curtains billowing all around me, I grabbed the shutter and had begun to close it, when the beauty of the storm caught my eye.

I stepped outside onto the terrace and, grasping the iron railings to stop my hands from shaking, watched as darts of lightning fell from the sky over the black mountains. My hair was soaked and dripping, but it didn't matter. The clouds grumbled so loud that it felt like the noise was coming from the belly of the house, almost from underneath it; at the same time the shutter came loose again and banged loudly on the wall. I jumped out of my skin.

There was somebody living in the villa. I was completely sure. It wasn't abandoned at all. I darted back inside, ran through the house and dashed to the car without looking back.

My hands shaking more than ever, while thunder, lightning and rain seemed to came at me from all sides. I just wanted to get the hell out of there. Now. But every time I tried to unlock the car door, the keys slipped through my fingers and fell into the mud. And each time I bent down to recover them, rivulets of rain dribbled down my face. I grabbed at the keys one last time, a fistful of freezing mud coming up with them. I went to try the door lock again, only to find a pale face crowned by a hood – a man's face – was looking at me from across the car, through the passenger window.

I screamed and grabbed the first thing I could get my hands on – a fallen branch, wet and slimy – and swung it as hard as I could at the man, who was now walking towards me on my side of the car. He lifted up his hands, shouting things I couldn't understand, as I took another swipe and knocked him into the mud. I dropped the branch, and was about to stick the car keys in the lock again, desperate to drive away from that place, when the noise of the storm subsided just long enough for me to hear what he was saying.

"*Sei pazzo?*" he shouted. Are you crazy?

"Stay away from me!" I replied in Italian, as he struggled to his feet.

"I'm the castle caretaker!"

I realized I'd dropped the keys yet again, but he beat me to it and bent down to pick them up.

"I'm Tommaso Carpentieri. I live there," he yelled over the noise of the storm. I followed his gesture, as he pointed to a gray stone cottage that looked like one of the castle's outbuildings.

"In the castle?" I shouted.

"Sort of. Look, we really need to get inside." Then he said something about *fulmini*.

Fulmini? Oh, yes: lightning.

I didn't want to be electrocuted on my first night in Italy, but I wasn't convinced.

"How do I know you're not a murderous maniac?" I shouted.

"As far as I can tell, it's *you* who hit *me* with a branch! Come on. Come out of the storm. But leave that behind!" he said, gesturing to the branch at my feet.

"No way. I'm fine. I'm going to Aquila Nera in the sq— *Aaah!*"

The loudest thunderclap yet broke through the sky. To my shame, I covered my head with my hands. The rain had become so thick, it was almost like breathing water.

"It's not safe out here!" Tommaso said. "We're high up and last year a pine was set on fire by lightning just a couple of hundred meters from here. Look, I'm soaking and covered in mud. You have thirty seconds to decide. Either come inside with me or I'll drive you down to the Aquila Nera now."

"Don't tell me what to do!" I shouted, rain dripping on my face.

"I'm not telling you—"

At that moment, a small branch fell on the roof of the car and missed me by mere inches, making me squeal.

"Fine! I'm coming with you!" I yelled, utterly defeated.

"Good call," the man shouted. He grabbed my hand, and we ran on slippery ground, soaked to the bone, toward a gray stone cottage.

CHAPTER 4

The first thing I saw was a glowing fire, burning in a fireplace topped with a stone mantelpiece. There were beautiful, lyrical paintings on the walls, full of greens and blues. The ceiling was low and vaulted, red bricks laid together in symmetric patterns. The sudden warmth of the room made me shiver so violently that the man – *what did he say his name was?* – noticed.

"Come. Sit at the fire," he said, and I looked at him properly for the first time. He was tall, taller than me; broad shouldered, with thick, dark hair and skin that was used to the sun. He had stripped off his hooded jacket to reveal an old-fashioned sweater and corduroy pants, now muddy, which made him look like he was from another time. *Outlander*, I remembered – the story of a woman who walks unawares into a circle of stones and ends up in another time.

"What did you say your name was?" I asked.

I couldn't tell his age, because there was a timelessness about him. He was older than me, for sure, but probably not older than thirty or so.

"Tommaso. Tommaso Carpentieri. Come on, sit, get warm," he replied. "And you are?"

"Callie."

"Call-ee," he said, in that Italian way that stressed the double 'l' and made the final 'ee' sound longer. I liked it.

Safe inside, I began to wonder what had possessed me to follow this stranger into his house. He seemed like a perfectly nice man, yes, but didn't it always start that way? Next thing you're on the news, discovered buried in his back yard.

Okay, maybe that was a bit far-fetched.

Whatever the case, I was too frazzled to think any longer. I did as I was told and sat on a comfy armchair in front of the fire. Another long, deep shiver traveled through me.

"Take those clothes off," Tommaso said.

I jumped right back up. "What?"

He blushed pink on his dark skin. "I mean: I'll give you some dry clothes so you can get changed," he explained.

"Did you just ask me to take my clothes off?"

"I didn't mean—" Another boom of thunder interrupted us, instantly followed by a strange sound from somewhere next door. A sort of yelp.

"It's okay. It's just thunder," Tommaso said, trying to reassure me.

"That wasn't thunder," I whimpered, doing my best to steal a glance into the other room.

"Don't be scared."

"I'm not usually scared of storms," I scrambled, trying to sound normal, but wondering how I could run out of the cottage and back to my car, all the while dodging lightning and fallen branches.

Another strangled yelp.

I looked toward the door, my heart pounding against my ribs.

"Everyone is scared of storms, deep down," he said. "It's instinct." Then, "Morella!" he called in a light tone, stepping into the next room.

I caught a glimpse of what was probably his bedroom, also with a low, red-brick vaulted ceiling and pure white walls. *Should I run away now?* I was frozen. In every way.

"Morella, *tesoro*, come out."

Tesoro meant sweetheart. Did he keep his wife under the bed? "I'm home. I'm back, okay? Okay?" He crouched on the floor, sticking his head under the bed. That sound again – the yelp.

"Come on! We have guests!" He made a clicking sound with his tongue and a black nose appeared from under the bed, and there was another yelp.

A dog! I laughed to myself, cursing my imagination.

"Come out, Morella. Come on," he coaxed. "*Papà è a casa,*" he whispered, and then turned slightly toward me, embarrassed.

I had to giggle. He'd just said, "Daddy's home."

Morella appeared. I'd never seen a dog that big; she was more like a foal. "Good girl. Good girl. Callie, meet Morella. Morella, Callie."

I smiled. "Is she good? Can I touch her?" I loved dogs and couldn't wait to pet her; but she was so big that I knew, should she decide to bite, she could take my arm off easily enough.

"Of course. She's great. She would never bite a friend. But if you're someone who's trying to get into the castle on shady business, that's another story."

"Unless there's a storm and she's hiding under the bed," I pointed out, and he laughed. Poor Morella was shaking all over. "Aw, come here." I reached out my hand to her. "Don't be scared." Slowly, she wandered up to me and I sank my face into her soft fur. She came up to my waist.

"I'll get you some clothes," Tommaso said, returning to the bedroom and opening a chest of drawers, while I cuddled Morella. The rain was battering the windows even harder than before, and it seemed that beyond there was only darkness.

"Who's a huge dog? Oh, you are! Yes, you *are!*" I said in English.

Tommaso paused in the doorway, a bundle of clothes in his arms. "You're American?" he said in English too.

"Yes, from Texas. Could you not tell from my accent?"

"I guessed you were not Italian. Why you come to Montevino?"

It seemed like he would struggle a bit with speaking English, so I switched back to Italian, for his sake. "Long story, but I'm looking for... well, relatives." I wanted to change the topic quickly, so I turned my attention back to the dog. "You beautiful puppy. You're enormous!"

"She's a Romanian Shepherd."

"Is she? She does a great job of camouflaging as a dog," I said, and laughed shyly at my terrible joke. Tommaso laughed too; not many people got my wonky sense of humor.

"You make jokes in Italian! That's really good, for a foreigner," he said pleasantly. "There," he added, handing me the bundle.

I would look like a scarecrow in his clothes, but at that point I didn't care. They were warm and dry, and that was enough.

"Your home is so... picturesque."

"It used to be the gamekeeper's cottage. Though I suppose I am a bit of a gamekeeper too. I take care of the deer, make sure hogs don't come in."

"I think I have to explain what I was doing at the villa—"

"Why don't you get changed first? Otherwise you'll catch something. When you're done, I'll be next door," he said.

Ten minutes later I was back, sitting in front of the fire in dry clothes – a pair of sweatpants that were too long for me, an enormous woolen sweatshirt and warm socks – with a cup of herbal tea in my hand, and Morella at my feet. My thoughts drifted to Misty back home. I knew there were a few others to feed and look after the little cat, but I still hoped she wouldn't be disappointed when she couldn't get into my apartment.

"Are you hungry?" Tommaso had changed too, into jeans and a plaid shirt. He seemed younger now, more twenty-first century.

"I suppose I am. I've been travelling all day. Or all night? I feel a bit... funny, actually."

"No wonder. You seemed terrified earlier on. You hit me with a branch," he said cheerily.

"I'm so sorry. But you freaked me out."

"Then I'm sorry too," he said. His eyes were deep, dark green, the color of moss or leaves. He had a way of looking aside when he spoke to you – not shifty, just shy. "Drink up, *signorina*. Let me make you some pasta."

Oh, *signorina*. I loved being called *signorina*!

"Thanks, but I don't think I can handle pasta. Sorry… Oh, wait! Pasta! I need to go back to the *nonna*, she'll worry…"

"What *nonna*?"

"The Aquila Nera one. I need to go, I suppose. It's so late, I have already checked in… What if they close up…"

"Hey, hey, hey. You can't go back out in that."

"I need to call them, then."

"Cell phones don't work up here. Use my landline. I'll call them, if you want?"

"That'd be great, thank you."

He did, and I listened to the quick conversation in Italian, in awe. They spoke so fast. He seemed to be friendly with Adriana; I supposed in a village as small as this, everyone knew each other.

"*Buonanotte*," Tommaso said into the phone. Good night.

"I'm sorry I left them hanging. Of course I'll pay for the room."

"I'm sure it's not a problem. Oh, by the way. I have a message for you from Nonna Tina. She says to eat dinner, that you're too skinny."

"Did I just gain an instant granny?" I giggled, but a part of me reveled in that feeling. Something warm, and loving, was beginning to bloom inside me, and it was so good that it was almost frightening.

"All Italian *nonnas* are instant grannies," Tommaso joked. He couldn't see or guess the emotion I felt, and I could never have put it into words – not with a stranger, not with anyone. "How about some bread and honey? The honey is from bees I keep here. It'll build you up a little."

"Thank you. You're very kind," I said. At this point, exhaustion and the heat of the fire were beginning to creep in and my eyes were closing.

I imagined giving Kirsten the lowdown on my day. *Yes, I found the house. It's actually a villa, but there's a storm so I'm waiting it out in a gamekeeper's cottage, and this mysterious Italian guy who looks after the castle is making me bread and honey.*

I pushed my gaze around the room again, and my eye fell on the lovely canvases on the walls. One in particular caught my eye: a black-haired little boy, against the backdrop of a grape-laden vine under a blue, cloudless sky. I wondered if Tommaso had painted them.

"There. A bit of sugar to perk you up," he said, as he came back, carrying a tray. "More tea, and a little grappa."

"Thanks. What's grappa?"

"A very strong liquor. It'll warm you, relax you and stave off colds." Tommaso's language was sophisticated, I thought, not basic; I could tell he was well educated, even with my imperfect knowledge of Italian.

"And get me drunk?"

"Not unless you're a super-lightweight," he said, lifting a crystal glass in which sat a tiny amount of honey-colored liquid.

"Sold." I wasn't a big drinker, but I could do with a little bit of courage now. I took a suspicious sip, then downed the liquid. It was like swallowing an electric blanket – in a good way. The fire crackled and danced, reflecting a warm glow on the walls. It smelled of resin. "Oh, wow! That did warm me up."

"There, now you're one of us," he joked, then hesitated. "So... I suppose it's the right moment to ask you what you were doing at the Stella house?"

I bit into the bread, suddenly ravenous. The honey was out of this world. "Mmm. Yeah. I actually own it," I said, and immediately regretted it. I wasn't ready to discuss all that. It must have been the grappa.

"Seriously?"

"Yes."

"How? I mean, you're American. Though your Italian is good."

"Well, I don't know about that! But, thanks. Yes, I've grown up in America. My biological mom was from here, though, and apparently, she left me the house. I just found this out two days ago. Like I said, it's a long story – and a little crazy."

He didn't argue with that. "Who was your mother, if I may ask?"

"Malva Stella."

Such a beautiful name. Malva Stella. And if my father, the man whose name I didn't even know, hadn't given me his last name, I was a Stella too. *Callie* Stella.

Oh. That feeling in the pit of my stomach, somewhere between pain and warmth and longing.

Belonging.

"Oh, yes," Tommaso said, breaking into my thoughts. 'My dad was a friend of the Stella family. Malva moved to America and" – he hesitated – "I never knew she'd had a daughter."

He'd been about to say something else. I was eager to piece together every part of the jigsaw, so I pressed him: "What were you about to say?"

"Well, I'm sure you… You *must* know, you probably don't want to be reminded."

"I don't know much about Malva. Actually, I don't know anything about her."

"Well, they went to America, and she passed away there."

I gasped and closed my eyes. My head spun. And so… *She was gone. I would never meet her.*

"I'm sorry... You didn't know?"

I shook my head.

Tommaso was silent. And then: "I'm so sorry it had to be a stranger who told you."

Malva was dead.

A heartbeat passed, then I found it in myself to open my eyes and reply. "Everything I'm learning about my family has been told to me by strangers." I tried to smile.

A roll of thunder shook the house, and Morella curled up closer to Tommaso. I barely noticed, lost in my own thoughts. Even such shocking news seemed to be far away – I felt a little numb. My brain was so full, I couldn't take any more discoveries. I needed to sleep, but first I had another question.

"Tommaso, I was told the house hadn't been lived in for years. But it's spotless. No dust, everything clean. The shutters are open. It even smells nice."

"I think Flora comes to clean it. It's only a guess, but I see her occasionally, coming up to the villa."

"Flora?"

"She's Malva's sister... Your... aunt?"

I smiled broadly. "I have an aunt?"

"Yep. You didn't know that either?"

I shook my head. My mother's letter had mentioned she had no family left.

"Wow. I'd like to ask you how you didn't know any of this, or why you never came to visit... but I'm beginning to sound like a village busybody. And you need rest."

I sighed. "Yes. Thank you. I wonder... why does Flora" – *another sweet name* – "come to clean if nobody lives in the old place? Why bother at all?"

He shrugged. "You'll have to ask her. You know, it's funny..."

"What is?"

"Casa delle Lucciole never actually *felt* abandoned. I mean, yes, the castle's gardeners keep the garden trimmed, I knew that, of course, and Flora cleans the place. But apart from all that, it always felt like there was someone there."

"That's exactly what I thought when I was inside."

"Maybe it's just my imagination, though. And you must have been frightened by the storm, and jet-lagged."

I couldn't deny it. My reaction in the house and outside it had been dramatic, to say the least. I couldn't explain what had happened, not even to myself. I stifled a yawn. Talking to Tommaso had been so easy, it was as though I'd known him for a long time, but my thoughts were fading, and sleep was taking over.

"You're exhausted. I'll make up your bed," he said and stood, followed by Morella.

"I can sleep on the couch," I protested.

"No way. I'm a gentleman. And she's a *gentledog*. You take the bed, Morella and I will sleep here."

"Thank you for letting me stay. I hope it's not too much of an imposition."

"No imposition at all. Really. It's a pleasure. I have girls from Texas appearing out of the blue, attacking me with a branch, then staying over all the time. It's routine."

"Don't remind me. I'm *so* sorry."

After Tommaso had finished changing the sheets, I wasn't even too self-conscious to let myself fall into the bed. I was too drained to focus on the fact that I was about to fall asleep in a stranger's house, in an isolated place almost in the middle of nowhere. The sheets smelled fresh and clean, and the warm blankets weighed heavily on me, cocooning me.

I had no time to think before falling asleep, the noise of the storm acting as a strange lullaby. I slept so deeply that if there was any thunder during the night, I didn't hear it.

CHAPTER 5

The feeling of something wet against my cheek woke me up. I opened my eyes to see an enormous black nose, belonging to an enormous dog, sniffing me. It took me a moment to remember where I was.

Italy... the storm... Tommaso...

"Hey, pup," I murmured, and reached out to stroke her head. I rolled over and gazed at the ceiling, with its red, intricate brick patterns. A soft light came through the window, pale golden, and the place was in silence.

The events of the day before, good and bad, came back to me. *Malva was gone. I would never meet my birth mother.*

Grief bit me, and I closed my eyes again, letting the emotion roll through every fiber of my body.

And then: *Firefly House. The family I might have left. Flora... Montevino... everything left to discover.*

I lifted myself out of bed, every muscle sore from travelling and tension, and tiptoed through to the living room as quietly as I could, in case Tommaso was still sleeping on the couch, but the place was deserted. On the table, I discovered a *caffettiera*, Italian-style, a dish covered with a cloth, a box of matches, and a note with a few words and a small sketch titled *Orissi*. What did that mean? It was a drawing of a girl with long hair brandishing

a branch, and a tiny man with a speech bubble that said *'Help!'*
The rest of the scrap of paper was filled by lashes of stylized rain.
I giggled. The handwriting in the note was almost indecipherable,
but after a lot of squinting and turning the note left and right, I
managed: *Help yourself. Please let Morella out.* Caffettiera *on the
stove, firewood in the shed. T.*

I followed Tommaso's instructions, turning on the ring
underneath the silvery contraption on the stove and observing it
suspiciously for a few minutes, until it began bubbling. The scent
was incredible, so much better than machine coffee.

Under the cloth I discovered a small cake; it looked home-made
and smelled divine. I was starving. Morella and I had a quick
breakfast, then I slipped my sneakers on, still a bit damp after
last night, and we walked out into the almost blinding sun. I
blinked as my eyes took a moment to adjust to it. I rolled up my
sleeves – Tommaso's shirt was huge on me – and stood outside
for a moment, contemplating my surroundings.

Reminders of last night's storm lay beneath my feet: the
ground was soaking and there were fallen branches all around – I
was thankful, now, that I'd accepted Tommaso's hospitality and
not attempted to drive – but it was a clear spring morning with
a bright blue sky and even brighter sunshine. I made my way
across the few hundred yards that separated Tommaso's cottage
from the villa with Morella, who went on her way, leaving me
alone to reverently step through the wrought-iron gate and into
the villa's garden.

Casa delle Lucciole. Finally, in the light of day, I could see it
clearly. The dark burgundy color of its outside walls, the frescoes
that decorated the walls, the terrace and the little tower on the
side took my breath away. The frescoes were delicate and slightly
faded, representing vineyards and fields dotted with men working
the land and women in long dresses carrying baskets of grapes

on their heads. I was dizzy for a moment – maybe it was because I'd been looking up for a few minutes, or maybe I was a little overwhelmed.

I pushed the wooden front door, left slightly open from the night before, and there I was, back in the hall, simply decorated with portraits, framed mirrors and a small antique side table. Through the first door on the left was the drawing room, bathed in light. Stony steps led upstairs, but I wanted to explore the ground floor first. Once again, the scents of vanilla and cinnamon hit me, and I was greeted by the feeling that the house was very much lived in. Now I could see properly how spotless it was, how well kept, with long white curtains hanging from the windows, the colorful antique rug, the blonde wood floors and immaculate white walls. I could so easily imagine a fragrant breakfast on the coffee table, clothes left around, hanging jackets and post in the hall.

This morning I could see that the focal point of the room was an immense fireplace, framed in wood and stone. The mantelpiece had a few knick-knacks on it, but no photographs. Seeing the fireplace reminded me of Tommaso's note about the wood – and yes, the place was chilly, even if the night before the heating had been on. I would explore everything first, and then try my hand at lighting a fire.

I kept wandering and discovering the rooms, my feet making no noise on the parquet. Another reception room at the back of the living room, and then, on the other side of the stairs, the kitchen. Like Tommaso's, it had a brick vaulted ceiling and white walls, and it was all made of wood and stone in a perfect mixture between ancient and modern. There was a fireplace in here too, blackened and full of soot. I opened a cupboard to see what was inside: crockery – some modern, some looking like they were made at the same time as the house – and utensils.

I was suddenly reminded of the *Mary Celeste*, this ship I'd read about somewhere, was found sailing the seas with nobody aboard and everything left suspended in time: food still on plates, beds unmade. It was like everyone had vanished…

I left the back door that led to the garden for later and moved down the hall. The small round tower I'd seen from the outside contained the study I'd been into the night before, and its shape made it look like a miniature castle. There was a set of stairs here too; I made my way upstairs on granite steps, the walls whitewashed like the first floor, the ceilings high and decorated with small stucco flowers and vines. I walked, silent and awed, among the antique furniture and paintings on the walls, until I found what seemed to be the master bedroom. There was a large cabinet against one wall and the four-poster bed opposite was made and covered with an immaculate crocheted bedspread. On both bedside tables were pristine crocheted doilies and painted glass lamps, and on the wall behind the bed hung a portrait of a woman.

Her face hypnotized me for a moment. It was white and round, with large black eyes and wavy black hair; the woman wore a cream blouse buttoned down the front and ruby earrings. She was beautiful, and there was a determined air about her, a gentle strength.

I tiptoed to the bed, still wrestling the uneasy feeling of being a guest here, of intruding on someone, living or dead, but desperate to look at the painting more closely. Gingerly, I took off my shoes and climbed onto the bed to get a better look. Then, as carefully as I could, I took the picture frame off the hook and turned it around. But there was nothing. No name, no signature.

The woman's eyes were incredible, I thought, as I placed the portrait back on the wall. They looked so real, so clear. *Elisa!* It had to be her. Yes, there was definitely a likeness to the woman in the photograph that I'd found in the diary, minus the glasses.

But that could be because the portrait had been painted to mark a special occasion, therefore she'd removed them.

I climbed down, and in doing so I moved the bedspread a little. The sheets were rough to the touch. I could see the threads criss-crossing as the loom had woven them, just like the linen cloth that covered the box my mother had left me. The sheets and pillowcases were embroidered in burgundy thread with two initials inside a flowery garland.

ES

I smiled, as if I'd found an old friend. That was the link, for sure – Elisa had lived here, and she had to be related to me. Maybe this had been her room. But how was she related to me, if indeed she was? I wondered, too, if her second name was really Stella. I could almost feel the eyes of the woman in the portrait looking down at me... *Elisa, who are you?* I called in my mind.

"Who are *you*?" A voice behind me spoke, loud and hostile. I was so lost in thought that I jumped almost to the roof. I clutched my chest and stood to face the stranger.

I blinked. The woman in front of me blinked too. It was like looking in a mirror. It had to be her: it had to be Flora, the woman Tommaso had said was Malva's sister. Same hair as me, same eyes as me, same heart-shaped face, and with a tall, slight build. We were like twins, apart in age. I began to shake all over.

"Flora," I whispered, and I sounded like a little girl.

"Who are you? What are you doing in this house?"

"I'm... Callie."

The woman's light blue eyes, identical to mine, widened under her eyebrows, thick and dark. She had a mane of black hair, curly and unkempt, and dangling earrings. I couldn't tell her age; she seemed young, and yet there was a sense of weariness about her that made me think almost of old age. Her smooth, olive face contrasted with the shadows under her eyes.

"Callie?" she murmured, like she'd seen a ghost.

"Yes. Your niece? You might not believe I'm… me…"

"I think it's pretty plain we are related," she said.

Of course. You couldn't fake such a resemblance.

I nodded. Words failed me.

"How… how did you find out? About this house? About… me?" she said. She sounded as shocked as I felt.

"I… I… My mother left me a letter, and, well, she left me this house. I only found out the truth two days ago… I had no idea I'd been adopted," I rushed on, half forgetting my Italian along the way. There was so much to say, so much. I couldn't possibly condense it all in two sentences. We had to sit down, and talk, then I could explain everything. But she wouldn't give me the chance.

"Your *mother*?"

"Malva. Your sister."

There was a moment and then the woman's eyes widened even more, and her lips parted in a silent '*O*'. Once again, I wondered why my mother said she had no family left.

I held my breath, hoping she would open her arms for me and hold me, and my wish would come true… *Not to be alone in the world anymore.*

"You need to go away and never come back. It's for your own good," I heard instead.

"What?" I murmured. Then a little louder, "*What?*" Tears began gathering in my eyes. It was as if something had thawed in me, the hard, icy wall around my heart melting slowly in the Italian sun. I pressed a hand against my chest. It was a physical pain, to be spoken to like that after so much hope.

"Yes."

There were a few heartbeats of silence. I could hear the blood rushing in my ears, emotion almost electric on my skin. But I took my courage in both hands. "There's so much I want to know. Why Malva gave me away, who my father is, where he is. Please, let's talk," I pleaded with her. "I know this is all so sudden, and I'm sorry I couldn't tell you I was coming, but I... I didn't even know you existed!"

Flora's mouth trembled underneath her iciness. "Go back where you came from, Callie. And don't come looking for me again." And then: "I'm sorry." She turned on her heels and left, leaving me frozen in shock, the spring sun scattering white rays across the floorboards, the scent Flora had carried with her – something fresh, herbal – vanishing slowly behind her.

This woman was my blood relative – my biological mother's sister. *My aunt.* The way we looked was a clear sign that the same blood ran in our veins. My wish, not to be alone in the world, had come true – but not in the way I'd wished for. Flora clearly knew of my existence; she'd recognized my name. But I was a ghost from the past, someone she didn't want in her life at all, now or ever. The thought I'd been tormenting myself with – that there was a reason why my parents had given me up – came back into my mind. Clearly, that reason was still valid, whatever it was.

I realized I was shaking; it took a few seconds to find myself again. When I could finally move, I ran to the window to see Flora's slight figure running out the house and disappearing beyond the gate. I found my way to the terrace and stood there, breathing deeply, more tears finding their way out of me. Like Alice in Wonderland, would I drown in my own tears? The ones I'd had stored away for years...

The same questions kept coming back, echoing in my mind: Why had Flora never looked for me? Had she met me as a baby? Maybe she had looked for me, but never found me. Or maybe she'd just deleted me from her life.

Only Flora Stella had the answers. Only she could tell me what had happened to my mother, and why I'd been given away. She was also the only link I had to my father, and the mystery surrounding him. I would not stop trying to get her to tell me the truth.

But for now, all that could be seen of the woman I had hoped would hold me close to her, was a dark figure running down the winding road toward the village.

There was no other way to move on from the shock and upset of meeting Flora: I had to keep going. I retrieved my luggage from the car, and had a look around for Morella – after her wander she had returned to the cottage and she sat, mellow and contented, on the doorstep. I assumed it was okay for her to stay out, as Tommaso had said nothing about shepherding her back inside.

I ran upstairs with my things and looked for a bathroom; to my joy, there was a clean, sweet-scented, all-white bathroom beside the master bedroom. The clean smell in this room made it even more evident that someone had been there very recently. I locked the door. Just in case.

After a long, warm shower I put on my own clothes – jeans and dry sneakers, a long top and a cotton scarf to protect me from the chilly breeze – and having brushed my hair and put some make-up on to hide the worst of the jet lag, I began to make my way down the road to the village armed with the documents for the Italian lawyer and more than ready for a second breakfast. No point in driving – I needed the fresh air to wake myself up. I also had to find somewhere my cell phone worked, because back at the Windmill Café, Kirsten must have been worried sick by my sudden disappearance. And, finally, I would go and apologize to

Adriana and Nonna at the Aquila Nera for cancelling the room during the storm.

As I walked, I breathed in the pure, sweet-scented mountain air, still full of moisture after yesterday's rain. Oh, the smell of rain and wet earth was incredible. It seemed that May here was still a little chilly, colder than I would have imagined, and colder than in Texas too; but the sky was now perfectly blue. The road was asphalted, sandwiched either side by dense woods, with an undergrowth of dead leaves, and walnut and chestnut trees whose new leaves had taken a battering. Their branches seemed almost to be woven into each other, making the woods thick and dark. After the storm there were broken branches and puddles everywhere.

At every bend, there was a small shrine with a religious statue inside, painted and decorated with flowers and candles. They were picturesque and somehow comforting, like constant reminders that you weren't alone.

It only took me twenty minutes to reach the edge of the village, where I passed a church and found my way to the main square. Montevino was picture-perfect. Everywhere I turned it was like being part of an enormous play, where the backdrop was this amazingly theatrical scenery – the small stream dividing the place in two, a stone bridge making the halves one whole place; the old cafés with yummy smells of coffee and freshly baked goods wafting from them; the narrow cobbled streets; and overlooking it all, the Alps. They seemed to be everywhere I turned, standing sentry to the busyness of life in this little corner of the world.

The moment I stepped onto the cobblestones of the square, my cell phone rang. It was Kirsten; her face appeared instantly.

"Hi!" I smiled and held the phone with both hands, tucking the documents under my armpit. "So good to speak to you! I'm so sorry, it's like the Bermuda Triangle here. Phones don't work

where I've been staying… and there was a huge storm last night."
A few people threw glances at me, hearing me speak English.

"Yeah, I was worried! It's like two in the morning here, but I'm up wondering how you're doing. So, how are you?" She was in her room – she lived with her parents – and in seeing that place, with the hanging lights behind her and the mountain of teddy bears on her bed, where we'd spent so much time hanging out, I was ambushed by homesickness. I stopped and sat down on a wooden bench, clutching the documents.

"I wish you could see all of this… wait," I said, and turned the camera around to give her a mini tour of where I was.

"Wow! It all looks so… old! Cool!"

I laughed. "I know!"

"So… Did you find your family? Did you see the house? Oh my God, show me everything!"

"Malva… my biological mother… I've found out that she passed away, sadly."

Her voice grew quieter. "Oh, honey…"

"Yeah. I know. Her sister – my aunt, I guess – is here, but she's… fierce… let's put it that way. As for the house, it's incredible! I'm going to be staying there. It turns out it's livable, not abandoned! And get this: there's a castle right across from me!"

Kirsten's eyes got huge. "A castle?"

"Yes! Very European, isn't it? The village is in the middle of nowhere! I'll send pictures as soon as I can."

"Is everything all old and beautiful? Is the food amazing?"

I laughed. "Pretty much everything is ancient, and I haven't had much chance to enjoy the food yet, but I did try some local liquor, and boy, it's good!"

"Liquor?"

"No, no, no, not that way. I was soaking after the storm, so this guy I met gave me a drink, I was staying at his—"

"*Callie?*"

"It's not like it sounds," I said, laughing.

"I'm sure there's a plausible explanation for drinking liquor with a guy you just met and staying over at his house," she said primly.

"It really wasn't like that." I rolled my eyes.

"Callie…" She tilted her head slightly.

"Yes?"

"You've changed."

"What do you mean? I've only been away two days!"

"There's something different about you. I don't know, I can't explain it."

I had to change the subject. I was already halfway between elated, because of everything exciting that was happening to me, and distraught because of Flora; I couldn't deal with more drama. "How are things with you?"

"You might've changed in like two days, but everything is just exactly the same here."

"I suppose so. Everything is so surreal for me at the moment. Anyway. I'm meeting the lawyer now to talk more about the house. Hopefully I'll understand the jargon in Italian. Have to go, you get some sleep."

"Okay. Speak soon, girl."

"Speak soon. Take care."

I touched the red button and the call ended. It was so good to talk to Kirsten, but the call had left a bittersweet taste in my mouth. She had to accept I wanted something better. A true friend would support me, even if she believed I wasn't doing the right thing. I supposed I had to give her time – everything had happened so fast.

Lost in thought, I began looking for Studio Tava. It sounded like some hip-hop recording place in downtown San Antonio, instead of a law firm somewhere in deepest Italy. The GPS on my phone guided me across the small stone bridge to the other side of the river. The water was white-green, pure melted ice, and ran furiously fast and foamy. Stone houses were built right on the water, and mossy steps ran from them to the shore. One of them hosted Studio Tava, as announced by a silvery plaque at the door. I rang the bell, and once again in the space of a week, I was soon sitting in a lawyer's office.

"*Ah, sì, la ragazza dal Texas,*" an older, larger-than-life man boomed at me. "My name is Corrado Tava. We got your email. It's a pleasure meeting the new owner of the Stella house."

"*Grazie,*" I said with a smile.

"You probably know that Anthony Baird" – his pronunciation of the name threatened to draw a smile out of me, then I remembered how funny my American accent probably sounded to him – "contacted me too, and asked to see all documents you were to sign. He gave his blessing. Did he tell you?"

"Well, I haven't read my emails since I arrived." Right at that moment, out of the corner of my eye, I saw a pretty, tiny Italian girl with a pixie cut looking at me from her desk. There was no mistaking the look in her eyes, though: it was vicious.

I wasn't having much luck with first impressions here.

"Why don't you do it now? Phones work in this particular spot. We are a bit behind here in Montevino!" He laughed. "Sofia, can you bring us a coffee? Coffee, yes?" he added toward me. Sofia, the girl with the scowl, stood with an expression that suggested she would have liked to slip poison in my cup. Maybe she was having a bad day?

"Thanks, I just had one," I said.

"*Oh, bene, bene,* so you'll have coffee then." Of course. Another Italian thing: you *cannot* refuse coffee. "I have someone in now, but I'll be with you as soon as I can. Is it okay to wait here for a little while?"

"No problem," I replied and took a seat in a small waiting room. The door between the waiting room and the office was open, so I was directly in Sofia's icy eye line. Great. I quickly checked my emails – yes, Mr. Baird had given me the all-clear with the documents he'd seen. Maybe I had some time to catch up with Elisa. I took the diary out of my cross-body bag and began to read again.

August 28, 1939

Caro *Diario*,

I've chosen to work at Leone's candy factory. At least it means I can stay home, instead of moving down the plains to the rice fields. I spend all day making candy, stuck in a room with other Montevino girls. Don't get me wrong, it's a good job. Well paid, and easy, and we get to take lots of candy home, to Pietro's joy. But I am meant to be a doctor, not a factory worker.

My first day of work, to add insult to injury, ended with Carlo Caporale waiting for me outside the factory. Word must have gone round that the haughty Stella girl who'd been accepted into university could not go, and he was jumping at the chance.

"Fancy a vermouth?" he asked in that way of his, like he is the king of the village.

"No, Carlo, thanks."

He jokingly laid a hand on his chest. "Aw, you break my heart."

"You'll pick up the pieces!" I said, laughing.

"Come on. Give me an hour of your precious time."

"It's not that I don't want to," I lied out of politeness. "It's that they're waiting for me at home."

"*Tomorrow?*"

"*'Bye.*" *I hurried away.*

"*What possessed you? Go with him!*" *The girls who'd come out from the factory with me were bewildered.*

"*You're welcome to him, girls,*" *I whispered, making sure he couldn't hear me. But the jolliness was a facade. I didn't want to show how gutted I was, spending my day making candies and chocolates and nougats when I wanted to be in university. Oh, this makes me sound so spoiled, when Mamma, Zia Costanza and Pietro break their backs on the farm, when Papa makes and repairs tools all day from his wheelchair, until he's so sore he can only lie down. This is a good job. Stop complaining, Elisa! And get on with it.*

I said my goodbyes and walked away, but one of the girls, Francesca, took me by the arm.

"*Be careful with Carlo,*" *she said. I shrugged and ignored her. What did she mean? Carlo was no harm. Just a boastful rich boy. I would be polite, of course – nobody deserves to be dismissed – but I would not give anyone the chance to say we were going out together. Even exchanging a vermouth and a chat with a man has a heavy meaning in Montevino, and I can't have that.*

After a week at the factory, I was so low I would just wake up with tears in my eyes. I was throwing my life away, I knew it. I did what most Montevino people do when they just don't know where to turn – I went to Don Giuseppe again. I begged him to ask the bishop for financial help, and he did, but nothing came of it. Any surplus funds would be to help the poor, not to send a woman to university.

It feels like the whole world is against me. Almost like it's not meant to be, because the obstacles are simply insurmountable. I should give up and move on, but I just can't. In spite of all my hard work in school, all my achievements, I will never be allowed to be anything more than an unqualified midwife like my mother – this sounds like I'm dismissing her, but it's not so! The work she does is incredible, but it would be even more incredible if she had knowledge of modern medicine, and more than herbs and poultices to work with. I would take everything she knows, everything she taught me, and take it further. I would do this for her, not just for me! And for my grandmother as well. For the women in our family.

I went to the High Woods to think and cry all my tears in private, and found refuge in the stone cabin that I'd used as a playhouse all throughout my childhood. It's the perfect place to think and be alone. There, I could let go of my strong facade, of the pretense I kept for my family so as not to upset them, and for my friends out of pride, and let myself go. I cried so much that I fell asleep there, among the chestnut trees, the woods enveloping me and giving me a little comfort.

When I woke up, Leo was there.

I hadn't seen him since the birthday party, since dancing together. Truth is, we haven't been seeing each other as often as we used to. Things are a bit awkward between us now. I can't explain…

Everything was easy when we were children. We spent almost every afternoon together; he'd come to my house and call me out with our signal. We thought it was a secret between us, but Mamma knew very well, always opening the door first and calling him in for milk and bread before we went out to play. We had this pact that we would marry one day, in a future so comfortably far away that it didn't worry me then. But now the future is here.

I awoke to the sound of him whispering my name. He kneeled beside me, and I could see at once that only propriety stopped him from taking me in his arms. I must have looked a tear-stained mess.

"I'm so sorry," he said, without me having to explain anything. "If I could help, I promise you, I would. Even if…" His voice trailed away. I knew he would have good reason to secretly rejoice if I stayed in Montevino.

"Thank you, Leo." Strange – I've known him since we were babies, and only now did I notice how long-lashed his eyes were.

"I know you're disappointed, but it'll get better, you know. When my father left and my mother almost seemed to give up on life, it seemed like everything was against me. There would be no way out. Just slaving away day in and day out, simply to survive…"

I stopped reading for a moment. The words on the page resounded with me to the point that my heart skipped a beat. I'd come so far, across the ocean, to read memories from people who lived decades ago and seemed to echo my own thoughts, and in this case, my memories.

I was ten years old and sitting on a plastic chair, my legs dancing. I was in a hurry to go home, but I was waiting for my parents; the people who'd brought me here had made it very clear I couldn't leave. In my hands I held my favorite Italian book, *Priscilla*, and on the chair beside me sat a brown teddy bear someone had given me the night before. I didn't want it. I wanted my own toys. I wanted home. Most of all, I wanted my mom and dad.

I'd been waiting for ages, when a short, plump woman came to sit beside me. She looked nice, but I really didn't want to talk to her.

"Honey, my name is Brenda," she said, and tried to hold my hand, but I held my little fist tight against my chest. Her kind expression didn't change. All these years later, I still remember the brilliant green of her blazer and the large hoop earrings that twinkled when her head moved. When she spoke, she sounded like she was whispering. "How are you, sweetheart?"

I eyed her. "I'm okay. Can I go home now?"

She looked at my anxious, swinging feet. "Well, we're looking for a nice, comfortable home for you as we speak. Are you hungry?"

I shook my head. "I want to go home to my mom and dad. Where are they?"

"Honey—"

"I'm not honey," I snapped. "My name is Callie."

"Callie. Sorry. Come into my office, okay? We're going to have a little chat and then guess what? We'll fix you milk and cookies from our special cupboard." She threw a glance to a tall, blonde woman who'd materialized at her side. The woman's eyes were shiny, but I didn't understand why.

"I don't want to go to your office. I don't like cookies."

"Honey…" Brenda began.

"I said my name is CALLIE!" I shouted and burst into tears.

That moment I knew I wouldn't ever be going home. My ten-year-old self understood that Mom and Dad were gone forever, even though I tried to deny it. Images of the smoke, the fear, the cries, a pair of strong arms lifting me up and taking me somewhere I could breathe again – they all told me the truth I didn't want to acknowledge.

Brenda wrapped her arms around me. I hid my face in her chest and sobbed. She whispered words into my ear that everything was going to be okay. Except, it was never going to be okay again.

Here I was now, eleven years later. And, yes, like Leo had said about his own situation... I'd survived. Probably not exactly thrived – but that was my fault, I supposed, with the chronic distrust of life I'd developed.

"...but then, I began living again. Even if I truly didn't believe that was possible."

I'd held my breath while he was speaking, because Leo rarely talked about himself, and I didn't want to break the spell.

He was right.

And he was wrong.

Because I will survive and move on, yes, but what I lost will always be there as the reminder of a broken dream.

"Thank you, Leo," I said gently. "Really."

"I have to be honest with you. It's good that I can see you more often again. Here at the cabin, or at your house. But if I could choose between this, and seeing you happy, I promise I would choose your happiness. I would choose for you to go to university."

That is Leo, generous to a fault. I didn't know what to say, because I felt he was trying to tell me more than he was actually saying... it was a way of asking me if we could see more of each other now; and I knew he didn't mean just as friends. "But, maybe, you can find other ways to be happy," he concluded.

I knew what he meant. I looked down at my hands, folded in the lap of my cotton dress. I could not reply.

What a day. The fireflies are dancing outside my bedroom windows, there are so many tonight! Everything is going so fast at the moment. Life charges on and I feel I'm half a step behind with just about everything.

Goodnight, Diario,

Yours, Elisa

The mention of the fireflies made my heart skip a beat: was she talking about Firefly House? I looked at the diary in wonder. I was sucked into Elisa's life like it was a novel. How were Elisa and I related? It was strange, to read these words written almost eighty years ago and yet find them so relatable even now. It was as if I'd just lifted the veil of time, and I could see the past unfolding before my eyes. So strange, and yet so simple.

She'd said that the Stella women were generations of healers. And I was a Stella woman too. A whole new life was forming in my brain, with new thoughts and new possibilities.

Elisa had been so sure of her life's purpose and unafraid to follow her path. Perhaps because she'd had someone like Leo in her life. I'd had guys asking me out, but had never said yes. Maybe I just hadn't given anyone a chance…

Sofia slammed a cup of coffee in front of me, interrupting my thoughts. "Tell your aunt to stay away from us," she hissed.

I looked up at her, gaping. *What…?* But I didn't have time to form any words, because Signor Tava called me into the office.

Still reeling from Sofia's words, I took the pen the lawyer offered and tried to concentrate as he ran me through proceedings in almost incomprehensibly fast Italian.

"Am I giving my soul away here?" I asked nervously, as I signed on one dotted line after the next.

"Italian bureaucracy," he said cheerily.

"Oh."

Once it was all done, I smiled through Signor Tava's hearty handshakes and warm welcomes to Montevino. With the deeds to Firefly House clutched tightly to my chest, a sudden, shocking revelation dawned on me. No wonder Flora was so hostile! I'd just told her Malva had left *me* our family home… I kicked myself for being so insensitive. She'd kept the place so well, year after year – while for some reason not living in it – and then I had arrived out of the blue to take it away.

I had to speak to her. I had to make sure she knew she was welcome at the house, that nothing would change. She was my aunt, we were family. I would explain that, and she would come round. I was sure of that.

Almost sure.

I'd taken a few steps along the ice-green stream, absorbed in my thoughts, when I bumped into a tall man, my head almost bouncing against his chest. "Sorry, I didn't—"

"Hey, Rissi," he said. It was Tommaso, in jeans, T-shirt, and with messy hair, clutching a folder just as I was.

I touched my chest. "Callie. My name is Callie." In seeing him I'd broken into a smile, but now I was a bit annoyed he couldn't remember my name.

He laughed. "I know. But you came with the storm. So that's what I'm going to call you. *Orissi* is storm in our Piedmontese language. Rissi."

I laughed. "I see, like in the cartoon you left for me! By the way, thanks for breakfast. And for rescuing me last night."

"You were a damsel in distress."

"I was in perfect and complete control of the situation, if you don't mind."

"Of course. You finished there?" He indicated the silver plaque of the lawyer's office behind us.

"Yes. All done. I am the proud owner of Firefly House," I said, my breezy tone turning more serious as the news sunk in.

"Congratulations! I am off to see those guys too. Long story. I have a bit of time, though. Coffee?"

More caffeine.

"Sure!"

"Leone's then. They do the *best* cake."

"You Italians are obsessed with food," I joked, following him along the cobblestones.

"I will not deny it, Rissi." Tommaso took my arm lightly and led me just off the square to a café that looked like something out of a travel magazine.

"Oh! *That's* Leone's!" I said, my nose up, looking at the elegantly painted sign.

"Yes! You've heard of it? I'm not surprised. They've been here forever. They make their own candies and chocolates, as well as having this café."

"Yes… yes, I've heard of it." I smiled to myself, remembering the mention of it in Elisa's diary.

The place was so stylish; from the glass cases that contained cakes and candy as beautiful as little sculptures, to the green velvet seats and the antique pictures on the walls. "*Established 1911*," a sign above the counter said. We chose our place on the velvet seats, and I wondered if Elisa had ever sat there.

"They have this cake here, it's called the Century Cake, see?" He showed me a chocolatey, hazelnutty thing with "1900" written in icing sugar on its creamy top. "It's a secret recipe. I'm serious, it has a trademark. Nobody knows how Leone makes it. Would you like to try it?"

"Yes, please!"

A young girl in a taupe apron brought us a slice of cake each and a cappuccino decorated with tiny chocolate musical notes. By the time I did go back to the States, I thought, I was going to be double my weight! But I didn't care. It was too good.

I took a mouthful. "Oh my gosh, Tommaso. This is amazing."

"It is."

"I won't fit in my clothes by the time I go home."

Tommaso shrugged. "Come to work with me on the castle grounds and you'll burn it all off," he said, smiling. "I do need a hand with some fences, actually."

"Sure. I'll get you some Sellotape," I retorted.

"I love your sense of humor. You make me happy," he blurted out, and then froze for a moment, as if what he'd said was too intense for the situation. His long, dark eyelashes fluttered against his pink cheeks.

"Yeah. Well, thanks. I… I met my aunt. Flora. She was at the house… this morning," I managed, changing the subject quickly.

"Ah… I can see from your face it wasn't the easiest of meetings."

"To say the least."

"Flora is like that. She's… thorny. A lot of people dislike her. But, well, in a way I understand her reason for being like she is."

"What reason would that be?"

"That she's unhappy. That's usually the main reason why people are horrible."

"True. Even the secretary there at Tava's… what was her name… Sofia, I think. Even she looked at me horribly when she realized I was Flora's niece."

"Oh, but she would have a good reason for that. You see, Sofia's dad, Marco, and Flora were an item. Word in the village is that Flora broke his heart badly. That would be Marco Leone, by the way. The owner of this place," he whispered.

"Maybe she had her reasons," I said defensively.

"Yes. But some break-ups are harder than others," he said, as a shadow of pain passed across his features, giving me the distinct impression that he might be talking about himself. I waited a moment to see if he wanted to elaborate, but he didn't.

"So, you have fences to repair but you're here hanging out with me?" I teased him.

"I came down to see Tava. Hopefully to sort out some stuff. Difficult stuff. I won't bore you with the details."

"Bore away. I'm sure you've had your fill of my family history!"

"Well, I'm trying to get my family business back. Vineyards mainly, but also some hazelnut trees. My father lost it all a few years ago, and... Well, I'm trying to make things right for him. We used to sell hazelnuts to Leone's, actually." He gazed out the window, before continuing, "My father... he was conned out of everything he owned. It was bad. Anyway. I don't even know why I'm telling you all this. Sorry."

"Don't be silly. A listening ear in exchange for cake? I'll do it any day. No, seriously, I'm here, if you need to vent."

"Thank you. It probably won't work... I will probably never get back what we used to own. But I need to try." He shook his head. "You know, I can't believe this."

"What?"

"A lot of people know about my family losing the business, what happened to my father, and all that, but I never talk about it. It's too raw. But then here I am discussing it with you. It's weird. Anyway. Enough about me."

"Well, I'll up the dysfunctional if you want. I lost my parents in a fire when I was ten. I grew up in care. Last week I found out I had been adopted and that a woman called Malva Stella from Italy was my birth mother. And here I am now."

"Wow! You win."

"Totally. Do you know where Flora lives? I need to go speak to her. Glutton for punishment, I suppose."

"Everyone knows where everyone lives here!" Tommaso laughed. "But you can find her now at the shop. I mean, she has a shop just off the square. It's called Passiflora, and she lives just above it. I'll show you."

Tommaso paid for the coffee and cake and led me outside and along a cobblestone road, where a neat line of nursery children were gazing through some shop windows, looking around and pointing things out to the adults who were trying to guide them along with bright yellow rope. Like a line of ducklings, I thought with a smile. The last child that passed was a boy of about three years old, wearing denim shorts and a dinosaur T-shirt. He had an adorable wonky walk, with his head turn sideways to look at Something Very Interesting in the road. He was precious. I looked over at Tommaso, who was staring at the little boy intently, almost hypnotized. Then he caught my eye and shook himself.

"Good luck," he said, and indicated a shop window surrounded by painted green wood, with a tin sign above that read:

Passiflora
Flora Stella, Naturopata

"And you... at the lawyer's. Shall we... regroup later?" I asked. I felt myself blushing. Like a teenager.

"I don't know. Things are crazy in my job, you know. Sorry, I have to go." And he practically ran off back down the street, leaving me bewildered and a little embarrassed.

I looked up at the sign above my aunt's shop: *Naturopata*. I'd never come across that word before, so I googled the translation: "Naturopath, a doctor specialized in holistic and natural therapies."

Hmm. That sounded interesting. I took a deep breath and opened the door. A soft chime resounded in the room, which was fragrant with the smell of herbs, flowers, and oils. I could detect lavender and daisies… oh, and rosemary as well.

I spotted Flora behind the counter, going over some papers, and was surprised when she looked up with a sort of resigned expression on her face – not exactly happy to see me, but not completely hostile like before. It was definitely an improvement.

"*Ciao*," I said tentatively. At that moment, she seemed to remember who she was, and who I was, and she frowned again. Color rose in her cheeks, and for a moment she looked so young and pretty. Her hair was down, and I noticed for the first time how long it was. Her clear eyes, as blue as mine, were made cat-like by eyeliner, and her nails were painted dark blue. Surrounded by herbs and potions and mysterious jars as she was, she seemed to me like a witch. But a good one.

She frowned. "What are you doing here?"

"I came to see you."

"Well, I told you. You need to go back home. I can't help you."

"Mmmm." I browsed the jars lining the shelves, plotting. "These are so pretty. And the smell in here is beautiful."

She huffed. "Thanks. They're not just pretty. They're useful. They're medicinal herbs."

"That one with the little flowers…"

"This one? Chamomile," she said, and handed me the jar.

"Oh. I've only ever seen it in teabags."

"I pick it fresh from the field near the graveyard."

"So, you *are* a witch," I whispered under my breath.

"What?"

"Nothing. Joking."

She shrugged. "The women in my family have always been healers of some sort. I'm a naturopath."

"In *our* family, you mean…" I said. I knew I was almost pleading. But I couldn't help myself. It was my family too. Flora didn't reply; instead, she armed herself with a cloth and began moving some tin boxes around and dusting the shelves they sat on.

I took a deep breath. *Let's start again.* "Did you call the shop Passiflora after your name?"

"Passiflora *is* my name. Flora for short."

"That's lovely," I said, and I meant it. How beautiful. "Malva and Passiflora. Both herbs, right?"

"Mmmm."

I paused, summoning the courage to take the plunge. "I went to Tava's today. I have the deeds to the house now. Everything is signed."

"Good."

I raised an eyebrow. "Good?"

"Yes. Well. It was our family home. I can't live there. Now you have it."

"But… Well, it's not exactly fair that I just sweep in, and take the house, and you—"

"It doesn't matter to me."

"But it must matter to you! You've kept it so well. It even smells nice. A bit like this place. You can come up whenever you want, and…" Words failed me. There was silence while I struggled to find a way to say what I meant. "I understand it's a lot to take in, with me turning up this way, but I had no idea I'd been adopted, and maybe if we could just sit down and chat—"

"Have they been good to you?" Flora interrupted without turning around.

"Who? The lawyers?"

"Your adoptive parents."

"Oh. Yes. Very."

"So… What do they think about you being here?" Still she wouldn't turn around. Now she was crouching in front of a low shelf, dusting. Her wavy mass of hair was shiny and so long it seemed to have a life of its own.

I said the line I'd repeated so much lately. "They died when I was ten."

Her arm stopped in mid-air. A moment of silence. "I'm sorry."

"Yeah."

"What happened to you after that?" Her voice was a little gentler now.

"I went to foster families. No horror stories, thankfully. It was okay. I live alone now, in my own place."

"I see." She began cleaning again, this time even more energetically.

I was at a loss. The words that were nestled in my heart – *why did you not look for me?* – were too raw, too difficult to drag out. This person was all that remained of my family, and at the same time, she was a stranger. The combination was disconcerting, to say the least. How much could I push? How far could I go?

"I'm sure you understand, Flora… I have quite a few questions."

"I can't answer them."

I snapped. "Why? None of this is my fault. I didn't ask to be abandoned, and adopted, and then to have my life turned upside down again. Why on earth are you being so horrible to me?"

"Because I'm simply not a nice person."

"That is such a cop-out!" I was exasperated and about to explode, when the bell chimed, and a customer came in.

"How can I help you?" Flora said brightly, though I could sense a brittleness in her voice.

Our conversation was over.

"We just wanted to leave these. Will you be there?" The woman, who was tiny and thin, was wearing a light shirt tucked into skinny jeans, and had a wad of brightly colored brochures in her hands.

"No," Flora simply said, without missing a beat.

Her tone was harsh, but the woman didn't seem bothered. She just ignored Flora, laid her brochures on the counter and turned toward me. She had jet-black hair and expressive dark eyes, her sunglasses acting like a headband. "You're the American girl, aren't you?" she said with a smile.

"I am, yes. I'm Callie." I smiled back.

Flora rolled her eyes. "Montevino grapevine," she grumbled, but the woman ignored her.

"My name is Paola. I'm from the Pro Loco," she said, and offered me her hand. "Do come tonight. It's the Montevino chocolate fair, see?" She showed me one of the brochures Flora had ignored.

Oooh. Chocolate. "Sounds right up my street!"

"Great! The whole village will be there. Well, nearly the whole village," she said, giving Flora a dark look.

"What's the Pro Loco?" I asked. The only word I could think about was *loco*, which meant crazy in Spanish.

"Pro Loco," Flora explained, "means gossips and meddlers." There was a mischievous light in her eyes. She was teasing Paola, who once again ignored her. I could tell that this dynamic between them went back a long time. They seemed to have familiarity with each other, and despite Flora's negative attitude, a sort of labored friendship.

"Pro Loco is like a citizens' association," Paola explained. "We organize events, make sure we keep traditions, plan all the village festivals and fairs and saints' days, you know."

"Food and church, to sum it up," Flora intervened.

"We just had the Day of the Dead," Paola said, undeterred. "You missed that."

"It must have been a riot," I said, trying to remain straight faced, and out of the corner of my eye I saw Flora hide a smile.

Paola continued, "Yes. But we have lots more. The chocolate fair is tonight, like I said, then we have a cheese and wine market in the summer, then it's mushrooms and game and berries in the autumn, then it's Christmas, then we have the salami festival."

"A salami festival?" I had to laugh.

"Oh, yes! These things have been held for centuries, you know. People used to slaughter the family pig, gather to make sausages and salami, and use up every little bit of the animal, then have a party. These things marked the agricultural year. Everybody enjoyed it; it was one of the few occasions to stop work and have fun."

"The pig was especially happy," Flora said dryly.

"She's a vegetarian," Paola explained.

"Vegan. Basically, around here, I'm a Martian," Flora added pointedly.

"And these traditions have been carried out for centuries?" I asked.

Paola tilted her head. "Well, maybe not for centuries, but for a few generations anyway. There's always Mass, a market, a lunch or a dinner with insane amounts of food, and music. We love a party in Montevino."

My fondness for this place grew even stronger. "I'll be there tonight for sure," I said. "And I can assure you I will not miss the cheese and wine market either... if I'm still here."

Paola nodded. "I heard you're up at the Stella house. Will you be staying here long?"

"To be completely honest, I don't know. I'm liking it here so far, though," I said, throwing a sideways glance toward Flora.

Paola grinned. "I'm glad to hear that. We always need helping hands, so if you want to help at the next event let us know. You'll get an apron and free food."

"Wow, an apron," Flora said sarcastically and met Paola's eyes. "You know I love you," she added and winked.

"Cranky old witch," Paola replied, somehow fondly. "See you tonight, then, in the community hall. Details are on the brochure. Bye, Flora. I just don't know why I bother trying to involve you."

"Because you love me too? By the way, I kept this for you. It's the last one of this batch. I have to make some more, so I thought you might want it," she said, and handed Paola a small dark bottle.

"Oh, thanks. You're still a cranky old witch, though."

"I know."

Paola smiled and left, with a last wave to me. I turned to Flora. "Was that a spell?"

"Almost. Arnica oil. She has a bad back."

"Ah... So, I won't see you tonight?"

"No way."

"You don't go to village things?"

"Over my dead body."

"I'll come and get you at eight then," I said, and stepped out without giving her time to reply.

Before I went back to Firefly House to do some more exploring, I had one last thing to do in the village. I wanted to apologize in person to the Aquila Nera ladies, and say hello to Nonna Tina. The place was empty – the lunch wave hadn't begun yet, then.

"*Buongiorno!*"

"Oh, here you are!" Adriana said. She was wearing her flowery apron once again and cleaning windows with newspaper. Nonna

Tina was sitting behind the counter, her homemade pasta laid out in the deli-style display.

"I'm so sorry I worried you last night."

"Not at all, you were with Tommaso, you were safe," Adriana said. That sounded nice.

"You'll have a coffee then," Nonna Tina offered. No, she didn't offer – she *told* me.

"Oh, no, thanks. I've had a few this morning."

"Sure, how do you take it?"

I could feel my heart racing overtime already, but armed with yet another espresso, Nonna Tina beckoned me through to the back. "Come, come, let's have a seat and a chat," she said. I followed her to a little courtyard, where a few tables sat, surrounded by potted geranium plants. From the enclosed courtyard, I could see a square of blue sky and a little corner of mountain. A sweet breeze was blowing, sweeping the courtyard; it smelled of pine trees.

"Drink, drink! It's good for you."

"Thank you." I stretched my mouth into a smile.

"You met Tommaso. Good girl." Nonna Tina had a vivacious, mischievous look in her eyes, like a little girl in an elderly lady's body. Her hands were wrinkled and weathered; hands used to work, I thought. "Tell me all. What took you here, so far away?"

"Long story." I'd said that quite a few times by now. "To sum it all up, Malva Stella was my mother."

"Malva? Oh… She was a lovely woman. So sweet, and yet… willful. I never knew she had a baby. But both your mother and Flora went to America for a while, suddenly, and nobody knew why. Your grandparents were sick and died not long after. When they came back, both Malva and Flora looked like they'd been through the mill… like the life had gone out of them. Flora was only a young girl, you know, sixteen or so."

"Really?"

"Oh, yes, I remember it well. Malva in particular was in bad shape, but then she'd always been sickly. She died soon after too, and Flora was left alone at such a young age." Just like me.

I bit my lip to contain the emotion I felt for these people I hardly knew.

"I'm so sorry, my dear. It's a sad story. But the women in your family are made of strong stuff. You know they pass on their second name, Stella? None of them take the name of their father. So, you would be Call-ee Stella." She pronounced it the Italian way. "Strange, isn't it? I don't know how their men accept it; they are so stubborn around here. Heads made of the same stone as the mountains!" she laughed. "But the Stella women have their way. They always do. Well, almost always. I don't think they had their way when they left you."

I looked down. "Do you know anything about… you know… the whole thing? My birth, my adoption?"

"No, I'm sorry. But something tells me Malva wouldn't have wanted to leave you. I am sure."

"But she did. And Flora could have looked for me."

I was overwhelmed, and it probably showed, because Nonna Tina placed her hand on mine for a moment. It was cool and fresh. I noticed a little bit of flour on one of her fingers. "There might be many reasons for her choice."

"Maybe. But I'd like to know what her choice actually *was*. And I don't understand why Flora is so… negative."

"Flora is like that with everyone. Something broke her, and nobody except her knows what it is. But she's only a part of your story. Because your story doesn't start and end with her." Nonna Tina's eyes looked so wise, so knowing. I was comforted, at least a bit. "Tommaso is such a nice boy, isn't he? I've known him since he came up to my knee! Also, my sister has an orchard up there on the hill, so she keeps an eye on him."

I smiled inwardly, thinking of the *nonna*-web that kept track of everything happening.

"We're distant cousins," Adriana called out. "Like most people in Montevino."

"Anyway. He just didn't have an easy life, you know," Nonna Tina continued. "Tommaso's father, Raffaele Carpentieri, died young. He was a brilliant man, but he had no common sense. Strange, because the men of his family have always been very grounded, you know, the salt of the earth. But Raffaele wanted more than his grandfather, and his great-grandfather, and anyone in Montevino way back ever had. He inherited the vineyards on the side of the hill, just down from the castle. He took on a solid, small business from his father and began expanding. But he went too fast and got into debt, and that's when Antonio Caporale came in."

Adriana made a snorting sound. I could tell this Caporale wasn't very popular... *Wait a minute, I'd heard that name before. Carlo Caporale was the name of guy who was after Elisa! Maybe the two men were related?*

"Signor Caporale pretended to be their best friend, their savior. He offered to have the vineyards put into his name for a while, so the banks couldn't seize them to pay off Raffaele's debts. Raffaele believed his offer of help was genuine. Or maybe he just wanted to believe, I don't know." She shrugged. "He certainly didn't have much choice. As I could have predicted, knowing Caporale, when the time came he refused to give the vineyards back. Raffaele lost everything, all but a handful of vines, and the stress of it all almost killed him. Almost. It was the drink that did it. One night, he got so drunk he drove off the road. They found him the next day."

"It was a huge shock for Tommaso," Adriana intervened. "He adored his father. They were so close."

"I'm so sorry," I said. I certainly knew how he must have felt.

"Tommaso took charge of what vines were left and does his best with them. There are just enough for one man to take care of. He barely makes any wine from them, so he rounds off by looking after the castle. He's actually a painter, did you know?"

"Oh, wow, no." But that explained the paintings on the walls, and the funny little cartoon he'd made for me.

"Even when he was small, he always had crayons with him, can you believe it?" Nonna Tina continued. "This toddler walking around with a drawing pad under his arm and crayons in his pocket, like a mini-painter!"

I laughed at the thought.

"Yes. You know what he did? His mum used to clean up at the castle. She took him with her while she worked. Well, he drew on the silk wallpaper in one of the sitting rooms. Wallpaper that was almost two centuries old!" She laughed.

I gasped. "Oh, no!"

"Oh, yes. Alice… his mamma… was mortified. He meant no harm, he said he wanted the wall to look nicer! It's still there. Visitors never notice that there's a little blue boat drawn in a corner…" She laughed some more.

"He's so talented. Self-taught," Adriana said. "He couldn't go to art school in Turin, of course. He wanted to take care of what was left of the vineyard. For his mother too."

All this information only made me like Tommaso more. "So generous," I responded. "That's what I call being there for your family."

"Oh, yes. He's certainly done that. He has his pick of the girls, you know? With his looks," Nonna Tina said. "More coffee?"

"Please, no. I mean, no, thanks." I said nothing about Tommaso's looks, but secretly agreed with Nonna. "So, he plays the field?" I asked with some apprehension.

She shook her head. "No, dear! Just the opposite. He's very shy."

"He was so nice to me. But then..."

Nonna Tina raised her eyebrows in a silent question.

"He grew cold suddenly. I was surprised."

"Tommaso was... well, he was badly burnt. He'll tell you himself, maybe."

There was an ache in my chest, half sad, half tender. I wanted to see him. I'd never felt such a strong desire to make someone better. I was left almost breathless.

Nonna Tina sat quietly, not looking at me, but I had a sense that she was aware of me, aware that something inside me had shifted.

"Are you coming to the chocolate fair?" I said finally, trying to change subject.

"Oh, yes! I never miss a chance to dance!" Nonna Tina said cheerily.

"I'll be there too. With my cranky husband who refuses to dance. You?" Adriana said.

"I will be coming, but..."

"But?" Nonna Tina said.

"I don't have anything to wear! I know, it sounds ridiculous. But I only have jeans and T-shirts, and a couple of casual skirts."

"It's not a dressy affair. Don't worry! Jeans and a T-shirt would... Oh" – she had caught sight of the disappointment on my face – "I see! You feel like dressing up a little!" She smiled.

"It's not very like me, but, yes." I laughed. "Usually, people have to force me into a dress!"

"That's easily sorted, dear. Look in the closets. In Firefly House, I mean. I think there are clothes there."

"Seriously? Whose clothes?" I wasn't sure that I liked the idea of wearing musty clothing from an ancient closet... and would they not be horrendously out of fashion? Would I end up looking, like, eighty years old?

"They belong to the Stella women. Flora's taken good care of them. Have a look, if you're not sure. And I can assure you, you won't look like an eighty-year-old."

What? How did she...? But I didn't have time to ask questions, because Nonna Tina spoke again.

"You know what you need, *cara*?"

Please, not another coffee. "What, Nonna?"

"Some fresh pasta."

Twist my arm, I thought.

She took me inside and busied herself at the counter. "There. Let me make you a parcel. Compliments of the house," she said, and wrapped some floury tagliatelle in brown paper. "Three minutes in boiling water. No more, or they'll *overcook*," she said, and made it sound like the apocalypse. "Oil and salt. Maybe parmesan. Nothing more. You'll thank me."

"I thank you already. *Grazie*, Nonna Tina," I said, and on impulse, I gave her a hug. "*Ciao*, Adriana!"

"*Ciao, tesoro!* Come back soon!" Adriana called, and I was touched. Yes, my own aunt was being less than agreeable, but I felt that Montevino was beginning to open its heart to me.

CHAPTER 6

When I stepped back into Firefly House, carrying my pasta parcel, I felt a shift around me. Something was different. I couldn't quite put my finger on it, but it was. Was it a scent in the air, the hue of the light, who knows? It was like my arrival had somehow changed the atmosphere.

I laid my precious parcel on the kitchen counter and silently made my way upstairs into the master bedroom. What Nonna Tina had said about clothes kept in the house had made me curious, so I headed up to the master bedroom and opened one of the heavy antique closets. It was empty. Maybe Flora had cleared everything away? I tried the chest of drawers, but I found only old, yellowed papers and bed linen, tidily folded and smelling of lavender.

There were still two bedrooms I hadn't explored yet; one was square, small and white. The other was housed in the tower, perfectly round and papered in powder pink. It was the smallest room, and the only one with a single bed. A semi-circular light-wood closet sat against the wall; I opened that too – and jumped out of my skin because a black-haired woman was looking at me from the side. And then I laughed at myself: the inside of the closet door had a mirror on it, so I'd jumped at my own reflection! Beyond the mirror was a rack of clothes, pressed together tightly to make room for all of them. It seemed Nonna Tina was right. Which Stella woman had these belonged to? Maybe... Malva? Could these be my mom's dresses?

Underneath the clothes was a box marked with the initials 'PC'. Not recognizing them, I turned my attention back to the rails. Each article of clothing was encased in plastic to preserve it from dust and mold. I took out one that was clearly vintage: sleeveless, made of cream-colored silk, complete with a long, flowing skirt. It was beautiful, very *Downton Abbey*, and completely not my style; but something compelled me to try it on. I ran my hand down the lovely, soft fabric, and held it up in front of me. The dress reached my ankles. A little thrill ran through me – was I not supposed to dislike dressing up? And dresses in general? But this felt different.

I took off my clothes and sneakers and slipped it on. It fitted me perfectly, except for being a little tight round the shoulders and hips. Whoever had owned this dress must have been slightly smaller than me, but it was definitely my size. I twirled before the mirror, like a little girl trying on a fancy dress – still in socks. I took off the socks, too, and wearing that dress in bare feet, in that old house full of memories, was so surreal. I felt I'd jumped back through time.

I hoped Flora wouldn't mind me wearing it this evening. I would wear it just this once... She couldn't be mad about this one time, surely? I just couldn't bring myself to take it off.

Looking deeper into the closet, I noticed there were a few pairs of shoes as well. I raced to try them on, but sadly none of them fitted me, so I resigned myself to wear my own black flats. I would most certainly be overdressed, but I didn't care. I'd probably already been labelled as the crazy American girl.

There was still a little bit to wait before evening fell, so I got changed back into my own clothes, laid the lovely cream dress on the bed, ready to slip on tonight, and headed downstairs to the living room. The couches looked soft and comfy; the fireplace was crying out to be brought to life. I ran outside and picked up some wood and kindling from Tommaso's shed, then kneeled in front of the fireplace. No problem at all. I would have the fire going in no time.

Forty minutes later, I was sweating, I had soot on my hands and, I was pretty sure, on my face, and some little baby flames were beginning to get going. Who would have thought that lighting a fire took so much skill?

"Well, fire: zero - Callie: one!" I said aloud. I washed my ash-stained hands, fetched the diary and settled down to read.

September 2, 1939

Caro *Diario,*

Something incredible has happened!

This morning Pietro came to Leone's, to tell me that the Conte wanted to see me urgently. I didn't tell anyone; I knew it was wiser to keep it to myself.

It could be that he was to send me on errands, like he sometimes did, but the formality and secrecy of having Pietro collect me made me wonder if there was something more.

I changed into my Sunday dress, brushed my hair carefully, curled it at the ends, and wore the ruby-red earrings. Inside the castle, almost shaking, I felt so out of place among all those precious things. The Conte sat in his study, a grand room with silk wallpaper and velvet-covered chairs. I remembered standing there at Christmas and on Patron Saint's Day when I was a child: he would give us a small parcel with oranges and a little chocolate. We hardly

*ever eat oranges, since they are exotic and expensive, but
chocolate! That's always a feast.*

*The Conte is good to us, in his own brusque way. He
saved our family from falling apart after Papa's accident.
When Papa eventually pulled through after weeks of hover-
ing between life and death, the immense relief that he was
alive overshadowed the shock that he could no longer feel
his legs. But without Father to work the farm, and my
brother still a child, we were destitute. We sold the house
to pay for the hospital; we lost everything.*

*The Conte offered to help, but Mamma refused at
first. Although she never said so openly, I'm sure it wasn't
just pride keeping her from accepting; it was contempt.
She always had a strange attitude toward him, but Zia
Costanza pressed her, reminding her that if we didn't accept
his help, I would have to go into service, and my brother
would most likely have to emigrate like many other men did.*

*Mamma was silent the day we moved into the Casa
delle Lucciole –*

Firefly House! So that was how such a poor family ended up in
this house. I couldn't believe I was in the same place Elisa had
lived in, that I walked the same rooms she had walked…

*– so different from the humble homes in the village. Now
she looks after this place as if her life depends on it. Pietro
has left school at eleven, like most children do around here,
and he helps her. The Conte often said to Mamma to leave
the small farm attached to the house, to let the laborers do
the work and just look after her home and family. But she
won't hear of it. She never charges the people she helps as
a midwife either, though they give her something anyway*

— eggs, apples, chestnuts, even a chicken or a rabbit, some-times. Mamma does her work on the fields and orchards surrounding the house to help support us and to repay the Conte for his generosity. This way she feels she's paying rent, and we're free, or freer, of obligation.

But why has the Conte done all this for us, and why did Mamma accept it with such reluctance? Tongues wag, and a possible reason has come to my ears, but I don't know if it's true, and I can't ask Mamma. They say that my grandmother, Mamma's mother, was more than just a nurse to the Conte's wife, sick with tuberculosis; she was also the Conte's lover, forever hidden and forbidden, even after the poor Contessa died, because the difference in class and status was too enormous to be overcome. Their love remained a secret and was never given the seal of marriage. Or so they say. Mamma, born not long after the Contessa died, has never uttered a word about it. It's a family secret, and quite a sensational one. Imagine! If it's true, I am the young Contessa! But I never think about that. I have other plans.

"Elisa. Please, sit down," the Conte said as I entered. I wasn't used to being addressed so respectfully by him; the last time we'd spoken properly, I'd been a child. Not that long ago, I suppose. Now he spoke to me like he was speaking to a signorina.

"I'm told you want to go to Turin. To university."

I gasped and searched for an answer, my mind suddenly blank. "Yes," I managed.

"Your grandmother would have liked to have been a doctor. She told me. And she could certainly give Dottor Quirico a run for his money."

I said nothing. What was the point in complaining that I couldn't go?

He chuckled softly. "When you were little, you used to be chatty, you know? Now it's like talking to that," he said, indicating a small marble statue in the corner.

"I'm sorry. I'm just surprised. Anyway, yes, I wanted to go to university, but my plans have changed now." I was desperate to say: "Will you help? I'll pay you everything back as soon as I can work!" But I couldn't betray Mamma's trust.

"Yes, I was informed of that." He turned away from me for a moment, and when he turned back he had an envelope in his hands. "This is for you," he said, and handed it to me. Inside the envelope was more money than I'd ever seen in my life. I felt the blood rise to my cheeks. I was sure I looked scarlet. As though this was a matter no more important than his daily market list, he continued, "You will receive one of these a year until you graduate."

"Thank you, but I can't accept it." I immediately returned the envelope… but oh, how desperately I wanted to take it!

"Fine. Just give up on the whole thing, then. I suppose pride is worth a lifetime of frustration, isn't it? I should know."

What had he given up out of pride?

My mind was a battlefield. I knew I had to refuse, but I was desperate not to. Imagine… university. Days and weeks and months where all I had to do was learn. And one day, they would call me Dottor.

"Take it, girl. To refuse it would be foolish." Then he leaned a little closer, almost whispering the last words. "Your mother will understand."

I didn't think on it again. I took it, stammering, "I don't know how to thank you."

The Conte shrugged. "Cure me when I get sick." He smiled. I wanted to smile back, but I was too overwhelmed.

"But… who told you?" I could only say.

"Does it matter?"

"It does to me."

His face changed then, becoming a little harder, sadder. "I can't tell you, I'm sorry."

"Another secret," I said, and for a moment I was quite shocked at my boldness.

"What do you mean, another secret?"

When I replied, my voice was so low it was almost imperceptible. "I believe there is a big secret in our family." I couldn't hold back my thoughts anymore.

"Elisa. I can only say I did my best to keep everyone happy. It didn't always work."

I lowered my head. "I'm grateful for all you did for us. And for what you're doing now."

The Conte smiled a smile full of sadness. "Vittoria couldn't give me any children," he said. Vittoria was his wife, the Contessa, who'd lived a short, painful life riddled with tuberculosis. "Now when I die, all of this will go to a distant cousin, who has nothing to do with this place." He seemed bitter. "I'd like it to be different, but tradition and expectation are our rulers, not our hearts' desires." Then his eyes grew darker, warmer. "Please know that your mother, your aunt, your father, you and your brother; you're all the family I have."

That was as far as he would go. I knew he wouldn't say anything more.

"Thank you," I said simply.

"Yes. Now go and make me proud."

I woke up to find that the light had changed, having darkened as the day went on. And then it came back to me… the dream I'd been having.

In my dream, I stood on the terrace, just as I'd done on the night I'd arrived, but instead of watching the lightning, I saw a summer garden at night, everything lush and in bloom, the scent of flowers and greenery drenching the air. Little lights flew all around in the darkness – fireflies, like a mini-galaxy in my garden. It'd been such a magical dream, it took me a moment to swim back to the surface, back to reality.

I rubbed my eyes. The fire was now just embers, glowing softly in the gloom. I laid my feet on the floor and sat up, peering at my watch. I'd slept for hours! It was time to go out. I was starving, and the idea of chocolate was a siren call.

I put on the dress, almost reverently – though my reverence had to give way to some jumping and contorting of my body when I had to do the zip up by myself. Then I took some make-up from my bag; just some simple, barely-there make-up. I felt that very little would look better with a dress that was a statement in itself.

As I looked at myself in the mirror, a sudden thought made its way into my mind: Kirsten was right, I had changed. I could see it in my eyes – it was almost imperceptible, and it would be impossible to notice for someone who didn't know me well.

I made my way out through the evening scents of the garden, two questions fighting for my attention: whether Flora would agree to come with me, and whether Tommaso would be there.

CHAPTER 7

The night was chilly, and I shivered as I stood in front of Passiflora in my borrowed summer dress. I should have worn my jacket, but it just wouldn't have looked right – and now I was paying for my vanity by having goosebumps all over. I was already halfway to regretting my decision to try to coax Flora out. I'd chosen to be a little pushy and direct, not accepting "no" for an answer, just as Paola had done.

I knocked. "Flora! Are you there?"

A voice came from behind the upstairs window, and her face appeared for a moment. "No!"

I had to giggle.

"I'm here to take you to the fair, Flora. Come on, get dressed."

"Flora? Why are you not calling me Auntie?" she called.

I could hear a slur in her voice. *Was she drunk?*

"Can I come in? I'll make you some strong coffee."

"Leave me alone," she said petulantly. "I don't need you to take care of me. I don't need Marco. I don't need anyone. I do perfectly well on my own!"

"It doesn't look like it to me, Flora."

"Sure. Nice of you to come here and judge me. You're wearing the right dress to do that!"

I sighed. "What do you mean?"

"That's Malva's dress. Your mother's. My sister's. And judging me was her favorite hobby."

"I'm not judging you! And how dare you talk like that about Malva." I'd never met Malva but protecting her felt like an instinct. I couldn't bear for anyone to speak about her like that, especially someone who should have preserved her memory.

"Go. Away."

"Look, Flora, let me come in. We'll have coffee and a chat and then I'll leave you alone, okay?"

"I've managed up until now without you. Or anyone." Her voice was getting louder.

"Nobody has to manage alone," I found myself saying, and wondered who I was talking about exactly – me, or her?

"I said go away. You are nothing to me."

I groaned, "Fine!" and left that sad, angry house and the sad, angry woman inside it.

*

My hands were shaking on the steering wheel as I drove, guided by the GPS, towards the community center. I was furious. And desperately worried for this aunt I'd just discovered I had. Did she not care at all that I was here? Did it really mean nothing to her to have a long-lost niece? It was as though she'd pushed me so far out of her memory that I had never existed. But then why would she care? I was just some stranger who had turned up on her doorstep, claiming to be her niece and to own the family house. Yes, I had the deeds, but surprisingly, she'd never asked to see them.

No, I realized, she'd taken one look at me, heard my name, and accepted it. I was sure that when she'd seen me, she'd recognized me.

Flora seemed so alone and lost. There was something desperately vulnerable about her. What had damaged her so much? The loss of our family? Something else?

Before me, the community center was all lit up, with bright rectangular windows and a lilac sky behind it. Soaring above were the ever-present mountains. A lively song was seeping out of the building, and from the windows I could see the silhouettes of people dancing. The party had spilled outside, as you would imagine on such a beautiful spring night, and there were clusters of people of all ages everywhere, chatting, sipping wine and holding small plates with chocolate morsels on them. Children chased each other and ran around the small playground next door. There seemed to be fairy lights everywhere, inside and outside.

I made my way to the entrance, and was enveloped, instantly, in warmth, music, and wonderful smells. I looked around. There was an area where small stands were covered in goodies, all variations on the theme of chocolate; the bigger table display, complete with shelves and a whole stand, was Leone's. The multicolored candies made me think of Elisa's diary... There were also a few Century Cakes under glass domes, sold by the slice, all lined up like sweet full moons.

A small band was playing in one corner, with an accordion player standing there as if his instrument weighed nothing. Some older people were dancing, and children were jumping around on the dance floor. Nonna Tina was there, dancing with an elderly gentleman, and Adriana, twirling away with a girl who looked like her daughter; clearly, she hadn't managed to convince her husband to brave the dance floor. I waved, and they waved back. There was a family feeling here – everybody seemed connected to one other, like the whole village was a family in itself. I gazed around for a moment, just to take it all in – I wasn't looking for Tommaso, of course not.

A black-haired woman came to greet me with a smile – Paola, my aunt's friend. "Hello! I'm so glad you're here." She took my arm gently and gazed at me. "*Bellissima!*"

"You make us look so frumpy, though!" another woman chimed. She was holding a tray with chocolate truffles. "Want one?"

"This is Michela, my sister," Paola said. Michela didn't look like Paola at all. She was wiry as Paola was soft, with bleached hair and way too much make-up.

"*Piacere. Oh, sì grazie!*" I took a truffle then looked over my outfit. "I know, this dress is a bit over the top!"

"It's nice to dress up once in a while," Michela said, but I detected a steely look in her eyes, that peculiar woman's look when she sees someone she vaguely compares herself too, unfavorably.

"I suppose so."

"Come, I'll show you around," Paola said. One hand gestured to the stalls set up around the room. "These are all local businesses. You see, there are lots of hazelnut woods around here, so we make this" – she stopped for a moment to grab a truffle from the tray – "special chocolate. It's called *gianduja* and it has hazelnut paste in it. Try it."

I didn't have to be told twice. Popping the *gianduja* into my mouth, I was instantly blown away by how creamy, dense, and mouth-watering it was. "Oh my gosh. This is heavenly!"

"Yeah, I know," she said proudly. "Chocolate and wine are our specialties, though we produce a lot more good stuff. We even have a University of Taste, you know? People from all over the world come to attend it."

"Sounds amazing."

"Come, I'll show you my brother's company. Here."

We reached a table covered in a lovely tablecloth, with baskets and small plates full of artisan chocolates in every flavor and shape I could imagine, all beautifully packaged in ribbon and lace. I had to take a picture of that for Kirsten.

"And this is my brother, Alberto." A man who looked like the male version of Paola stood behind the table. "Alberto, this is Callie."

He extended a hand. "Nice to meet you. You're the American girl! Word travels fast."

I smiled. "Born and bred. But my birth mother was from here. I was adopted as a baby."

"Oh… who was your mum?" Paola asked.

"Malva Stella."

"Oh, yes. She was my mamma's friend. I'm so sorry… she died too soon. It was so sad."

"Thanks. Well, I never met her, and I only found out I was adopted a few days ago. It seems incredible to think, but it's true."

"That must have been a shock," Paola said. "Oh, and now you're here all alone!"

I shrugged. "Kind of used to it."

"No, wait," she said, holding up a finger. "You're not alone. Malva was Flora's older sister, wasn't sh— Oh."

"Yeah. We're working on that." I would not start complaining about Flora to a total stranger. Okay, technically, Flora was almost a total stranger too, but still.

"Actually, believe it or not, Flora has a very sweet streak. She just… Well, she has demons."

I remembered the conversation with her earlier and nodded. "That she does. Anyway, I love this place. Alone or not, I'm having a great vacation, if you can call it that."

"I'm so glad! So that's why you never visited before? Because you didn't know—"

Before I could reply, Michela leaned in to whisper something to Paola. Paola nodded, and allowed Michela to lead her away to another table.

"Sorry, Callie! Work to do! Later," she called over her shoulder.

I liked Paola, but I was grateful not to continue that conversation. Alberto, who'd been quiet throughout our chat, gazed over the table he was manning. "You want to try something?"

"Oh, yes, why not?" I said, looking for my wallet, but Alberto put a hand on mine and stopped me.

"On me," he said. "Choose whatever you like."

"Are you sure?"

He smiled, patting my arm. "Of course! It's a pleasure."

"Thank you!" I swept my gaze over the selection. "Wow. There's so much! I couldn't possibly choose!"

"A bit of everything, then," he said, and handed me a few small organza pouches, elegantly sealed with a ribbon and tiny flowers, full of chocolates.

"Oh, my goodness! This will certainly keep me going for a while!"

"When you try one, you'll realize they won't last a while." He laughed. "Anyway, it seems you like it here."

"Oh, yes. It's beautiful and so different to what I'm used to."

"Where are you from, exactly?"

"Texas."

"Cowboy hats?" he said with a smile.

"Of course! We all wear cowboy hats and line dance all day!" I rolled my eyes.

"Just like we eat pizza and sing opera all day over here!" he said, laughing. "Well, maybe I could show you around a little?"

"Sure, why not?" I said, and caught sight of Paola, who was busy at the next table, throwing furtive glances in our direction and smiling. Well, obviously she was smiling because we were at a party and all that – but it seemed to me that her expression was somehow linked to me and Alberto chatting. Was she hoping to set her brother up?

I didn't want to give him or Paola the wrong impression, so I turned to him quickly and said, "Well, actually, I'll have a look around by myself. You take care of your stand! I'll speak to you again later – and thanks for the chocolates."

He stammered a protest, but I didn't reply. Instead, I made my escape as diplomatically as possible, choosing to go to another stand a few tables down.

I was at a different table trying some incredible chocolate cream cakes, when I spotted Tommaso on the other side of the room.

My heart smiled. And then I hastened to hide my delight – also, I probably had cream on my face!

When he saw me, he raised a hand and gave me a shy smile. He didn't come any closer, though. I remember how cold he'd suddenly been, earlier, and hesitated for a moment; but it was him who came to me. His mood seemed to have shifted again, thankfully.

"Rissi." The nickname he'd found for me made me smile. "You look beautiful." *Bellissima* was the word he'd used, and for some reason it melted me. It sounded different to the way that Paola had said it. Maybe because Paola wasn't a gorgeous six foot something black-haired man with the longest eyelashes…

"Hey. Thank you. But it's not me, really. It's this dress." I gave a little curtsy. "I found it in a closet at Firefly House. There's lots of stuff that belonged to Malva and her – my – family. It looks almost untouched. Can you believe it?" I was rambling.

"I beg to differ," he said, and then he mumbled something else, something I couldn't really make out.

"Sorry?"

"I said, I think it *is* you," he mumbled a bit more clearly, looking somewhere over my shoulder, out of the window, at his feet. One thing was sure: he was shy, just like Nonna Tina had said. And he wasn't the only one… I was sure I was turning the color of a strawberry.

"Oh. Well. Thanks. How did it go? The lawyer's?"

He shrugged. "No joy. Some key documents were destroyed, nothing we can do… surprise, surprise… I'm back to square one."

"I'm so sorry."

"Mmmm. Don't worry. I'll be fine. You like *cioccolata*?"

"I could live on it. Do you?"

"Only dark and bitter."

"Like you," I joked, and he hesitated for a moment, making me worry he'd taken what I'd said seriously, when I was just messing with him. But thankfully, he had a good sense of humor, as he'd proved already before.

"Exactly." He laughed. "Also, I never say no to a glass of wine and a little music."

I smiled. "Seconded." He seemed to have thawed again. I wondered what had caused him being so offhand with me earlier. Probably just a moment.

"Was Alberto flirting with you?" Tommaso asked suddenly.

I shook my head. "Not really. He just offered to show me around. I bet he does that to all the tourists!"

"Mmmm, well," he said, and I followed his gaze across the room to the Alberto guy. He was still looking at me. He waved to Tommaso, and Tommaso waved back without much conviction; he leaned in and murmured, "Want to dance?"

I raised an eyebrow. "The whole village will see us and talk about it."

"Well, let's give them something to talk about!"

Without waiting for me to respond, he took me by the waist. The touch of his fingers on my hips made me tingle. I was ready for him to step closer to me, to inhale his scent – smoky wood, I thought. His arms circled me and mine instinctively went around his neck. The music swirled about us, and then we began to move. He might have been a shy man in everyday life, but he wasn't a shy dancer. I let myself get carried away by the swell of the song and the heady lure of this moment with Tommaso. I allowed myself be led by him, to respond to what moves he was making.

I let all my tension go and dissolved into him. For a moment, my worries dissolved too, and nothing else seemed to matter except the two of us, there together on the dance floor.

I became one with Tommaso, with the music, and even if my head was spinning, it didn't matter. His arms were strong, and he would catch me if I fell. His body was very warm, so much so that I forgot how chilly the night was, and how light my silk dress. He heated me up, and his fingers pressed gently on the bare skin of my arm, where there was no barrier to be found in the silk of the dress.

He was shy, yet so secure in himself, somehow. Our eyes locked and we didn't look away for the rest of the dance. His gaze wasn't shy anymore, but determined, yet soft. Weird. It was like those mossy green eyes were saying to me, "Trust me…"

Suddenly, everything stopped. Someone was calling my name.

"Callie! Here I am. I came, see? You happy now?" It was Flora. She stood near us, close to the dance floor. She wore what looked like sweatpants and a T-shirt that had seen better days. Her hair was tousled and her eyes unfocused. She was staring at us, swaying from side to side with the music, and almost everyone was staring at her.

"That dress!" she crowed, looking me up and down. "You look just like your mother." She almost spat out that last word, and it made me shiver. It was like she'd hated Malva, and now she hated me.

"Here we go. Drunk again," I heard somebody whisper, a young woman with a mocking look in her eyes. It was Sofia, Marco's daughter and the nasty secretary from Studio Tava. I threw her a desperate glance, embarrassed by Flora but also upset by how vicious this young woman's words were.

I decided my best bet was to humor Flora. "I'm happy now that you're here, yes." Then I held out my hand. "But it's probably better if we go home now, okay?" I was surprised at my own meekness. At that moment, a tall man in a checkered shirt crossed the room toward her.

"It's okay. I'll help her," he said.

"Dad, come away," Sofia hissed.

"No!" Flora swiped at the air. "Marco, go away." *So that was Marco Leone!* Flora's words were slurring badly now. "Don't look at me. Go away!" she repeated. The place was almost silent now. Even the band had stopped playing.

"Come, Flora. Come." I took her gently by the arm and Tommaso wrapped an arm around her shoulders. I was grateful that he was there.

"I'll drive you," he said, once we were out in the cold air. Paola and Michela tried to reach me, but I practically ran out, thinking only about getting Flora back to her house.

Reaching his car – a battered Jeep – I climbed into the passenger seat, while Flora was slumped over in the back. "You can get your car tomorrow, Rissi, or I'll get it for you," Tommaso said.

I nodded. "Thanks."

"Aw!" A muffled cry had come from the back seat – Flora had slipped down.

"Wait. I'll go in the back," I said, hurriedly switching seats. When Flora saw me, I reached out to her, lifting her up. She didn't protest. Instead, she rested her head on my shoulder, like a child. Even if the smell of spirits seeped off her, her hair still smelled sweet and herby, and she fell asleep almost immediately.

Now that I saw her so vulnerable, I realized she was younger than I'd originally thought. Never mind aunt and niece; we could almost have been sisters.

"What's wrong with her? Why is she suffering so much?" I said, thinking aloud. "Don't take this the wrong way, but are Italian women always so dramatic?"

"Italian women *and* men are more dramatic than most, yes. But Flora... well, you guessed. She is suffering."

"But why?"

"All I know is what I've heard through the grapevine," Tommaso replied. "Let's just worry about getting her home."

"What happened with Marco?" I whispered.

"I've known Marco a long time, but he never really elaborated much on the whole thing."

Flora curled up closer to me. "Callie," she said softly.

"Yes. I'm here," I said.

Thankfully, Flora's house was unlocked. Tommaso carried her upstairs, and, after some maneuvering through the flat to find a bedroom, we managed to put her to bed. This must've been her bedroom, with an unmade bed with clothes and tissues strewn across the floor. While she managed to keep Firefly House spotless, that clean streak didn't transfer well to her own home, it seemed.

I took her shoes off and tucked her in. There, up close, I studied her, feeling a rush of emotions: slightly foolish for being here, given the way she'd treated me, and at the same time comforted by the fact that whatever the circumstances, here I was, looking at the only living member of my family.

I found Tommaso in the living room, where he was waiting for me, his arms crossed, studying some botanic prints that were on the walls. Unlike Flora's bedroom, this room was clean, except for some empty bottles on the coffee table. Mysterious jars full of dried herbs were everywhere. The air was laden with the same lovely scents as were in Flora's shop: vanilla and lavender and cinnamon, and others that I couldn't place. Candles crowded the room too – some of them burning. I went to blow them out, worrying that Flora would come in here later, accidently tip one over, and the place would go up in flames.

I began to close the curtains against the darkness outside, and Tommaso switched on a table lamp. "I'm sorry we spoiled your night, Leo... I mean, Tommaso! *Tommaso!* *What the hell?*

"Don't be silly. It's no problem." Thankfully he hadn't heard me calling him Leo. We were whispering, so as not to wake Flora.

"Do you think... do you think Flora is an... *alcoholic?*" I said it in English because I didn't know the Italian word. "Do you understand what I'm trying to say?"

He nodded. "Yes. My answer is: I don't know. I've never seen her like this. But then again, there's something wrong, for sure. Sometimes she doesn't even open the shop."

"Really?" I was shocked. I'd had just one visit there and I could see the love and care she put into it. I remembered its shelves, full and clean, the lovely scents, and the overall polished look of the place. It didn't seem neglected at all.

"Yeah. She's struggling to pay the rent. Michela told me, you know, she owns this place. She lives up the hill, not far from us."

"Is Flora not getting enough customers? I saw a lot of orders in brown bags with names on them, ready to go, when I was there."

"I don't think the number of customers is the problem. Passiflora is quite renowned in the area. People come from other villages as well, even from Turin. It's that she keeps it closed a lot, so she doesn't get as much business as she should."

"I see. Which makes me think..."

"That she's home drunk? Maybe. But let's not jump to conclusions."

"I suppose you're right."

"It's hard being on your own with no family... Oh, sorry," he said. "I didn't mean to..."

"It's okay. Well, Flora *has* got family. I'll help her."

"Do you believe in fate?" he said, surprising me. I was suddenly aware of the faint sound of music coming from the chocolate fair.

"What do you mean?"

"Well… I'm not sure exactly how much you know, but my life took a few twists and turns. And sometimes I ask myself… Were certain people meant to leave my life so I could find others?"

I wondered who he was thinking about at that moment – his father?

"Life is pretty crazy in general," I replied. "My parents was swept away by a faulty plug, for one. I've thought a million times: 'What if…?' What if my parents had decided to get the wiring checked at some point and fixed the problem? What if we hadn't had too many electrical wires plugged in? What if my mom hadn't used her hairdryer? Or the microwave? Or the fan, or whatever it was that started the fire? *What if? What if? What if?*" I took a breath. "Maybe they'd still be alive. Maybe I wouldn't be here now. Or maybe all of this would've happened anyway… I think I want to believe that all the twists and turns take us to where we need to be."

"If that is true, you were always meant to be here. You were always meant to come find your family and look after them."

I thought of Flora, asleep in the next room. "Maybe, yes."

Tommaso barely knew me, and yet he seemed to have summed up what was on my mind, and then put it so delicately. He'd been tiptoeing into my life instead of storming into it, even though he'd literally appeared during a storm.

Then the spell was broken. "Let's go, Rissi," he said, moving toward the front door. "Flora needs a good night's sleep."

"And a vat of strong coffee in the morning."

"That too."

I checked on Flora one last time – she was sleeping soundly. I switched off the light and walked out into the night.

*

We were parked in front of Firefly House, the garden sweeping and whispering all around us. We'd spoken little on the ride there, but when we arrived, we took our time saying good night. "Thank you for the dance earlier," I said.

"I'm only sad it didn't last a little longer. You know... it takes a lot for me to trust. And I'm trying not to trust you."

I didn't need to ask why. I felt the same. "Maybe you can try to let go a little, instead?" I whispered, and once again, I realized I was talking to myself, as well as to him. Maybe I could let go a little too.

In the next moment, Tommaso reached across the seats, taking me in his arms again, like when we were dancing. I didn't resist. Instead, I let him lay a hand on the back of my neck and kiss me on the forehead. It was a small ritual that meant so much, a message passed through the lips that needed no words: I am here for you.

He murmured, "Good night, Rissi."

*

Inside Firefly House the master bedroom suddenly seemed vast, and the bed cold and empty. I took some sheets and blankets out of the chest of drawers and made up the bed in the round pink bedroom instead. I lit some simple white candles I'd found in the kitchen – making a mental note to buy some more down in the village – and took the silk dress off. I still couldn't believe I'd worn Malva's dress. Looking at it, feeling it, wearing it had been bittersweet. If only she could have been here.

"I'll look after Flora for you," I whispered to the dress, as though Malva's spirit were inside it.

After a short search in the closet of wonders, I found a pretty aqua nightie, short and lacy, scented with lavender from the little fragrant bags scattered in the drawers. My mother seemed to have been so feminine in her taste. In the perfect silence, I snuggled under the covers and began to read the diary from the point where I'd drifted off that afternoon. Once again, Elisa's story carried me away.

When I told my parents about the Conte's offer, there was deadly silence. I know Mamma so well, and yet, this time, I couldn't read her. Papa simply looked at her. He was usually the one to have the last word on all matters of the family; but this time, I could feel that the final decision was deferred to her.

Except, I was determined that the decision had already been made; that the decision was mine, and nobody else's.

I was ready for my very first battle with my parents, a battle that I knew I'd won already, because I was going to go, whether they wanted it or not. Mamma gazed into my father's eyes for a moment and unspoken words passed between them. Then, she looked straight at me.

"Costanza and I will make you two new skirts. And you need a coat. A thick one. Who knows if your place in Turin will be warm enough?"

I threw myself into her arms, and then Papa's, and then into Zia Costanza's!

I'm going to university!
Your happy, happy, happy, blessed,
Elisa

September 15, 1939

Oh, caro Diario!
Today is the day I leave for Turin, and I'm stealing a bit of time at the desk to write in your pages. I still can't

believe it. People like me don't go to university. Women don't go to university. Women don't become doctors, least of all women from poor families.

I feel like a queen, even if my woolen dress is a hand-me-down from Zia Costanza, my coat has been mended a hundred times, my stockings were bought with the money Zia Costanza and I made washing sheets in the freezing river water. But there's something else I need to tell you: the goodbye between Leo and me.

We met at the cabin, though Mamma did bring up a couple of times that it's unsuitable for a nineteen-year-old woman and a twenty-year-old man to spend time alone in the woods. But we needed a moment to ourselves. He leaned against the stone wall, while I stood, careful not to ruin my outfit.

"You don't even look like you," he said. "It's like in two days, you have changed…"

He was right. Gone was the simple cotton dress I wore almost year-round, except for winter days when wool would take the place of cotton. My shirt and skirt outfit, together with a fitted jacket and black high-heeled shoes (walking with them in the forest had been so hard!) made me look like a city girl. I wore a small felt cloche, with my hair gathered in a bun at the nape of my neck.

"I won't be away forever."

I knew he was conflicted. He was happy for me, I knew it in my heart of hearts, but it was hard for him to see me go.

And, yes, I admit it. It was hard for me to leave him behind. Very hard.

"Who knows where you will end up working after university," he said, idly running his fingers along the contour of the stones. His working hands, strong and square. His *slow, deliberate ways, like someone who's used to waiting for things to grow.*

"Well, by the time I graduate you'll be nice and settled with a lovely wife… she'll look after the house for you and she'll give you lots of children. You'll have forgotten all about me by then," I said.

I was trying to keep the conversation light, but I must have caught his strange mood, because I sounded a bit forlorn. The forced lightness of my tone couldn't hide a hint of regret.

It makes no sense. I need to become a doctor. I've always dreamed of that, always. How can I regret not taking another path? It's an illusion.

An illusion, maybe, but I feel it even now, as I write these words.

The ache of things that could have been.

I know that Leo wants to settle down, have a family, fill the space left by the loss of his father and the absence of his mother. I also know that he is too wise, too sensible, to ask me to be that woman. The silly, childish pact we made as kids is not something either of us can hold on to; it would be absurd to consider a child's promise an engagement. He needs someone who will help on the farm, who will look after him and the family she gives him, and I can never do that.

Maybe one day women will be able to have a profession and a family as well… but that's not possible now. No man would allow that.

I have made my choice. I know it's right for me, but it doesn't change the fact that as I watched Leo leaning against the cabin today, the light of the rising sun in his dark hair – the way he is, so reserved and yet so tender – a strange ache bloomed in my chest.

I wonder what his wife will look like; how I will feel when I attend his wedding, and then go back to Turin, to my studies?

Without him?

No matter. I will be too absorbed in my work to be upset about it.

"I'm looking forward to meeting your fiancé," he said suddenly. His tone was distant, forced.

"What do you mean? What fiancé? You don't mean Carlo, do you? Because—"

Carlo Caporale! Once again, I wondered how he was related to the Antonio Caporale who'd stolen Tommaso's lands. They had to be related – the villages around here were so small, and like Nonna Tina had said, everyone was somebody's cousin. It felt strange to read names mentioned in the diary, and then hear them mentioned in real life, now. It made time seem weightless, like the past was always present. Like Elisa's story and mine had had a reason to come together the way they had.

"No, not at all!" Leo smiled, though it was, somehow, a sad smile. "I know you can't stand him." He didn't look at me, but up to the canopy of trees, inundated with golden rays. "I mean the fiancé you'll meet at university, I'm sure. Some highly educated, intelligent man who can have proper conversations with you, not about the farm and the harvest and chickens and how much our wine will sell this year."

"I have no plans to find a fiancé or ever marry, for that matter. You should know me well enough to know that."

"I do. But this is what you think now. I don't know the woman you'll become. You'll be living in Turin, going to

*university, becoming a doctor. I don't know the woman you
will be when you come back to Montevino, if you ever do."*

"When I come back... in a month's time?" I tried
to laugh. "You know, I'll only be a few hours away. I'll
come back at least once a month... Have you ever heard
of trains?"

He didn't reply, and my heart sank a little. Would I
change so much, like he predicted? Had I already changed?

"Leo, please. This is a happy moment for me. My dream
is coming true. And I've worked so hard for it. I must pinch
myself to believe this is happening. Don't spoil it for me.
Don't make me feel bad about leaving."

"You know what? You're right." He ran his hands
through his hair and smiled. "This is your moment and
I'm just thinking about myself. But there are things I need
you to know, I suppose. Before you go."

I know, *I wanted to say,* you don't need to tell me...
but I remained silent.

"Listen to me, Elisa." *He took me by the shoulders and
fixed his eyes on mine.* "My days will be empty when you're
gone. I won't see you every evening or sit with you after a
day's work and talk, or just enjoy silence with you there
beside me." *He leaned closer to me, his voice faint.* "You
know, don't you, Elisa?" *he said, echoing what I'd been
about to say.* "You know that you've always been more
than a friend to me." *Not much of what he thought and
felt had ever been spoken so openly as what he'd said in the
last short while. A place that had been locked and shut was
now ajar, for me to glimpse the warmth inside.*

*For a moment, I swayed. My heart longed for him,
but my duty and dreams were within reach and I couldn't
let them go.* "I can't be a wife and mother on a farm.

Most women don't even get a choice. I'm not the woman you need."

"How do you know what I need or who I need? Don't I get to decide that for myself? Who says I want a farmhand?" He was almost cross now, and his anger rubbed off on me.

And so, I wrenched it out of me, the thorn in my heart, what I knew had been happening and couldn't stop.

"What about Agnese?"

Agnese, the sweet, blonde daughter of Martino Fossano from Camosso, the next village up the mountain. Her father is a friend of my papa, to add insult to injury. Gossip from both villages agreed that Leo and Agnese were meant for each other. They'd danced together at last year's fair, I'd noticed.

"Agnese is… nice. Many say she would be the perfect wife for me. But there is only one thing wrong with that."

My voice came out in a whisper, so afraid was I of his answer. "What?"

"My heart is taken already. By you."

I touched my neck where Tommaso had touched me, and relived the moment when we were dancing, with his hands around my waist… Oh God! Had I really called him Leo? The embarrassment. Oh, well. He didn't know who Leo was. I closed my eyes and allowed myself to dream a little.

CHAPTER 8

I opened my eyes in the golden light of a spring morning, too comfortable to move. I never usually slept late, but since I'd arrived in Italy it was like I'd been in a trance. Maybe it was the mountain air.

I had barely begun to switch my brain on, and was still in the kitchen, sipping coffee from a mug, when the doorbell rang. I put down my mug and went to answer the door.

Tommaso was outside, legs planted on the ground like a tall tree, with an ax at his side. He was wearing a checkered shirt, the sleeves rolled up, and jeans. His dark skin was flushed and there was sweat glistening at his temples. Despite the hardened lumberjack look, though, there was a smile in his eyes.

I glanced at his side. *What in the world is he doing with that ax?*

"Do you know the expression 'ax murderer'?" I said, crossing my arms.

He laughed. "No. I know about cutting off a tree damaged by the storm, so it won't fall on people, though."

"Want to come in? Without the ax?"

"Actually, I wanted to invite you for lunch. I'll just have a quick shower..."

"...while Morella sets the table." I laughed. "That'd be great, I have some pasta from Nonna Tina."

"And I have homemade pesto. Made with basil from my herb garden."

"You have a herb garden?" I raised my eyebrows.

"Of course. To be fair, most people grow stuff around here. And you'll try some red wine from my vineyards?"

"Honey, cakes, wine… an aromatic garden… Is there anything you don't produce yourself?"

He laughed and lowered his eyes. How a man could look bashful while carrying an ax was beyond me, but somehow Tommaso managed to do it, with that strange mixture of self-assurance and shyness he seemed to have.

I continued, "Anyway, I only drink white wine."

Tommaso's eyes danced. "My Barolo will make you change your mind. I promise."

"What's Barolo?"

"Deep, lush, supple red wine. You'll be amazed. Promise. Come," he said, and turned away into the late summer morning. The crickets' song had just begun, and the temperature was beginning to rise.

"Supple? How can a wine be supple?" I asked, throwing my jacket on and following him outside. The sky was white but blue lurked at the horizon.

He said honestly, "It's a sommelier term. You'll see."

"Sommelier? Now you're just showing off with your big words!" I teased him, and I was rewarded with a laugh. "Anyway, it's lunchtime!"

"Just a small glass. It's good for you."

"I woke up like, an hour ago."

"The breakfast of champions!" he joked. "I'll give you a sip, just to try, and line your stomach first."

"I count on it. I'll grab Nonna's pasta and come over."

"Deal."

*

When Morella saw me, she jumped up and nearly flattened me, making puppy noises that sounded out of place in such a giant body. That enormous, scary-looking dog was really a pup at heart. I held her paws and put my nose to her nose, cooing, "Good girl!"

Tommaso grinned as he watched us, then wandered in the direction of the kitchen. In moments he was back. "And here's what I was telling you about," Tommaso said, a wine bottle in his hand.

The bottle's glass was a deep green color. There was no label circling it. "The wine you make?"

"Exactly," he said. "Here, try." He was already pouring me a glass.

Tommaso was right. It was delicious, even to someone like me who didn't have a clue about wine. I pointed to one of his paintings. "That's Montevino, isn't it? The other side of the hill."

"Yes. The vineyards that belonged to my family. The ones that Caporale stole. More wine?"

"Yes, please."

He filled my glass to the brim, and I laughed. "Are you trying to get me drunk?"

"Don't worry about that. It's impossible to drink too much of this."

"If you *were* to get drunk, you could just ride Morella back to the house."

We both burst into laughter.

Our eyes met; I felt my cheeks flush. I was about to tell him about my meeting with Nonna Tina when there was a low jingling outside – the sound of keys finding a lock – and the door opened.

A striking woman stood in the doorway. She had natural blonde hair that defied the idea that all Italians are dark; she was dainty and petite in high-heeled shoes and a simple, short skirt.

She was stunning, with the innocent, clean-faced look of an angel, but my first thought was how on earth she had managed to walk on the dirt paths around the castle in those high heels. The moment she saw me, her smiling face altered.

"Federica?" Tommaso said.

"Tommaso. I'm so sorry." Her eyes stayed on me briefly, but she ignored me and moved toward Tommaso, her heels clicking on the floorboards. "I… Your mamma said you were away for work in Milan… I thought…"

Tommaso went to block her from coming in any further. His arms were crossed. "I *was* in Milan. I came back a few days ago. And I've asked you not to go and see my mamma. And not to let yourself into my house."

She sighed. "I wouldn't have used the keys had I known you were here."

"No. You shouldn't have. Let's not drag this out. What do you need?"

"I see you have company."

Tommaso's voice grew firmer. "Federica. Why are you here?"

She sighed again. "I'm sorry. Only… I need Gioele's nursery folder. I forgot it."

I tried to make myself look busy as Tommaso opened a drawer in the tiny kitchen and fished out a bright red folder. His movements were quick, tense, different from the deliberate, relaxed body language he had had before. He handed it to the woman, then took a few steps back, as if she was infectious or something. "Well, there it is."

"Oh. You swept the place."

"Yes," he said, unapologetically.

"I'm sorry," she repeated. "I won't bother you again." Her face was suddenly tired, underneath all the make-up. "Next time I need something, I'll come when you're working."

"You won't come at all."

"Okay," she said curtly, and I could see she was annoyed. "By the way, Gioele is good. He's learned to write his name."

Tommaso's face was stormy now. "Federica…" he warned her.

"Okay. Okay. You're busy now."

This was too uncomfortable. "No, no, not at all. Don't mind me," I said, rising from the chair. "I'm going."

Tommaso's face fell, but if this girl Federica was in any way satisfied with having interrupted what was going to be our lunch, she didn't show it. "You don't need to go," she said.

"Don't go," Tommaso blurted out, and he seemed surprised at his own force.

Federica looked at him, and an emotion I couldn't decipher passed over her features.

My gaze moved from one to the other. "Thanks, but maybe it's better if I let you finish the conversation alone," I said, and the blonde woman stepped aside to let me pass, Morella at my heels. Strange, I thought. Morella hadn't even got up when Federica arrived.

Walking toward Firefly House on the soft grass, I realized my hands were shaking a little. I had a lump in my throat. We'd been having such a good time, Tommaso and I, and I'd felt… happy. It was as simple as that. But seeing him and Federica together had told me more about them than I wanted to know. Yes, Tommaso had been clear with her, about not letting herself in, not coming back at all.

But.

But I could feel the ties between them. Funny how love, sometimes, looks a lot like hate.

I was unnerved, and though I didn't want to admit it, disappointed. I made myself a quick lunch, and dived straight into Elisa's diary, with the plan to lose myself for a little, and then to go and see Flora.

CHAPTER 9

January 19, 1940

Caro *Diario,*

I haven't written much, I know. Sorry, Diary. But I've been so busy. I'm in class all day and I study all night. Turin has swallowed me whole. Leo was right, I can't go back to Montevino as often as I'd like. I can't even sleep as often as I'd like. Sometimes, dawn comes and I'm still studying.

Today the usual group bothered me again. The men on my course – or should I say boys - who think a woman's place is in the house, not in the university. They do childish things, like stealing my pen and hiding my books when I go for a cup of coffee. Having a woman on the course doesn't sit well with some people.

Sadly, it's not just these boys who believe I should not be here; some of the teachers too, it seems. There's Professor Coppi, who routinely acts like I'm not there. When he asks questions, he scours the room with his eyes, which grow vacant as they pass over me, focusing again when they fix on the student next to me. Once, he deliberately asked me a question about a subject far more advanced than all we'd been studying, and made a big show of my ignorance when

I couldn't answer. Of course, he didn't put the same question to anyone else, so as not to embarrass his clever fellow men.

Some other professors speak to me patiently, as if I were a child, or somehow dim. Or fragile; like in our first autopsy, when the lecturer made sure I stood near the door, in case I needed to leave quickly, my womanly senses being overwhelmed by the gore. A fellow student ran out; one fainted cold on the floor and had to be revived with smelling salts. But this "little fragile woman" didn't run and didn't faint; they should have given the place by the door to someone else.

There's this one professor, though, Professor Bacher, who seems to believe in me. He treats me with respect. He's so short-sighted he can't see a hand from his nose, but he has the reputation of being the best cardiologist in Italy. Thank goodness for him. Thank you, Lord, for little mercies, like Zia Costanza says. And now, back to my books.

Buonanotte, *Diario,*
Elisa

March 14, 1940

Caro *Diario!*

Finally, I made it home!

The atmosphere has changed in Montevino. Those Blackshirts, Mussolini's henchmen, are everywhere now. They watch everyone closely, more closely than they used to. It's disquieting. Part of me thinks I should be careful about what I write in this diary, but part of me thinks, what nonsense! Who would read these pages? It's not like they search homes to look for dissenters. And I'm not a dissenter.

I don't like them, don't get me wrong; Mussolini seems to me full of hot air and pretenses, with those stupid faces and gestures he makes, like he wants to give the impression he owns the world, and instead looks like a clown. But there's no way I'm rocking the boat or speaking out. No way. I must finish my course. Politics can sort itself. It usually works that way – governments come and go, and we little people get on with our lives.

Papa disagrees, though. He's developed a keen hatred of the Blackshirts.

I was home on the weekend, and I saw the Conte had people over for dinner, men in uniform and their wives. I was in Papa's workshop in one of the outbuildings chatting to my parents. The Conte looked like someone who was walking on thorns; I could tell he wasn't exactly happy to be entertaining these people in the castle. He was showing them the grounds, the women's heels sinking into the grass, the men affecting military stances, looking around like generals on a campaign. A thin, tall man seemed to be the leader – I suppose I would have recognized him had I read the newspaper more, because he seemed to be someone high up in the ranks. They passed by Papa's workshop, but the Conte steered them away. I was thankful. Papa is just not one for holding his tongue.

"That lot!" Papa grumbled.

Mamma was sweeping the floor. Is there ever a time when she is idle? Because I don't think I've ever seen her sitting down during the day, except when she sews or mends.

"Shhh, Luigi, please," she urged him. To no use, of course. Papa is a sensible person, usually, but he believes that a man should be able to speak his mind in his own home. Which would be right, if we didn't live under a dictatorship. Because we all know that this is what it is.

"Don't shush me, Maria," Papa said crossly. "They're bullies. Bullies in black shirts and fancy boots. And if we don't do what they say, we get thrown in prison. I cannot believe we all have to hold their party cards!"

"Without a card, we don't get the rations," Mamma reminded him. "And now, hush, please..."

"I don't care about that! I'd rather starve. But if they put me in prison, who will provide for the family? I'm just happy I'm too old to go to the front. At least I don't have to fight on their behalf. And not because I'm a coward! Because what they fight for is wrong. It's wrong!"

"It's not. They're defending us, Papa. They want Italy to be self-sufficient, to be powerful! To have an empire!"

Silence fell. My brother's voice had uttered these words. He'd appeared, standing in the doorway. None of us could believe it was Pietro, little Pietro, who had spoken. He's not even fourteen, the age that is still deciding whether to remain a child or become a man.

"Defending us from who? We need defending from them, if anything!" Papa replied when he found his voice again.

I heard my mamma whisper another helpless, "Hush, please."

Pietro ignored Papa's outburst, saying instead, "Soon I'll get my cartolina. *I'll be called to the front and I'll be able to do my duty for my country..."*

I had to stop reading and ponder the meaning of the word *cartolina*. It meant "postcard", but it had to be a call to the army. My heart sank as I read those words. What was going to happen to Elisa's little brother? These must have been such terrible times.

And still, Elisa's diary was full of life and hope and strength. I hoped with all my heart that the whole family would survive the war. I glanced up from the diary, needing a moment to process it all. I looked around the cozy, sweet tower bedroom. Funny how, in the space of just two days, Firefly House had gone from feeling spooky to feeling like my own. I sighed and immersed myself in the diary once again.

My heart sank; my brother, in the army? But he was just a child! Had he gone to someone in the village, one of the Blackshirts, and found a way to lie about his age? I searched his face, and he looked away. I resolved to ask Papa later, and Leo.

Leo and I had never talked about the war…

"They enrol children now?" Papa tried a laugh, but it didn't really work.

"Oh, Gesù!" Mamma looked up to the sky and murmured a quick prayer.

Papa glowered at Pietro. "And why do you think fighting is the best way to do your duty? Our duty is to work the best we can, to look after our homes and villages, not to go killing people. Our country was doing very well before the war began."

"Luigi, please be quiet," Mamma pleaded. "Someone might hear you."

Papa snorted, but suddenly, voices outside startled us. I thought they'd passed by!

"And what do we have here?" the thin, tall man said aloud, stepping into the workshop.

"My tenants," the Conte said curtly. He had followed the man into the workshop and now stood beside him. "But let's not delay, I did order dinner for seven on the dot," he added. I knew he was trying to draw the man away from us.

"It's… it's amazing to meet you," my brother stammered. He performed the fascist salute, and I could feel my stomach knotting. I didn't dare look at Papa.

"And you. What are you doing for the country, young man?" The guy had assumed a radio broadcasting tone that would have been ridiculous had it not been so tragically real.

"I hope to receive my cartolina soon," answered my sweet, idealistic, thoroughly deluded little brother.

The Blackshirt looked him over. "How old are you?"

"Fourteen." I wasn't looking at them, but I could feel my parents pale. I must have paled myself, because I knew what the man was going to say next.

"Still young, but I'm sure something can be done about that, don't you think?" He caught the eye of a third man who had been standing silently beside the Conte. Two women had also arrived, and were whispering to one another in the doorway.

"Of course. Young and strong, that's how the army needs them!"

The women turned to look and laughed.

Like I knew would happen, Papa growled, "Get out of my workshop and never come back."

"My good man, is this your workshop? Are you the Conte?"

The Conte was quick to intervene. "Please forgive him. The accident" – he said, gesturing to Papa's legs – "ruined his mind as well."

"My mind is not ruined! And you're just—"

"Luigi! Please!" Mamma begged. I was frozen.

"You are just a bunch of murderers," Papa said evenly.

The women gasped, and the thin man looked at him coldly, almost indifferently. There was no rage in his eyes, which scared me even more.

"Luigi! I told you many times not to speak when we have visitors at the castle! Maria, please, see to him. Poor man, he was ruined, ruined," the Conte said and patted Papa on the shoulder, wearing a little smile, like the fool in the wheelchair could only be laughed at and not taken seriously.

"You'll be hearing from us," the thin, tall man said to Pietro. "Conte Montevino will tell me all about you," he concluded. Pietro beamed, while Mamma was white as a sheet.

There were angry voices from my parents' room that night, and Pietro didn't sleep at the house. Papa has been a fool, but how could I blame him, with the scum of the earth acting like they owned us all? And Pietro, not quite saying he was disowning us, not in as many words – but it was clear what he was doing.

It was a terrible, long day. I'm too tired to keep writing, I'm even too tired to worry. Will there be consequences for Papa's tirade?

I worry that the Conte's intervention wasn't enough. And that what they'd said to Pietro – that something could be done about his young age and his desire to join the army – would be the easiest, cruelest way to get to us. But I can't even think about that, it makes me shiver.

Yours,
Elisa

I sighed. Elisa must have been terrified when those Blackshirts, as they called them, visited the castle – just yards from where I was sitting down – and her father not being able to hide his political convictions. There seemed to be a fracture in the family, with Papa and Pietro going down two different roads…

My heart was heavy for them.

*

The day was slipping by and it was time to make my way down to the village to go see Flora. Hopefully, she would have slept her hangover off and Passiflora would be open. I walked down the hill enjoying the pure air and the sunshine, dappled through the tree-lined road. As soon as I stepped into the square, I heard a voice calling me.

"Call-ee!"

"Nonna Tina!"

"*Ciao, bella!* Come, come. I made some fresh basil pasta, I'll prepare a parcel for you, and we can have a chat."

"Nonna, Call-ee must be busy…" Adriana appeared from behind the door of the Aquila Nera.

"I'd love to. If I'm not imposing."

"Not at all. I'll get you some…"

"…coffee. Thanks," I said, smiling.

"Come and sit with me, *tesoro*." Nonna Tina lead me to the back courtyard, and I wondered how much these stones and houses had heard from Nonna Tina and the people who opened her heart to her. "You seem worried."

I rolled my eyes. "A lot has happened. I met someone called Federica." Something told me that Nonna Tina would know who I was talking about.

"I know."

"You know I met her?"

"Yes."

I was a bit taken aback. How did Nonna Tina know everything? Did she have a telescope up there in the castle?

She seemed to read my mind, because she said: "My sister told me."

"Your sister. Okay." I gave her a mischievous look. She really brought gossip to another level. I imagined Montevino had old ladies with binoculars all over the place, standing sentry in crucial places.

"Remember what I said to you last time we chatted, that Tommaso had the pick of the girls? Well, he didn't seem to want anyone. Then, Federica happened."

"I see."

Nonna Tina shrugged as she spoke. "Federica is not a bad person. She's just... well, a bit stupid." She tapped her temple with her finger. I gasped; Nonna Tina wasn't very diplomatic. "Isn't she, Adriana?"

I heard Adriana laugh in the background. "Nonna! Behave!" she called out.

I suppose elderly people can be direct, but Nonna Tina was taking it to another level. "Let me tell you about her. Federica was – well, still is, I suppose – one of the prettiest girls in Montevino. She's a few years older than Tommaso, you know. She burst into Tommaso's life like a whirlwind. He was head over heels. He and Federica moved in together and got engaged, quicker than anyone could say, 'Be careful.'"

"Right."

"Except, she was still involved with Caporale."

"Antonio Caporale? The guy who stole the vineyards?"

"His son."

So, the Caporales stole Tommaso's land *and* his girlfriend. He has quite an ax to grind with them, to say the least.

"Can I ask you... do you know, by the way, what Antonio's father was called?"

"Let me see... Carlo. Yes, Carlo. Carlo, Antonio, and now Denis, the man who broke up Tommaso's marriage."

"*Marriage?*" I gaped. "*Tommaso is married?*"

"He was. But let me tell you everything in order. Tommaso is too kind for his own good. When he found out that Federica was still seeing Denis Caporale, she said she was confused, and he forgave her. He knows too well how devious the Caporales can be. Tommaso and Federica stayed together for a while, then she left him. Then she came back." Nonna Tina was explaining all this with generous gestures of her hands. Had I not been so sad and outraged for Tommaso, I would have found it funny and endearing. "And then, little Gioele came along."

The boy Tommaso and Federica had been talking about this morning. My heart skipped a beat. If ever there was a reason to stay away from that dark-eyed Italian man with a complicated history, little Gioele was the one.

"Tommaso's son," I said, and looked down at my feet.

"No. Gioele is not Tommaso's son."

"But—"

"Tommaso took for granted the boy was his, like anyone would. When Gioele was born, Tommaso was over the moon. And then Federica dropped the bombshell, that he wasn't Gioele's papa."

"Oh, no. That is just terrible!"

"Tommaso loved the boy so much, he couldn't let him down. So, once again, they stayed together."

"That's completely masochistic!"

"What does that mean, dear?"

"That he likes to suffer!"

"Maybe. But remember, for the first two years of Gioele's life he believed he was the boy's father… He was so proud of the child. He paraded him around the village like he was his biggest achievement! It would have been heartbreaking for Tommaso to part from him."

Wait. The nursery children. The line of kids that had passed in front of Leone's café yesterday. Tommaso had seemed almost hypnotized by them…

Today, Federica had come looking for Gioele's nursery folder, so… maybe Gioele had been one of those children! That must be why Tommaso had seemed so cold with me after seeing them. He was upset.

"It wasn't just about Tommaso and what he wanted," Nonna Tina continued. "It was also about Alice, Tommaso's mamma. The birth of the boy who she believed to be her grandson had given her a new lease of life. She was happy like I hadn't seen her in years. Not since Tommaso's father died."

"I understand. I suppose Tommaso could have children of his own one day, but hey, people aren't interchangeable. It's not like you let a son go, you just make another one."

"Exactly. Also, he knows himself what it's like growing up without a father; he didn't want that to happen to Gioele too, he didn't want history to repeat itself."

"I can understand that," I said. "I grew up an orphan."

"I know."

"How…? Never mind. So, Tommaso and Federica stayed together."

"But they're not together anymore. Federica ended up leaving Tommaso for Caporale. She took Gioele with her."

That was beyond cruel.

"Apparently, she doesn't let Tommaso see the boy at all, because Gioele would 'get confused about who his real father is,' so she says."

My voice came out in a whisper. "*She doesn't even let them see each other*? How could she do that to Tommaso? And to Gioele too! They both must be devastated."

"Oh, they are. Tommaso can't find peace."

"But…"

Nonna Tina tilted her head, looking at me with knowing eyes. "What's on your mind?" she said.

"Well, when I was at Tommaso's house, Federica said something about Gioele learning to write his name. And she'd left a nursery folder belonging to him. It was as if she was trying to bring the child back to Tommaso's mind…. as if she was trying to keep him in the loop, somehow. But Tommaso wouldn't have any of it."

"And rightly so! Tommaso is done with her. I'm sure of it."

"I'm so sorry. You see, when Federica turned up, I left quite abruptly."

Nonna Tina shrugged. "It'll be fine. Just cook him a nice meal. That'll make up for it."

I laughed, taking in the archaic advice.

"She thinks everything begins and ends with food," Adriana said, and winked at me.

"For Italian men, yes!" Nonna Tina said.

"That's a bit sexist," I replied.

"What?"

"Sexist."

"Oh, yes. Sex too. But wait until you're married."

My eye met Adriana's over Nonna Tina's shoulder as I nodded seriously, with Adriana giggling behind her.

*

Passiflora was open, thankfully, and Flora was looking over some papers at the counter. She was dressed in gypsy style, with full make-up, although her eyes were circled with blue. The place was tidy and full of fragrant herby smells. I was glad to see she'd slept the hangover off.

She looked up when the door chimed. "Oh, *ciao*," she said when she saw me, without interrupting her work.

"*Oh, ciao* back. Don't sound too happy to see me." That wasn't an easy thing to say in Italian – I suspect I must have said something wrong because she raised her eyebrows, confused.

"I suppose I should say sorry and thank you for last night," she managed.

"No need to say sorry. But thank you would be nice. However, I can think of a better way to thank me. You could offer me a cup of tea and sit me down and tell me more about our family. For that… I would be grateful," I said, and my voice came out small.

"Okay."

"I have so many questions for you, and…" I stopped. "What did you say?"

"I said okay. I'm not short of tea," she said, and indicated some shelves full of herbal teas in tin boxes.

I couldn't believe this. "Really? Oh! Oh, good."

"Yeah. Tea is one of my main sellers."

"No, I mean, it's good that—" My words were interrupted when the chime above the door rang out as a man in a baseball cap stepped in. "I have a delivery for" – he looked down on a piece of paper in his hand – "Flora Stella?"

"That's me. Come round the back," Flora said, leading the man out of sight.

I hovered in the main room for a few minutes, then decided to take a tour around the shop. It had every herbal combination you could think of, it seemed. Lotions and candles and bath soap too. Before long, I decided to try to find Flora to see if she needed a hand. Her voice was coming from beyond the counter, somewhere deep in the back of the shop. I followed the sound and soon came to a small back room, almost entirely taken over by a dark wooden table and shelves. The shelves were cluttered with more jars full of herbs and various equipment. Tucked in one corner of the room was a small stove with several pots on it.

Beyond that was another room, painted white, and bare but for a few boxes piled along one wall. It opened out to a courtyard – did this shop ever end?

Here the delivery man, under Flora's watchful eye, was moving box after box off a van. Nearby, Flora was signing a form. She quickly handed it back to him, and then brought a hand to her forehead, her eyes closing for a moment. She looked tired, strained. I couldn't imagine what it was like owning and running your own business alone.

Opening them, her eyes settled on me. She instantly straightened, composing herself, and went to lift one of the boxes. "Is this new stock? Here, let me help you," I offered.

"Or maybe… not," she said, ignoring my outstretched hands and making her way through the back rooms to the main shop area again. She laid the heavy box down on the counter by the register.

I was furious. What gave her the right to speak to me like that? Whatever the situation of my birth or my family, I hadn't chosen any of it. "Look. You might have your reasons for being so negative towards me, but there's something called manners that you don't seem to have!"

"I didn't ask you to come here!"

"I didn't ask to come here either! I didn't ask to be given up for adoption and then orphaned. Twice. And to know nothing about who I really am for twenty-one years of my life! Do you think I planned any of this?"

Her eyes flashed – and then she seemed to deflate suddenly, like some heavy thought had the best of her. "I don't need your help, Callie. I really don't."

"You did last night. And you're going to have to accept it again, because I'm not going anywhere."

"Do you realize how annoying you are?"

"Well, we're related, so what do you expect?" I retorted.

Was that a smile on her face?

"I suppose you're right. Malva was the sweet one. When she was born, she snatched up all the sweetness in our family. I was left with the bitter," she said unexpectedly, and without looking at me. "Or that's what our mamma always said. That I was sour. And she was right."

"I was told that too. Not in those exact words, but yes, that was the gist," I said, thinking of the Whittiers, my last foster family – and their opinion of me. "But I was just defending myself. You learn that skill, growing up in care." She looked at me, almost surprised.

There was a moment of silence, then Flora spoke in a softer tone. "Here, take these out of their boxes and put them on those shelves," she said, shifting the box over to me and pointing to a line of shelves.

"Okay. Sure," I said, feigning indifference, but secretly smiling.

We got down to work, and I was immediately fascinated with the content of the boxes. Some were organic products – body lotions, all sort of creams, shampoos and shower gels – beautifully packaged in dark bottles stamped with what looked like hand-painted labels, and with a string bow tied around the cap.

"These bottles are beautiful."

"A friend of mine makes them. She does toiletries. I do the healing side of things – salves, brews, herb extracts. Come, I'll show you," Flora said, and she abandoned the boxes to go back inside to the small room with dark wood table and shelves.

"This is my laboratory," she said.

"Like a mad scientist?"

"Would that not be a lair? Anyway, look." She took a few books down from the shelves. *Physiology, Principles of Naturopathy, Healing Herbs*... the titles themselves were fascinating. "Remember I told you... the women in our family have been the local midwives and healers for a long time."

I remembered. Exactly like Elisa had said.

"I would love to know more," I replied, thumbing through the pages of one of the books.

"Want to borrow them?"

"I'd love to. Thanks."

"Sure. Just look after them."

"Okay, I was thinking of jumping on them and then throwing them out the window, but I guess I don't have to," I said deadpan and without looking up.

She laughed briefly – progress, I suppose – and while returning to the boxes, she asked: "What do you do? Back home in America?"

Shocked at her sudden interest, I replied, "I'm a server, a waitress. But I've been saving up to go to college. I don't know what I'm going to do yet, though."

"Mmmm. I'm sure you'll figure it out." *Was she really being nice?* "Listen, I'm parched. What about that tea I promised you?"

"That would be great."

A few minutes later, we sat in the back room in front of a steaming cup of herbal tea, which she had prepared on the stove. It smelled like a meadow.

"What is this?" I couldn't place the flavor.

"Flowers."

"Seriously?"

"Yes. I collect them in the summer and dry them. It's nice to drink sunshine all throughout the year."

"I heard somewhere that buttercups are poisonous."

Flora fixed her eyes on me and said ominously, "Well, we'll soon find out, won't we?"

I laughed, then took a deep breath. "So…"

"Yes. You want to know about Malva. My sister."

"And my father. Who was he? How did they meet? Why did they give me away?"

"Your father was called Paolo Caporale." Her face darkened, as if even just saying his name aloud disturbed her.

"Caporale?" I was breathless for a moment. I couldn't believe it. I felt my legs give way, and I had to sit down, my hand on my chest.

"Are you okay?" Flora asked, alarmed, and moved to sit across from me.

I nodded. "It's just… It's just I heard terrible things about the Caporale family."

"With reason, yes."

"You said *Paolo* Caporale… not Antonio?"

"Paolo and Antonio were brothers. Denis, Antonio's son, lives in Camosso. Nice family, eh? Antonio was a nasty man. But Paolo took it to another level."

For a moment, I couldn't think of anything to say. I was desperate to know more, and at the same time, I didn't want to know.

I lowered my eyes. "Where is he now?"

"Dead. Car accident. He was in Monte Carlo. He loved his gambling, though nobody knew where he got the money to do that. Of the two of them, Antonio was the wealthy one. Funnily enough, Antonio's house was broken into at some point, a lot of stuff was taken, but nobody was charged. After that, Paolo got a new fancy car and went to live it up in Monte Carlo. Coincidence?" She shook her head. The bitterness wafting off her was palpable. "I think there's still some stuff of his up at Firefly House. I just can't stomach going through it."

"Nothing good about him, then?" I asked in a small voice.

"Nothing, Callie. Except, he fathered you."

I almost gasped, hearing Flora saying something so nice about me. *Then why, why, did you not look for me?*

"So why did my mother fall for him?"

"Oh, that's easy. He was handsome, and a charmer. My sister was the loveliest person you'd ever meet. She was easy prey, I suppose. Malva was... naïve."

"But she didn't want to give me up. She said so in the letter. So why—?"

"She had no choice. She got sick," Flora said, and got up, busying herself with washing mugs and pots, as if every job was urgent.

"Did my father abandon her? And me? And how did I end up in America?"

"Our parents sent us there so that Malva would forget about Paolo Caporale... so that she would leave everything behind. She found out she was pregnant, and so she decided to stay there. With you. I came back to Montevino, and never saw her again. She passed away not long after, without ever contacting us to say she was dying. Then my parents – your grandparents – died too... Rosa and Claudio, those were their names... and I was left alone, without a clue how to find you. End of story."

"But why? Why did Malva not call you when she was sick? Why did she not give me to you, instead of having me adopted?"

I have no family left, Malva had written in the letter she'd left me. But she had a sister! Something must have happened between them.

"I don't know."

You do, I thought to myself.

"And my father?" I asked instead.

"Your father, among other things, spent some time in prison for trying to extort money from various people. Like I said, a real gentleman."

I rubbed my forehead. "God."

"I know."

I took a moment to try and digest all that Flora had said to me. "I'm so sorry," I said.

"You're *sorry*? You feel *sorry* for me?" she snorted.

"Yes. It couldn't have been easy, being left alone like that."

"No. It wasn't. But I don't deserve your pity. And I don't want it."

"I didn't mean…"

"I think you'd better go," she said in a low, hard tone.

I stood and scribbled my number on a piece of paper that was on her desk, for her to do as she saw fit. "Thanks for the tea," I said, and left with a heavy heart.

*

It had been a difficult day. Back up the hill I went looking for Tommaso at his house, but the lights were out. He wasn't home, and Morella wasn't either, because there was no barking. My heart sank further.

I was too tired even to cook and eat dinner. I made myself a cup of some tea I'd bought in Passiflora to accompany a small packet of brown sugar biscuits from Leone's, and took refuge upstairs in the little pink bedroom. I lit some natural-scented candles I'd bought, and the room was filled with a soothing lavender scent. I opened the window slightly, and a soft breeze danced in – no fireflies yet, but I could hear some crickets singing here and there. I had tea, biscuits, candles, and the diary. It was perfect. For tonight, I would forget everything – Flora's mood swings, the mysteries surrounding my adoption, the suspended dialogue with Tommaso.

Who my father had turned out to be.

For tonight, I would just immerse myself in Elisa's story. The next entry in her diary was written a long time after the one before.

June 18, 1941

Caro *Diario,*

Here I am, back in Montevino, after all this time. It's now the middle of the night and I'm writing in my room, in bed, by the light of the candle. Pardon the time away, but I promise I have a good excuse for all this silence! My grades should be written on here, in place of all the missing entries. I only have a few exams left before I can start my training. It's all so exciting. I'm hopeful training will happen somewhere near the village. We will see.

I've barely been home recently, so consumed by my studies, and I missed everyone. It's nice to be back for a time. But I'm constantly scared for everyone here. Montevino is a different place, with the Blackshirts patrolling the streets every day watching what everyone says and does. A group of them sit in the square all day, acting out their pretend power, which has now become very, very real. And today, when I arrived from Turin, one of them came near me.

"Hello, Elisa! Do you not recognize me?" he said.

I didn't look him in the eye. "Of course, I do, Carlo."

"Well, I'm glad you remember me. How's your course going?"

I was taken aback. Of all things, I wouldn't think he'd ask about my studies.

"Good. Good, thank you."

"I'm glad. No marriage on the horizon?"

There it was.

"No, Carlo. No. You? Surely you must be at least engaged by now? I don't keep up with gossip much, being in Turin."

"No. Someone broke my heart once, and now I shall never marry!" he said, laughing, a hand on his heart.

Huh! Always the jester.

A couple of Blackshirts from Carlo's company turned around and looked at him. It wasn't fitting for a man wearing the fascist uniform to behave in such a way; they had to command strength and dignity in all circumstances. But Carlo obviously didn't care.

"I'm sure you'll recover," I said, giving a small smile.

"I don't think so," he replied, and for a moment, he seemed serious. But it couldn't be. I must have been mistaken.

"Well, goodbye."

"Goodbye. And Elisa—" He caught my shoulder, more gently than I expected him to do. "About Pietro…"

I felt my pulse quicken. My baby brother, still a child, is now a soldier. The thin, tall man we met in Papa's workshop had made good on his promise: they enrolled him in the army on the false pretense he was sixteen. We don't know much about how it happened – false documents, or maybe just a quiet whisper in someone's ear – but he was accepted and sent south. What will happen next, we don't know.

Carlo leaned close to me and whispered, "I might have news."

"What?"

"I heard he—" Suddenly, he stopped, continuing in an unnaturally loud voice, "Good to know you're doing well!" A smile was plastered on his face. His comrades were coming closer.

I desperately wanted to leave, but I couldn't ignore the possibility of him having news of our Pietro.

"He's being sent to Ethiopia," Carlo whispered quickly.
I froze inside. "Thank you. For telling me."

"Don't worry. I'll try to keep an eye on things. For anything, come to me. Hey, time for some wine, I say!" He shouted to his comrades, changing tone completely. I looked at him for a moment, before walking away. Could I trust his kindness? I had no time to think of that. I had to decide whether to tell my parents about Carlo's news of Pietro or whether to keep it to myself. If they knew Pietro was to be sent to Ethiopia, they would go mad with worry.

Back at home, I had dinner with Mamma, Papa and Zia Costanza, and it was so good – such a normal thing to do. Now that everything has changed, both in my life and in the world, time with them has become a gift, a privilege. And still, even in the peace of our home, sipping Mamma's familiar rice and milk soup, there was something terribly wrong: the empty seat where Pietro should be sitting, and our forced cheerfulness.

The word "Ethiopia" kept whirling in my mind. We'd heard of how things were for our soldiers there: the heat, the thirst, the brutality. My heart bleeds for Pietro, for all of us. I can't tell Mamma, I can't…

I thought we'd go to our neighbor's cowshed after dinner, like we always do on autumn and winter nights. It's warm, and whole families and friends gather there to chat and tell stories. But tonight, it didn't happen. I know why: Mamma is scared that Papa will say things that will get us into trouble.

Mamma spoke to me while we were washing the dishes. Zia Costanza was close by. Even now, I'm still trying to digest all that Mamma said.

Papa was in his workshop, but she whispered anyway, as if someone could overhear us. Things haven't been the same between them, since the incident with the tall, thin man and Pietro's call to the army.

"They'll soon send him to the front, I think," Mamma said. There was no need to specify who she was talking about. "Probably to Africa. Me and Costanza pray and pray, Elisa!" I wouldn't tell her what Carlo had said, confirming her fears. I was stricken to see a tear roll down her cheek. She dried it with the back of her hand.

It feels like I've been living a parallel life, absorbed by my studies, while my family sinks deeper and deeper into difficulties. Pietro is conscripted, Papa is tempting arrest.

And Leo?

I miss him terribly. We've barely seen each other in the last year or so. Since that day in the cabin, he's turned his back on me; we've only met at village celebrations, or by chance, and he's always pretended not to notice me. It makes me sadder than I can ever say, but what can I do? Word in the village is that he's engaged to Agnese.

I can't blame him.

He has the right to move on.

But it hurts

Here the narration was interrupted. It seemed like Elisa didn't have time to finish the sentence, or even add a full stop.

I'm back. I don't know if I'm deliriously happy or terrified. Both, I think.

I can't quite believe what happened.

Mother, Zia Costanza and I were sitting in the kitchen. I was studying and writing, as usual. Suddenly, there was a knock at the door. Mamma jumped, and I held my breath too. Gone are the days when a knock at the door meant someone dropping by to say hello, to buy milk from our cows, or one of Pietro's friends calling him out to play...

Zia Costanza's eyes were wide, but she put her rosary down and went to open the door.

I couldn't believe my eyes. Leo was standing there, his cap over his face, a strong hand holding the door frame. My heart did a somersault. I could feel both Mother and Costanza letting out the breaths they'd been holding.

I steeled myself.

"Leo," Mamma said with a strained smile. "Have you eaten? Would you like some warm milk and bread, my boy?"

"No, thank you, signora. *I was just..." His eyes swept across the room, searching.*

"Yes, she's here," Mamma said knowingly.

I felt myself blushing, and I pretended to be busy marking the page on my book and putting it away.

When I looked up, his gaze was on me.

"Hello, Elisa. Would you like to go for a walk?"

"Not to the woods," Mamma admonished, and, for a moment, I felt like a child again.

"Alright. We'll go down to the village, Mamma," I reassured her. I was trying my best to sound aloof. Leo had ignored me for a long time. I didn't want it to look like I would just jump to his bidding the moment he called. I took my apron off and threw on my coat, while Leo stood awkwardly by the door, under Zia Costanza's cool gaze.

"Come," he said to me as soon as I was outside, and took my hand, almost proprietarily. I was torn between excitement and annoyance.

"You shouldn't hold my hand," I said, thinking to pull it away from him. What would our neighbors think?

He squeezed it gently. "But I will anyway."

I didn't find it in me to protest. "The village is not this way," I noted, my eyebrows knitted together. I still couldn't quite soften with him, not after the way he'd treated me.

"I know. We're going to the woods, silly. Don't worry. No one will see us. I promise."

I stopped abruptly, but didn't let go of his hand. "What are you doing here, Leo? You've barely spoken to me in months. And now you come and—"

"I had good reasons."

"Why? Because I chose university over marriage? Because Agnese is with you and…"

He shook his head. "Neither. Come away, please, in case—"

"In case someone thinks we are together? What? You don't want to be seen with me?" I flared, wrenching my hand away.

Leo turned to look at me. "Just trust me, Elisa."

I wanted to shout, to tell him how angry I was. But I also knew I was being unfair. It had been my choice not to turn our friendship into something more. But still, he was behaving as if… as if… As if I belonged to him. And he could let me go and then take me back whenever he wanted.

"Trust me. Please," he repeated, and I tried my best to keep my wits about me and not to be melted by the look in his eyes.

In Turin, I had to be tough – the only girl in a world of men – working doubly hard not just to pass the course, but also to be accepted. But here in Montevino, here with Leo, my barriers were down, my soft core exposed once again. I nodded and took his hand.

It was chilly here, colder than in Turin. There was a full, white moon in the sky, with an eerie halo around it – in fact, I can still see it from the window right now, still free of clouds...

We stepped into the cabin. Our cabin, as I'd grown to think of it. "I thought you might need this," *Leo said, and took out a blanket that had been tucked under his arm. He arranged it around my shoulders, and the small, feather-light touch of his fingers made a shiver travel down my spine.* "Better?"

"Better."

In silence, he lit a small fire for us, circled with stones, and we sat side by side.

"You haven't been home for a long time," *he began.*

"I had a lot of work. But..."

"But?"

"You seemed so far away, like you didn't care."

His gaze lingered over me. I felt a rush of blood to my head, and I was sure I was blushing. "I know I've avoided you, Elisa. But things have happened. I had to."

"Agnese," *I said, heartbroken, though I was trying to hide it.*

"Forget Agnese. No, I told you, it's not her..."

"It's because of my choice, isn't it? I went to university, and..."

"No! I would never stop talking to you because of that. You've always been so ambitious and strong-willed. It's one of the things that makes you special."

"What then? Why did you turn away when you saw me last? Do you have any idea how that felt?"

He looked pained. "I hated doing that. Elisa, listen. You made a choice, yes. You went to university. And I made a choice of my own."

I gasped, my thoughts racing. "You're going to become a priest!"

He laughed suddenly, and the sound was strange, in such an intense conversation. For a moment it felt like our old intimacy was restored. "No, I'm not going to become a priest. You're daft."

"What's going on, then?"

"Look," he said and took out a small, battered card from his pocket.

"What is this?"

"I'm a partigiano. Montevino division."

"You…"

"Yes. I joined the Resistance, Elisa. Against Mussolini. They don't own this country. They don't own us."

When he said that, I had a horrible flashback. Only yesterday, at the train station in Turin, I'd overheard a group of men talking in loud voices – a Blackshirt and two civilians. "Criminals. This is what they are. They can call themselves haughty names like partisans or Resistance, but they are criminals. They should all be locked up."

"Locked up? You're joking, aren't you? They should be shot. One by one." The Blackshirt laughed and wanted the last word: "A bunch of men in rags, playing soldiers. We'll squash them like bugs."

My breath had caught in my throat.

"This is madness, Leo," I said, the memory fading and the present returning once again.

"Do you think so? We can't work if we don't have a party card. We can't eat if we don't have a party card. They take most of what we produce. They decide what we can and what we can't say. They drag us into idiotic wars that aren't even ours…"

"I know all that. I agree with everything you say. But you can't oppose them! What are you going to do? Throw stones at them? This is an army we're talking about! The Italian army! The fascists have all the power, you can't—"

"We'll take it from them bit by bit," Leo interrupted. "Yes, we are few, and we are poor. We are not as well armed as they are, but—"

"Leo, please," I begged. "You'll get yourself killed. That is all you will achieve."

"Come," he repeated, like he'd done back at my house. He rose to his feet and offered me a hand to help me up. Grabbing a spade that sat by the far wall – he must have put it there, because I'd never seen it before – he led me into another clearing whose entrance was almost unnoticeable, unless you knew where to look.

Then he began to dig in the hard ground. "Look," he called me after a time.

I took a step towards him. He was holding something up. A jute sack. There were more of them in the hole he'd dug, covered in soil. He opened the thin rope keeping the sack he held shut, and took out a shotgun – and another, and another. "We do have weapons, and ammunition. And where I'm going, we have explosives too."

"Explosives? Leo… where are you going?"

"I can't tell you the exact location. In fact, it's better if you don't know anything. That is why I've been keeping away from you, Elisa. I couldn't come near you. Your family is exposed as it is, with Pietro off fighting and your father's opinions drawing some attention. I couldn't put you or your family in any more danger."

"Leo…"

He looked at me with a ferocity in his eyes I'd never seen before. "I'll be fine. I promise."

But I didn't want to conversation to end like that. "Tell me more about the place you're going to at least."

"It's up in the mountains. Not far from France. A few of us from Montevino are going: Davide and Lorenzo..."

"Davide Carpentieri? The mayor?"

"Exactly."

"And Lorenzo Pigna? He's only..."

"Fourteen. Pietro's age."

At the mention of my little brother, my anxiety increased. They were enemies, now, weren't they? Leo and Pietro. Fascist or partisan, there was nowhere the people I loved could be safe.

"Your father knows," Leo said.

"What? Is he one of you?"

"Not officially. But he helps us."

I swallowed. "You're all crazy."

"No. What's crazy is bowing to them!" Leo burst out. "How can you not understand?"

"I'm not bowing to anyone. I'm learning to save lives, not blow people up!" I was almost shouting now.

"You'll end up putting back together people who've been blown up by someone else! Nobody is happy to be doing this. I'm a farmer, for God's sake! I never even thought I would hold a weapon. But what choice do I have? Elisa, I've been called to the front."

"What?"

"It was bound to happen."

"But... But I thought they didn't call widows' only sons?"

"Now they're calling everyone who's left. I'm not afraid, Elisa. I'm not afraid of fighting. But I'm not going to join

Mussolini's army. I'm not going to wear the fascist uniform and kill for them."

There was a moment of silence, where I could hear my own erratic heartbeat. Then, before I knew it, I'd thrown myself into his arms and pressed his warm body against mine. He found my mouth and kissed me desperately, like it was our last kiss, even though it was our first. He held me so tightly it hurt. He felt strong, invincible, but I knew how easy it was for a man to die, for a heart to stop beating, and I was terrified.

"I love you, Elisa," he said.

In such circumstances, I didn't care about conventions. The only choice I wanted to make right then was to follow my heart.

"I love you too," I said, and it was like a long-buried truth had finally come out. I was so relieved. I hadn't realized how hard it had been to hide my feelings for him, to push them down, until I finally allowed them to breathe.

We kissed for a long time beside the uncovered weapons, and then held each other, clinging tightly, because we knew our separation was imminent. My heart was breaking in two, and yet I was so happy.

When I finally spoke again, the only thing I could think to ask was, "When are you going?"

"Tonight. We'll be there by dawn."

"Tonight? But..." I couldn't find any more words to say. I desperately wanted to make him stay with me, all through the night, and go with him when morning arrived. But I knew it could not be so. "When will I see you again?"

The pained look returned in his eyes when he finally met my gaze. "I don't know. I'll try to come visit some time, but as from tonight, I'm a deserter. I could be put in prison or shot."

I shivered, remembering the Blackshirt's words: We'll squash them like bugs.

CHAPTER 10

I awoke a couple of hours later to the sound of someone calling my name, somewhere. I blinked and tried to come back to the surface. Was it a dream? Or was someone calling me?

"Callie! Callie!" A male voice. Tommaso. He was shout-whispering, that way when you're trying not to shout but you need to be heard.

The sound came from the open window. I looked at my phone: *4 a.m.?*

I dragged myself downstairs, freezing in the cold house, and flicked the light switch before opening the door to Tommaso, who was wearing his trademark checkered shirt and a woolen hat that accentuated his deep, dark green eyes. Around his neck hung a camera, and he had a backpack slung over one shoulder. "Sorry it's so early, but I want you to come somewhere with me," he said, almost echoing Leo's words to Elisa – I was still half asleep, and hearing those words aloud after having just read them felt strangely natural.

"But it's... four in the morning!"

"I know. The earlier, the better."

"For what?"

"Trust me. Get dressed in jeans and good walking shoes and take your jacket. We're going on an adventure."

*

Twenty minutes later I was sitting in Tommaso's Jeep, sneakers on my feet – *did they count as good walking shoes?* – still groggy and disorientated. We hadn't mentioned Federica yet: it was too early for words, so we drove around impossibly steep curves, up and up the mountain in a comfortable silence. When Tommaso finally stopped the car, there was no more road ahead of us. Now it was just grass and flowers, rocks and trees. *Where were we?*

As though sensing my apprehension, Tommaso turned to me. "I promise you this will be good."

I nodded and stepped out the car. Suddenly, a gust of wind hit me. It was laden with natural perfume, of herbs and dew and wild things.

"Follow me," Tommaso whispered.

We walked through some trees, reminding me of the High Woods Elisa and Leo often ran away to, and soon arrived at a clearing where a small bench beneath a protective wooden roof beckoned. Tommaso headed straight toward it, plopping himself down and shifting the backpack into his lap. "Breakfast time," he said and took out a Thermos and two plastic cups. I all but snatched the steaming cup from his hand as he handed it to me.

As the coffee made its way through my veins, I began to feel more human and enjoy the moment. It was barely five o'clock now, and the sky was still inky, but there was a corner of lilac-pink in the east. Dawn would soon break.

After a while, Tommaso ventured, "Better?"

I smiled and nodded vigorously, tightening my hold on the cup. "A lot better. So, where are you taking me to?"

"We're going to walk farther ahead, just a little way, but we need to whisper if we talk. We don't want to scare the wolves."

*

After hiking in silence for a short while, we finally stopped before a large lake, surrounded by trees teeming with leaves. The surface of the lake was the clearest I'd ever seen, reflecting the gray of the clouds above. The mountains towered above, seeming to reach the sky. I'd never seen a landscape so beautiful, so perfect. I was speechless.

"Lake Nourissat," said Tommaso.

"Wow," I managed.

"I know," he whispered back. "And now we wait."

We crouched beneath some rocks beside the lake, staying as still as we could, our breath turning to steam in the cold morning air. I could feel the warmth of Tommaso's body beside mine. In the stillness and silence, I watched the pink and gold of the rising dawn reflected in the glassy lake water.

Just as I was about to lose all feeling in my legs, something stirred in the distance. The flicker of a movement. I felt Tommaso tense; his lips parted slightly, and his eyes narrowed a little. I followed his gaze, and my heart skipped a beat as a wolf appeared out of the trees, its coat gray and tan, moving silently over the grass and rocks towards the water's edge. It sniffed a trail along the ground, then lifted its head to check the air.

The wolf turned its head in our direction, but didn't approach. I couldn't believe this was happening. Soon, more wolves followed, their coats in hues of gray and brown. Then I saw another behind it, and another one, and another; five wolves, one pack.

Beside me, Tommaso lowered himself even further to the ground, his camera poised. I heard the quiet snaps of pictures being taken. The wolves all moved so well together, like a dance. I could've watched them forever.

"That is a male," Tommaso whispered, pointing at the leader of the pack, the first wolf we'd seen: he was a strong-looking, sinewy beast with a regal air about him. "And that's one of the females." The animal he indicated this time was smaller but still strong, exploring the grass and stones for scents and possible sources of food.

I heard Tommaso suck in his breath. "The pack is bigger now than when I first saw it. One more wolf… a female. Very young. Two males and three females," he whispered. "Usually there's an alpha couple, a beta couple, and several omegas, the younger ones."

It was easy to see which one was the alpha female. She was the smallest, with a coat that was a slightly fairer shade of gray, and the one who appeared to be the most alert. She seemed to gravitate around the alpha male, with a mixture of respect and self-assurance. Her dark eyes shone in the dawn light. She was beautiful. The pack seemed to have a language of its own, communicating effortlessly through touch and smell as they moved in harmony. I held my breath, overwhelmed by the natural miracle in front of me. I never wanted the moment to end.

The alpha female was the first to notice us; alert all of a sudden, she ran a short distance along the lake's shore, stopped, and stood waiting for the others. The pack, seeming to sense her urgency, followed her at once. Once they'd all caught up, they stopped as one and looked in our direction for a beat before sprinting off, disappearing along the shore and past the lake, scaling the rocky ground, quick and agile. Tommaso and I exchanged glances.

"That was amazing! I can't believe how close they were. Those were *wolves*, Tommaso! Real wolves! You weren't kidding. That was incredible. Thank you!"

His familiar grin flashed across his face. "You're very welcome, *signorina*." Then he grew serious. "We're the lucky ones. Some people spend a lifetime trying to see them. They collect paw prints, find tracks, but never actually see them in the wild."

I didn't need to be told what a gift this was. "I don't know much about wolves, but what I do know is that they live in packs."

"Yes. Small packs. A couple usually, male and female, and a few other members."

"Yes. I'd love that," I said, almost to myself.

"To be a wolf?" Tommaso smiled.

"To have a pack."

"You know," Tommaso continued, "a while ago, I had a really hard time in my life. It's still hard, in many ways, but back then I was… broken. I couldn't find peace anywhere. I started coming up here almost every day. I wasn't even looking for wolves. It just happened. There's something about being with them that brings me… freedom. It's like these creatures make me see there's another way to be in this world, and it's just about being alive. Making survival your only burden."

"Yes. I see what you mean."

He shook his head, glancing at me apologetically. "Sorry. I didn't mean to get all heavy on you."

"Tommaso… I know. The whole story. About Federica, about Gioele."

He looked at me, surprised. "You do?"

"Nonna Tina told me."

"Well. What doesn't kill you, makes you stronger." Before I could think, I slipped my hand in Tommaso's, and he held on to it without looking at me.

"I rocked that boy to sleep. I gave him his bottle. He called me Papa. And now I'm not even allowed to speak to him."

The whole thing was too painful for words. "I'm so sorry."

"Yeah."

We were still holding hands – mine was lost in his, it was so much bigger than mine. "I'm better now," he said after a moment. "Nothing will ever make me forget him or stop longing for him. But things aren't so bleak. I think… life is in color again."

"What happened?" I tilted my head on one side.

"You came," he said, and I had no reply but a smile.

CHAPTER 11

We made our way back to Montevino in Tommaso's Jeep, driving away from the magical, rarefied atmosphere of the mountains and back to real life. The wolves, the glassy lake, Tommaso's presence: it had all given me new courage, new determination. Tommaso and I, that morning, had shared our struggles and our dreams, both looking for a resolution; I wasn't alone.

"Could you let me out at the community center? My car is still there."

"Sure."

Outside the community center, Tommaso parked just down the road from the red Fiat, then turned toward me. "Was it worth it then, to be woken up in the early hours and dragged up a mountain?"

I laughed. "More than worth it. It was amazing. I never thought I would see wolves so close to me. It makes me think that" – I hesitated, looking for the right words – "that life is *surprising*. Really surprising. If you only allow yourself to take a risk, to stray from your safe routine... I mean, last week I was in Texas, right? And this morning I'm crouching behind rocks in the Alps, watching wolves with an Italian guy!"

"I can't even begin to imagine how it must feel to be in your shoes. My life has been eventful enough, up to now, but yours...

finding out all that about your past, ending up in the other side of the world…"

"I can't either. I mean, I don't really know how it feels to be in my shoes, if that makes sense! I don't think I've fully digested all that has happened."

"It will take time. Time is a great healer. Do I sound like some kind of wise man?"

"A little like Yoda."

"Who?"

"Never mind. Thanks for this morning. Really." Once again, I hesitated. I was about to say "I hope to see you later," but I stopped myself, not wanting him to think I was expecting to see him again soon.

"No problem. I hope to see you later," he said, and a smile started from inside me and spread to my lips. I opened the door and got out of the Jeep before he could ask me what was funny.

I still had the scent of mountain wind in my hair as I walked up to my car. A couple of people said hello, and I replied pleasantly with *ciao*, without having a clue who they were, but it made me happy to be recognized in the community. I wondered if any of those strangers had known Malva. In this village there were people who'd been closer to her than I ever could be…

I drove home, got out of the car and went back into the house, but I soon found it impossible to stay inside. The morning had blossomed: blue sky, poplar seeds dancing in the air, flowers swaying in the warm breeze. In the brief time I'd been in Montevino, spring had turned into summer.

I fished a blanket out of a chest of drawers and headed back outside to a grassy corner underneath a chestnut tree. I sat with my back against the tree to read, a soft breeze blowing the branches and my hair. I had the eerie feeling of being in a secret garden, in a timeless, enchanted place, as I dived into Elisa's story once again.

July 9, 1942

Caro *Diario,*

Finally, the exams are finished. I passed, which is a miracle considering how much I had on my mind, and the chaos the university is in. Some students were thrown out of courses, and some professors too, because of the Racial Laws. They're Jewish and therefore, the Laws say, not Italian. Initially, they were allowed to continue studying if they'd enrolled already – no new Jewish students would be accepted. But later, they all had to leave.

Professor Bacher is among the ones who were thrown out. He refused to leave, so was escorted out by a few Blackshirts: tall, burly young men dragging an old and fragile man by the arms. I can't think about that without bubbling with rage inside: nobody can stay out of this conflict, nobody can avoid taking sides. Pietro has chosen to go to war, Leo has chosen his side, but Professor Bacher has spent a life of healing and teaching people: he has no place in this war. All he wanted was to do his job.

And the worst thought is, I don't know where they took him. Home arrest, I hope, but he wouldn't be the first to just disappear.

Professor Bacher worked hard all his life, he saved so many lives. Anybody in their right mind would see the injustice of all this. But people are not in their right minds anymore, it seems. People have been taken over by a sort of collective madness. And Papa, out of all of us, saw it first; even before Leo.

Underneath all this darkness is a little light. I'm going to spend the summer at home, helping my parents before starting my training with Dottor Quirico. In spite of the chaos around me, I feel this deep sense of satisfaction every time I think of how I'll be following him to people's houses, bringing children into the world, curing illnesses and offering advice. I'm going to learn so much from him and do a little good in a time of such great evil.

"Not as much as you can learn from your mother," Zia Costanza would say if she read this, deadpan as always. She might be right, but I don't think she can see the progress that medicine has made, everything that a doctor can do nowadays. I want to make a difference in Montevino. There are so many people who suffer here. I still cannot believe I've been given this chance. I'll be busy every minute of the day, and sometimes nights too. Which is good, because I think about them all the time, always at the back of my mind, always there like a hole in my heart.

Pietro, and Leo.

I haven't seen Leo since the night he left. I'm so afraid for him. I tried and tried to convince Papa to tell me where the partisans are based, so I could walk up and see Leo, but he refused, for my safety and theirs. He knows I would never betray them, but we've heard things about how they convince people to reveal what they know. Yes, it's better if I am left in the dark. But I still fear for Leo, for Papa, for Pietro. All are weighing so heavy in my heart. Papa's friends come to the house more and more often, and they shut themselves upstairs, discussing business we are to know nothing about. I know for sure that there are more of those jute bags I saw up in the High Woods, going back and forth between our homes and the mountains.

Oh, Leo, my love. Where are you?

July 12, 1942

Caro *Diario,*

So much has happened. I'm so happy, and so scared. And everything in between.

Dawn is breaking, and in an hour or so I'll have to go to work. I haven't slept at all, but I need to tell you everything in order. I can barely believe it all myself.

Leo came for me last night. I heard our old signal outside my window – the three owl hoots made by blowing into his cupped hands – and my heart stopped for a moment. I couldn't believe it was him! I lit a candle as quickly as I could, slipped downstairs in my dressing gown and let him into the house. I heard Papa's low voice and Mamma's footsteps on the stairs. I knew she'd seen us, but she let us be. Bless her.

When I finally managed to light the petrol lamp, I saw how thin Leo looked, how ragged his clothes were. But his eyes, those black eyes I love so much, they were still the same, even after months of living in perpetual danger. He took me by the waist and held me to him in a way that was almost desperate. Like I was about to vanish. I should be ashamed to write this but I'm not. We kissed there and then, and I didn't care about my parents or Zia Costanza hearing us, I didn't care about anything. My Leo was with me at last.

"Elisa, I don't have long. We came down for a few hours only, just to see you."

"We?"

"Davide Carpentieri is with me. I asked him to join me. I need him tonight."

"What do you mean?"

"Anything can happen. I could be dead tomorrow."

"Don't say that. I don't want to hear that."

"But it's true. Elisa, I asked Davide to be our witness tonight. In the church."

"Witness? You mean..."

"Yes, my love. I want to marry you tonight. If you say yes. If you'll have me."

What do you think my answer was? Yes, yes, a million times yes!

I ran to Mamma, who lay awake in her bed, listening out for me by the light of the petrol lamp. "Leo came for me. We're getting married!" I whispered.

"Oh, Elisa!" she said, and her eyes were shiny.

Papa's face was a picture. Even in the danger of the moment, his look of total surprise made me giggle. And then I spoke seriously. "I have your blessing, don't I, Papa?"

"You do, daughter. You and Leo have my blessing... and my permission, which he didn't ask!"

I bent over and embraced him, and he wrapped his arms around me. At that moment I knew I would remember this instant for the rest of my life.

"Mamma, please come and be my witness. Papa..."

"I understand. Too dangerous to maneuver me and the wheelchair around. Go, sweetheart," he said, while Mamma was hastily getting ready. I got dressed too, grabbing the dress I use for church and slipping on my ruby earrings quickly. I left my hair down, not having time to arrange it. With one last kiss to Papa and one to Zia Costanza, who stood in the corridor with her arms around herself, her expression and her thoughts a mystery, as they often were, I joined Leo outside.

We sneaked into the church like thieves in the night – Don Giuseppe and Davide were there already, and it was *all so hasty, so hushed, that when it ended, it was like I'd been dreaming. Yes, I would open my eyes and realize I was in my bed, that it was almost time to go to work...*

But the feeling of his lips on mine, a quick, chaste kiss under Mamma's and Davide's eyes, told me this was real. Leo was a man who kept his feelings buried deep down, and usually would not express them in public. But he held my hands in his and looked at me in a way that said it all – our fingers intertwined, and it sank in at last. Leo and I were husband and wife.

At that moment, a memory swept through my mind: a summer of long ago, when I must have been no older than ten years old – Leo climbing a cherry tree to pick cherries for me, and then arranging one around my ear, the two red buds peeping through my dark hair. Maybe that had been the moment I knew about Leo. About what I would always feel for him, even as young as I was. Now, as he held my hands, I was so happy that I forgot all about the imminent separation. Our moment was brief, and yet eternal.

We had no time left. He had to go. I held him to me, clinging for a moment before forcing myself to let go. I gave Davide a peck on the cheek. I was so grateful to him for doing this for Leo, for us. I knew the danger he'd put himself in coming down from the mountains, the risk they'd both run. I watched Leo and Mamma embrace, and then stood arm in arm with her, our hands laced, and watched him go back to the mountains...

A shrill, sharp sound interrupted my reading. It took me a few seconds to come back to the here and now, so absorbed was I by the story.

More ringing.

Oh, yes, my cell phone… I'd found a windowsill upstairs where there seemed to be signal, and I'd left it there. I dried my tears, cursing modern technology and having to be wrenched away from such a romantic moment – one including a Carpentieri – as I carefully put the diary down and ran back to the house and up the stairs to answer. It was Flora. She'd used the number I'd left her.

"Hello, Flora." My cheeks were still wet. I wiped my eyes and my face.

"You okay?"

"Yeah. Yeah. Just a bit of hay fever," I lied, breathing deeply to try to disperse the memory of the diary and come back to earth. I didn't want to tell Flora about it. I felt it was my thing, at least for now; I wasn't ready to share it.

"Just wondering how you were. You haven't come to the shop today."

"I thought you weren't that happy to see me there. And you don't need my help anyway," I teased her.

"I don't need it, as such. Only, I have a few things for you."

"Sounds good, thanks. Want to come up here for lunch?"

"Why not? I'm on my lunch break anyway. Be there in a moment."

Well, that was progress. I went outside to fetch the diary and the blanket, then began preparing for Flora's arrival. I must admit I was nervous. I did all I could to make the table look pretty, there in the kitchen of what was our family home. I put some water to boil for pasta – I knew that Italians don't seem to think it's a meal unless there's pasta involved, and I was now one of Nonna Tina's regular customers.

Not even half an hour later, Flora was at the door.

"Hey, come in," I said. It felt strange that I should invite her in when she'd come and gone as she pleased up until I'd arrived. Unfair, somehow. I had to find a way to bring the issue up during lunch.

"Thank you. Something smells good," she said.

"Well, I'd like to take the credit, but it's Tommaso's pesto."

"Oh, Tommaso. I see." There was a half-smile dancing on her lips. Beyond that prickly, harsh exterior lurked someone else; someone she kept carefully hidden away from the world. Maybe someone she used to be, long ago. Someone she could be again.

"No, you don't," I said, smiling back. "There's nothing to see," I said, as we made our way to the kitchen.

"Nah, you're right. Tommaso is *absolutely not* smitten with you. At all," she teased me.

"Smitten is a strong word. And anyway…"

"Anyway, you'll be gone soon," she said, and as the words came out, her eyes widened. But when I looked into her face and saw her expression, I realized she didn't mean to be nasty. She was simply stating a fact. And, to my surprise, it seemed to be a fact she didn't particularly like.

"I suppose so. Take a seat. Lunch'll be ready in a minute."

"Thanks. By the way, I brought you these."

"Oh… lavender candles! I love them, thanks!"

"No problem. Wow. It seems strange… to be here with you. This house feels almost… new. No. *Renewed*."

Was that a good thing?

"Well, not for long. Like you said, I'll be gone soon."

"Do you have to leave?" she said, somehow impulsively, as if the words had come out by themselves. I turned around, and she looked away. "Of course you do," she added hastily. "You have a life in Texas, people who're waiting for you, a job. All this… must seem like a dream to you."

"It does, actually. And I do have a home. The place I bought when I got out of care. It means a lot to me."

An image of the apartment back home shot through my mind – the small lobby, with the linoleum floor and fire extinguisher on the wall, and a vase of fake flowers beside my neighbor's door – the one room I lived in, with cheap furniture and constant noise outside. It seemed so mundane, so modest, compared to this. And yet, I loved my little apartment back home; it was in that anonymous building block, in an anonymous part of town, that I had gained freedom and the ability to get to this moment.

"I have a best friend. Kirsten," I said, throwing a handful of pasta into the boiling water and remembering, with a pang of guilt, the missed calls from her that I'd seen when I'd ended the call with Flora.

"No man?" She rested her chin on her hand, a silver ring on each finger.

"No. No guy, no family." *Because you didn't look for me.* The angry thought came and went, making me lose my concentration.

"So... what about Marco?" I thought it would be okay to ask such a personal question, as she was doing the same.

She raised her eyebrows. "How do you know about him?"

"Chocolate festival, remember?"

Flora placed a hand on her forehead. "Oh, God, yes. I'd rather forget."

"So... Marco?"

She shrugged. "He's too good for me. And he will see sense, sooner or later. His daughter hates me, by the way."

"Well, she's wrong. How is Marco too good for you, anyway? You're beautiful, funny. Interesting."

"Yeah, interesting is a way of putting it. Anyway. So, your job is waiting for you back home, yes?"

An abrupt change of topic, if ever there was one.

"Yes, I do have a job waiting for me. It's a good place to work, with nice people, but it won't take me anywhere. I'm really only there to save for college, and I'm living off my college fund to be here. So, that's not good."

"I understand." There was a moment of silence, broken only by the pasta pot rumbling in the background, and by birdsong outside. A warm, golden light seeped in through the open window – gentler than the Texas light, somehow. And then Flora spoke.

"So, if you had a job here you could stay longer?"

I shrugged. "I don't know... Maybe. There are so many things to consider. I don't even know what I want to study yet."

Flora stood and went to the window, gazing outside. "Okay, you'll say no, and I completely understand," she said in a casual tone. "But... well, you offered to help me at Passiflora. If you want... there's a job there for you."

I was taken aback. That was pretty much the last thing I expected Flora to say, especially after the way she'd welcomed me.

"Me, work with you? At Passiflora?"

She shrugged. "Well, you're going to have to study those books I gave you, and there's a lot to learn, but, yes. You offered to help me, didn't you?"

"Flora, I offered you my help for free. I didn't mean you should pay me."

"I think the pasta is ready," she replied.

"Wow. Is that some Italian pasta sense? A sixth sense for spaghetti?"

Flora laughed. "I guess so."

I drained the pasta over the sink and mixed the sweet-scented pesto into it as Flora began pouring water from a jug into glasses I'd set out on the table.

"I think it's a good idea, you know," she continued. "The pay won't be much, but hey, who wouldn't want to work with me?"

I laughed. "I'll help you, but you don't need to pay me."

"If I don't then you'll have to go back. And we're right back at the beginning of this conversation."

"Look, don't take this the wrong way but… Tommaso told me you're struggling to pay the rent as it is," I said, handing her a steaming plate of pasta. I had no idea how she would take that, but I had to say it. It was the truth. There was no way I could allow her to have even more financial problems because of me. Because of wanting to keep me near. Was that what she wanted, to keep me near?

"That is true. But… Well, I haven't been able to open the shop every day. I've been… unwell."

"Yeah," I replied in a small voice. "Come on, eat up. Don't think about that."

But she laid her fork down and took a moment. "It's just to explain to you. The reason why the shop is struggling is that sometimes… sometimes… I don't know, it just feels too much, getting up in the morning."

"Oh, Flora…"

"Well, never mind. It was a silly idea. Sorry for bringing it up," she said.

It was decision time.

"You know what? Actually, it's a good idea. I can help you open the shop every day, you can get back on your feet… and I get to stay a little longer. I don't know if they'll keep my job open back home, but—"

"You make a mean spaghetti, you know?" Flora said suddenly, contemplating the plate in front of her.

I held my breath for a moment, then burst out laughing.

"Eat up!"

"Thanks," she replied, and twirled the spaghetti around her fork like the natural she was.

"So, yeah. Job accepted."

My thoughts went to Kirsten and Shanice, and my life back in Texas with all its familiar routines and places I knew. It would be hard to tell them about this. And they'd be shocked at how quickly I'd decided, how suddenly this had come on.

Had it, though? Because right now, change seemed like a long time coming.

"Well. Good. I'm happy," Flora said, and her eyes went to the window.

"Better hit the books, I guess." I couldn't wait to learn more about naturopathy. Especially the use of healing herbs – I couldn't believe I never got into something like that in Texas. After all, I'd been looking for a direction and this was something that felt right.

"Yeah, I suppose it is the right time for you to be changing things." Flora put my thoughts into words.

"You can say that again."

Sooner or later I would have to ask her the fundamental question that burned inside me, more painful than I could ever say. But not now, not yet. I decided to clear the air about something else that had been on my mind for a while – something I was surprised Flora hadn't brought up.

"Flora, listen. I'm grateful to my mother for leaving me this house. I've been here for such a short time, and I know it's strange, but I feel so at home already."

"Yes. I can see that," she said, and I studied her face for signs of bitterness, of resentment. There were none.

"The thing is… it's the Stella family home. You've kept it clean and well maintained all this time. It should be yours too. I don't understand how you could accept that it's mine so easily. I mean, you haven't exactly been welcoming, but you never actually protested about me owning the place."

"It's because I think it's right that you own the place."

"But you'd been coming here and cleaning it and putting the heating on. You'd been maintaining it like someone still lived here. Then, I arrived. Out of the blue. And you sent me away, remember? You said to go and never come back."

"Callie—"

"That doesn't matter, really. We've moved on from there. I understand why you didn't doubt who I am. I mean, it's like looking in a mirror…"

Her brow furrowed, as if the fact pained her.

"…but you never said this house shouldn't be mine. You never said this house should be yours."

Flora shrugged. "Because I don't think it should be mine."

"Why? You're a Stella woman. Like me."

"I don't deserve it."

"*What*? Please don't tell me it's more of the Flora self-hatred thing, because I've had enough of it since the chocolate fest."

She gave a brittle laugh. "Wow, you Americans are blunt. I like it."

"What do you mean you don't deserve this house?"

"Ah, nothing. You know, I talk nonsense from time to time. Well, thanks for this."

I knew from her face that this conversation was over, that today I would not be allowed to go any further.

"You Italians talk about food to avoid awkward conversations," I observed.

"We Italians talk about food as often as we're allowed to," she said, picking up her bag.

"So…" I began.

"Yes?"

"I'll see you tomorrow morning? At Passiflora?"

She smiled. "That'd be *meraviglioso*. Wonderful. Keep working on those books."

"For sure," I said.

It was a curt goodbye, Flora style, without an embrace or any sentiment. I watched her walk away from Firefly House and disappear, her figure looking suddenly tiny out in the big world.

So many questions were still unanswered. But at least I had a little more time to unravel the Stella secrets.

*

I cleaned up, my mind racing with all I had to do now I'd made the decision to stay. The enormity of it was beginning to hit me. I would call Kirsten tonight – she deserved to know before Shanice. What would I say to Shanice? To replace me for a while, or to look for someone else? And I would tell Tommaso.

I wondered what his reaction would be when he knew I was staying.

I was also desperate to ask him if he knew of Davide Carpentieri from Elisa's diary, since they shared the same surname, and eventually I would have to tell him that my father was Paolo Caporale. Surely he couldn't hold it against me, could he? He would accept it, I was sure.

Out of the blue, a sudden wave of happiness flowed over me, a feeling I hadn't experienced for a long, long time – maybe not since I was a little girl, before everything fell apart. I grabbed the books Flora had given me, and Elisa's diary, and headed outside to spend the rest of the afternoon reading and studying.

I started out with the topic that attracted me the most: herbalism. *Curare con le Erbe – Healing with Herbs –* a dark green, fabric-covered tome with beautiful illustrations. I began thumbing through it.

> Malva (*Malva sylvestris*) is a spontaneous European plant. Its name comes from the Latin *mollire*, to calm.

In the Middle Ages, it came to symbolize calm, love
and sweetness. It was so powerful and commonly used
it came to be considered an *omnimorba*, which means
"a plant that can cure all ailments."

Malva's name symbolized sweetness. Was she really as sweet as
everyone thought? Why had she not given me back to her family,
when she knew she was sick – and instead had me adopted?
The usual pang of loss and longing filled me as I thought of my
adoptive parents. It was impossible to keep resenting them for
having hidden the truth about my birth from me. I just wished
I could tell them all that had been happened. I was desperate for
them to know that I'd found my way home.

I asked myself what Malva and my adoptive parents had
wished for me. Happiness and love, for sure, but what were their
dreams and ambitions for me? The time spent together had been
so short, maybe too short for them to even think of how my life
would shape up. Flora had said that healing was in our blood; had
Malva hoped that I would follow the family tradition somehow?

Passiflora: (*Passiflora incarnata*) is linked with passion
and tragedy. A legend says it grew on Jesus' cross after
His crucifixion. A South American legend talks about
the tragic destiny of Maracujà, a noblewoman engaged
to a captain but in love with a young indigenous man
instead. She was confined in her house and watched
her beloved from the window, until one night he didn't
come. Word reached her that he'd been killed by Maracujà's fiancé, the captain. Crazy with pain, Maracujà
begged an old woman from her beloved's tribe to pierce
her heart with an arrow. From the wound grew a strange
and wonderful plant, whose petals opened to the sun

and closed to the moon: Passiflora. Passiflora is said to be a remedy for heartache and loss.

Trust Flora to have some tragic story behind her name. I went on reading until the chilly evening wind began to blow. It was time to go inside. As I gathered the books, a small leaflet fell out of one of them.

> *Naturopathy Academy, Turin*
> *Three-year course, accredited Naturopath*
> *Anatomy, Physiology, Pathology*
> *Way of Nature: herbal traditions*
> *Natural Nutrition*
> *Aromatherapy...*

And it went on, a list of subjects that sounded like a whole new world, a curtain opening on something that was alien and yet familiar. I thought of what Elisa kept writing in her diary over and over, about helping people and healing people. On the corner of the leaflet were some scribbled details of dates, and what must be train times between Turin and Montevino. This must have been the college Flora attended, I deduced.

A thought began making its way into my mind – something I didn't want to put in words, not yet – and I set it aside to mull over. I tucked the leaflet back into the book, and opened the diary once again.

Elisa's brother was in the army, her love had joined the Resistance, and she was left in what would soon be a place at war. I couldn't quite put her story in context, because back in school, we'd barely touched on the details of the Second World War in Europe, concentrating on the American side of things. Now I regretted it, because I didn't know what would happen next in

Elisa's story. All I remembered was that battles would be fought on Italian territory.

Now I noticed that Elisa had skipped her usual introduction. The tone was frantic and her handwriting, usually deliberate and beautiful, was rushed and messy.

It's like a rising tide. Every day something happens, and we can't keep up with the news. Tonight, when we switched on the radio, Mussolini's familiar booming voice didn't fill the room as it usually did. It was General Badoglio, once Mussolini's right-hand man, the hero of the Great War. According to propaganda, he had bent the savage people of Ethiopia to our superior will and contributed to the creation of the Italian colonial empire, of which he'd been proclaimed vice-king. I knew enough of fascist propaganda not to believe a word of praise sung about him, but what he said tonight was astonishing.

"... The Italian government, recognizing the impossibility of continuing the unequal fight against the overpowering enemy forces, in order to preserve the nation from further and even more terrible hardships, has petitioned General Eisenhower, commander-in-chief of the Allied armies of England and the United States of America. Our requests have been accepted. Therefore, any hostile act by the Italian army against the Anglo-American forces must cease everywhere. However, they will react to attack from any other forces..."

I gasped. Mamma turned from the sink and searched for Papa's eyes. Zia Costanza laid down her rosary slowly. I swear that even from this isolated place, we could hear the rising voices in the village.

"Does this mean that Pietro will come back?" Mamma burst out.

"Shhh! There's more!" Papa said, and we kept listening while the news sank in. An armistice had been signed with the Allies, our enemies – was it over? Was the war over? Were we free again?

Would Leo and Pietro return to me, to us?

We looked at each other, not knowing how to express the complicated mix of joy and disbelief. And then, a crackling noise, and the official transmission was halted. Another voice began to speak, one we'd never heard before. The signal was disturbed, and Papa wheeled himself nearer the radio to listen.

"Italy will not surrender; Italy will keep fighting. We will stand by the German side, as we've always done, and open our doors to them as friends and liberators from the treacherous snakes who sold us out. Our proud army will never stop battling the Allies, and we urge all civilians, men and women, to join the fight…"

There was more, and we listened to every word, without being able to make much sense of it. Finally, the message was over, and the usual transmission began again. It was just music now, an incongruous end to all that upheaval.

"Luigi…" Mamma pleaded. She's always been a woman with her own mind, but since Pietro left there has been a subtle, yet clear change in her. Now she looks to Papa to make sense of this chaotic world; she looks to him to guide us, when nothing around us makes sense. I think she uses all her strength to believe that Pietro will come back unscathed.

"I think it means civil war," Papa said, and a chill went down my spine. "Badoglio and his people want the war over. But the staunch fascists will not accept that. The war will be here, now. In every village and in every house."

"People will divide in two," Costanza said. "And they will fight."

"But will Pietro return?" Mamma implored again.

They exchanged a long look. Papa didn't answer.

August 10, 1943

Caro *Diario,*

With almost all men – even the youngest and the oldest, even the sick – called to the army, medics are almost nowhere to be found. Dottor Quirico and I seldom go to patients together now: we wouldn't be able to see to them all. A quick way to convince people to trust women doctors, I suppose... If only there were more around here than just me. People might stare and grumble less when they see me, but they have no choice but to accept me. Thank goodness for my mother and the women like her, or people would have nobody to turn to. Only now I realize how hard Dottor Quirico's job must have been before he bought a car, when he went everywhere on horseback, or cycled up and down the valleys in every type of weather. But there are places we simply can't reach by car or bike – only a horse, or on feet, will do. Thankfully the community is helping: the Conte has allowed me to borrow one of his horses, a mare called Vento, so many times that he said I can call it mine; and Leone provides me with coffee and sweets to bring to the patients, and keep me going too. God knows where they find coffee and sugar, but bless them that they do.

I try my best and work as hard as I can, but it seems like everything we do is a little drop of goodness against the rising tide. News comes so fast that we can barely make sense of it.

The Germans are coming. The Americans are coming… We don't know what to expect, we don't know where to look.

We have no idea what Pietro's fate might be, and none of us can find peace. Before everything fell apart, they would send a telegram to tell families of wounded or deceased soldiers; but now, in this chaos, nobody knows anything… And my little brother's whereabouts remain a mystery.

Oh, caro *Diario.*

I'm writing this almost with my head on my elbow, I'm so exhausted. But I made it, I saved Patrice's life. She's only seven. And to see her like that, eaten alive by the fever. Thank goodness I remembered something Professor Bacher said to me at university…

But I'm not making sense, I know! I'll tell you all. Dottor Quirico is away for two days, south of Montevino, almost near Turin, so my work has doubled.

I've barely managed to lay my head on the pillow because there has been a small flu epidemic across the local villages, and I haven't stopped for a moment. We heard calling at our door, in the middle of the night – a woman's voice.

"Dotor! Dotor!" She spoke in a mountain dialect, more similar to French than to our own Montevino sound. I heard my mother letting her in while I got dressed as quickly as I could. I ran downstairs and saw a woman wrapped in woolen shawls, pale and with huge, frightened blue eyes. She must have come from very far, her dialect and her clothes told me. It was only then I realized she was unshod, and she didn't even carry a petrol lamp.

"Please come. My daughter is dying," she said, and the lack of emotion in her words was contradicted by her trembling body and her bare, bleeding feet.

"Where do you come from?"
"Nourissat."

I paused. Nourissat? That's where Tommaso had taken me to
see the wolves. Imagine walking all that way in the dark, without
shoes, and with wolves roaming the forests... That poor woman!

*"Nourissat?" I was astounded. That is high up, and the
only way to get up there is by dirt path — when there are
any. Otherwise, it's stony ground or fields. "Did somebody
bring you? You came on horseback?"*

*The woman shook her head. "Please come." Her voice
was hoarse with exhaustion. Beneath the dirt and the
tiredness that lined her face, I guessed she was very young,
maybe younger than me.*

"I will. Don't worry. Who's sick? Who needs my help?"
"My daughter. The fever is not going away."

*Mamma and I exchanged a glance, and Mamma ran
out of the room while I grabbed my bag and wrapped myself
in a shawl. Mamma returned with a pair of stockings for
the mountain woman, which she refused. "We must hurry."*

*"Keep them," my mother said, and pushed them into the
woman's hand. We strode out into the dark, and I led her
towards the Conte's stable. I readied Vento, and we were off.*

*It took almost three hours, and even Vento struggled.
We finally arrived at a small wood cabin, dimly lit from
within. A stony-faced man let us in, murmuring something
under his breath. Mountain dialects are similar enough to
Montevino ones for me to understand that he thought doctors
kill their patients more than sickness does. Thank you, sir.*

*The little girl was clean, unlike everybody else in the
cabin — two other children, barefooted and wide-eyed like*

their mother. She was burning hot, a fever so violent I realized at once this was not the flu that had been raging in the villages. My medicine bag looked desolate, half empty and mostly made up of remedies my mamma had made for me; not the strong, modern medicine I'd dreamed of using when I'd started my course. Two things I'd learned, in my brief time as a doctor: that poverty and ignorance do even more damage than sickness; and that war kills in many ways, not just by catching a bullet in your body.

"What's her name?"

"Patrice."

"Patrice," I repeated, and gently swept her hair away from her forehead. Her chest was rising and falling frantically, and her heart was racing.

An infection of the brain, maybe.

"Has she been complaining of a sore head?"

"No."

Tuberculosis?

"Has she been coughing?"

"No."

Her father began pacing up and down, throwing his hands in the air. "I told you this would be no use! Dotori know nothing! And this is not even a dotor! *She's a* fémna!*"* A woman. *I ignored him. His daughter's life was more important than anything this man could throw at me.*

I laid my hand on the girl's forehead and held her hand. I closed my eyes. Silence fell on the cabin. Maybe they thought I was performing some superstitious ritual, but I was just concentrating.

And then it happened. The girl began to cool right under my hands, and her skin, which was dry before, began to sweat so hard it was almost leaking fluids. Cold sweat. I felt the little girl's temperature crash with every second that passed.

I knew what it was.

And I also knew I had no medicine to cure her, no way to save her.

The mother must have read my expression, because she yelped like a wounded animal.

"A basin of fresh water, please," I asked. The mother made a quick gesture, and one of the children ran out with a carved wooden bowl only to return a moment later. The water was freezing cold, straight from the glacier streams. I washed my hands and dried them on a clean cloth I'd brought with me.

"You need to wait an hour or so, then wash her down. Be careful she catches as little cold as possible; keep her covered as you wash her down. Then wrap her up warm, very warm, until the fever comes back."

"The fever will come back?"

I nodded, looking straight at her. "It has happened before, hasn't it?"

"Yes."

"How many times?"

"Many times." The woman looked at her husband, a gaze that was full of resentment mixed with fear. Clearly, he'd stopped her from calling a doctor. And the girl had malaria.

It seems impossible that malaria would strike someone who lives in the mountains. But the girls who went to work in the rice fields would catch it, and in spite of the mountain air, bring the contagion back. It would be rare for someone to catch it so high up, but quite common somewhere like Montevino. Or it used to be, but the authorities worked *long and hard to eradicate malaria. They stopped rice fields from being too close to villages and they distributed quinine free to the rice girls and the general population. Quinine is quite simply the bark of a tree that grows overseas. Before the war, you could get it everywhere; you could buy it in the* drogheria *– the chemist – and drink it in an* acqua tonica *at a bar, mixed with water, gin and sugar. This meant that malaria went from killing many, many people, to being almost eradicated.*

Almost. Like I said, war kills in many ways.

"How often does the fever come?"

"Every four days."

I nodded. That is how malaria works. The fever comes back and then falls in different cycles, from one to four days.

"She'll die?" *the woman said, without feeling, though her face was a mask of pain.*

"I can't say, right now."

Yes, but it will take a while. And a lot of suffering.

"Is there no medicine?"

There is. War took it away from us.

"There is, but I don't have it, and the other doctor in the village doesn't either. But I'll do my best to find it. I'll send someone around, even to Turin. I promise you, I'll do my very best. I'll be back soon." *I was sure the Conte would ask one of his men to go by car, scour the pharmacies, beg other doctors to part from their precious quinine… I had to find a way.*

*

Days passed. I received bad news after bad news. There was no quinine to be found. I didn't believe that, of course; I knew that it was there, but nobody wanted to part with it.

Those who had some kept it for themselves or their family and friends. They did not want to give it away to a woman doctor in a mountain village, just to cure a little girl from a castaway place.

One afternoon, I had to take myself away from everything, and went to the cabin in the High Woods where Leo and I used to go. I punched the stones until my hands bled, but I didn't care. Three hours north a little girl was dying, her internal organs ravaged by parasites. And there was nothing I could do.

It was then that I remembered Professor Bacher giving us a lecture about the effects of malaria on the heart. He said that before quinine was widespread, they tried to use…

Methylene blue.

I had to try.

Finally, after a two-day search, the Conte's man drove back from Turin with a dose of methylene blue. I made my way back to the cabin straight away, praying that I would find the place again when I'd only seen it in darkness, and praying the girl was still alive. Methylene blue should ideally be taken with quinine, so I had no idea if it would work. But we had nothing to lose – without medicine, Patrice was dead.

When I arrived at Nourissat, I found Patrice's father standing outside the wood cabin, pale and drawn. For a moment, I was afraid he would not let me in, but he opened the door for me, without saying a word, and followed me inside. I found the rest of the family gathered in one of the two small rooms the cabin was made of – a sort of nest had been made for Patrice, with warm and soft blankets, in front of the fire. The woman was kneeling beside her, rosary in hand; when I arrived she turned her enormous blue eyes towards me, and she lit up – hope was here. Except I had no idea if what I had would work. I could kill the girl by giving her too much blue, or too little. Or maybe the malaria was simply too advanced. Maybe what I had brought with me wasn't hope, but just illusion.

I was frightened, like I'd never been before, at university or as a practicing doctor. And still, I kept my expression strong and secure, and my hands steady, as I injected the girl's thin, white arms with blue. I could feel the woman's terror and the man's hostility as the blue slowly suffused the girl's skin, creating what looked like a faint azure cloud on her arm. Night was falling outside, and I would not leave Patrice. I sat on the floor beside her, unable to stop looking at her. Quietly, without saying a word, the girl's mother brought me a chair, and then a cup of warm milk and a piece of bread. We all sat and waited. The day turned into night, the soft words of the rosary comforting as we waited to see whether Patrice would live or die.

After a while, Patrice began to moan; we took her blankets off, as her fever was rising. The cycle was beginning again. I abandoned my chair and kneeled on the floor. Without being asked, Patrice's mother had brought a basin of water and a cloth, and began dabbing her daughter's head.

The fever rose. And rose. And rose.

And stopped.

And receded.

The fire that had burned within her had been dampened.

The woman looked at me. In an unexpected gesture, she quietly slipped her hand towards mine, and squeezed it hard. My emotion was buried deep – I was a doctor, and I couldn't show how scared, how hopeful, how broken I felt in that moment.

Patrice's breath changed, and she fell in a comfortable sleep. The smell in the room changed too, imperceptibly. I know it's absurd to say it, and unscientific – but I did not smell death anymore.

I let myself rest my head in my hands on top of Patrice's nest of blankets, and without realizing, I fell asleep.

I was woken by a male voice shouting, and some horrible, brute force lifting me up and pushing me against the wall. My eyes met Patrice's father's face, contorted in fury.

"What did you do to her? What did you do?"

Oh my God. Patrice had died. She had died in the night. And I had fallen asleep.

Patrice's mother was shouting too, trying to pull her husband away from me; out of the corner of my eye, I saw the other children cowering in the corner, in terror.

The man slapped my face; it stung. I was terrified, but also numb with Patrice's death. Somewhere in my consciousness rose the thought that the man would kill me, and I was simply not strong enough to defend myself.

"Stop! Stop! Patrice is cured! Look, she's cured!"

Cured?

I turned my head, in spite of the man's arms clasping my shoulders – Patrice lay with her eyes open, a soft blush on her cheeks, her hair dirty, but dry. She was curled up, like someone who's finally slept and rested after a long, long time. She wasn't dead. She wasn't dead!

Only, her eyes were blue. The white of her eyes was blue.

"You did some magic on her! You called the devil to cure her! And look at her now! The devil! I'd rather her be dead—"

But he didn't finish the sentence, because Patrice's mother hit him over the head with the fire poker, and he fell cold on the ground.

I steadied myself for a moment, and ran to Patrice. My face stung and my shoulders hurt, and I'd been so scared, but I didn't care. Patrice was alive. I checked her heart, her temperature, her breathing. The cycle had been broken.

Her mother's eyes and mine met, and she smiled. Quite surreal, as her husband lay on the ground with a bleeding head. I checked him too; he would live. He was just asleep for a little while.

"Patrice's eyes will go back to normal. It's just the remedy I gave her. I promise you, this has nothing to do with the devil. It's medicine. Science. Not magic."

She smiled wider, and I saw that half her teeth were missing. She took both my hands and kissed them.

It was really, really hard not to cry then. But I didn't.

"I'll be back tomorrow," I said. "Your husband'll be back on his feet then, so keep him away from me," I added, making a mental note of taking the Conte's man with me for protection, just in case.

On the way home, riding on Vento in the chilly morning, I thought of Professor Bacher. Where was he? Where had they taken him?

Wherever you are, thank you, for saving Patrice's life, *I prayed under my breath.*

And now, bed. I swear, I could sleep for a week…

Good night, Diary. Or good morning. I'm not sure what time it is!

Your drained and proud and happy,
Dottor Stella

August 23, 1943

We need to try to be strong, now. Pietro has been taken to Poland, to a work camp. It was Lorenzo Pigna who told us; he was with Pietro, but he escaped. He says he walked almost all the way from Poland; that he walked for months. From the state of his feet, I believe him. He's like a walking skeleton.

Mamma told me that since he'd been taken, his mother had lit so many candles in the church that they sprawled on the floor, and Don Giuseppe didn't have the heart to stop her. She lived in the church more than at home. And now, her Lorenzo is back.

But our Pietro is not.

Mamma cried and cried, Papa retreated in silence, the way he does. I must be strong for them. Yes, strong the way women are supposed to be…

She'd written the word "strong" three times in a few lines. My heart went out to her. My struggles and troubles, how small they seemed in comparison! At least that poor boy, Lorenzo, had come back. Maybe Pietro would too…

"Rissi!" a voice behind me called out and I turned to see Tommaso, standing behind the wrought-iron fence, looking fresh and cool in jeans and T-shirt.

I laughed at the use of my nickname, unashamedly happy to see him. "Come on in," I called back and he jumped the fence with ease.

"So… how did it go with Flora?"

"I'm not even going to ask you how you know that Flora was here today."

He laughed. "I was repairing those fences I told you about, when she passed right in front of me. She seemed lost in thought. May I join you?"

"Sure," I said, and he sat on the blanket beside me, crossing his long legs. "Well, you know, she offered me a job. Believe it or not."

"In Passiflora? That's great! I mean, if you accepted."

"I did, yes." I took a breath. "I'm someone who didn't change a thing in three years of life, and now I'm changing everything at once!"

"You get those moments, don't you? Suddenly, everything is turned upside down. But probably it means it's the right thing. That your time has come."

"Mmm. I didn't even say I was going to think about it. I just said yes. In the space of like, ten minutes of conversation."

"What makes you want to stay? Obviously, the family you just found. But... is it the place as well? Do you like it here?"

I laughed and decided it was better to avoid his eyes, in case he realized that, well, he was one of the reasons why it felt good to stay. His presence was something that made staying here even sweeter. Tommaso knew what I was thinking, I was sure, because he laughed and looked away too.

"Well, yes, I love it here! Who wouldn't? Look around you. And I love my home. *And*, you see, there's... these." I showed him the books scattered on the blanket.

He picked up the one I had been studying and thumbed through the pages. "That's what Flora does, isn't it?"

"Yes. I need to learn all this to work in the shop, you know. Back in Texas I was wondering what to do with my life. This has really hooked me."

"That's good. I think that when you find the right thing, it resounds with you. That's what happened to me with painting.

It'll never be my job as such, but it's something that keeps me going. It's one of the things I wake up for in the morning."

"I love your paintings... they're beautiful. Especially..." I paused. I was going to say "especially the painting of Gioele", but I stopped myself. He must have guessed, because sorrow seemed to pass over him, like a cloud on the hills.

Without saying a word, he came closer beside me and slipped his arms around me. He leaned against the chestnut tree, taking me with him, and we just sat there, snuggled together.

My heart was jumping out of my chest. I'd never been so close to a man before.

"You know, Rissi, I think you're amazing. You're in a foreign country, a foreign culture, all by yourself, and you're making your way. Figuring it all out." The sound of his voice in my ear made my skin tingle. I wanted to close my eyes and just listen to it.

"Oh, I don't know about figuring it all out," I managed to say, though I was very much distracted by his scent. This was going too fast. Definitely too fast. But it felt right, and I didn't want to stop it. I'd been so cautious, since I came out of the care system. Anything could upset my hard-earned, brittle balance. But now I seemed to have forgotten fear and just embraced life. I hoped with all my heart that I would not end up face first on the ground.

"It seems that Flora has begun to open up a little. Did she tell you anything more about your family?"

Was it the right time to tell him that my biological father was Carlo Caporale's son?

I had to. He would find out, sooner or later.

"Tommaso, have you heard about someone called Davide Carpentieri?"

"Well, yes. He was my grandfather."

"He was a kind man."

"How do you know?"

I smiled. "Never mind. Listen, Tommaso... Flora told me something quite... upsetting, actually."

"She did? I'm sorry," he said. I appreciated the fact that he wasn't asking directly what it was but waiting for me to speak.

"My biological father, Malva's husband... he was Paolo Caporale," I whispered, and then stilled, waiting for his reaction. With the way we were sitting, I couldn't see his face. I felt him contract, and I turned around.

He looked aghast.

"The Caporales took everything away from me, Callie." He hadn't called me Rissi. My heart sank, and I wrenched myself from him. I was kneeling on the grass, while he was still sitting with his back against the tree; but not for long, because he stood, his face white.

"I never knew my father, Tommaso. As far as I know, he abandoned me. He's dead now."

He nodded. I could see he was making a tremendous effort to control himself, to pretend this didn't matter; but there was no need for words. His upset was plain to see. I followed suit and stood, trembling all over.

"It's not my fault. I didn't even know who he was. I didn't know any of this..." I opened my arms.

"Callie. I'm sorry. I... I have to go."

"Tommaso—"

"I'm sorry. Just... give me some time."

"Fine. Fine. You know, Tommaso, I have nothing to do with that man. Flora said he destroyed my mom and he abandoned me. And now you give me the cold shoulder because... why? Because I might have inherited some of his nasty genes?" I was angry now. It was all so unfair, so undeserved.

"You came looking for your family. You found them. The Caporales are your family too."

"Like, who? My father's dead! Sure, had he been alive I would have wanted to meet him. I can't deny that. I know he was bad. I know it from you and from Flora, and I believe you. But I would have wanted to look him in the eye, at least. But he's gone... I have nothing to do with the Caporales now. Nothing."

"You still have a cousin. Denis. The nice guy who took *my* family away!" His fury shocked me. "You were looking for someone who shared your blood. Well, you found him."

Something in me deflated. I was floored. "You think I might be just like him? Just like them?" My voice came out small, laden with disappointment.

He looked down. He didn't deny it.

"Just go, Tommaso."

He turned away, jumped over the fence and disappeared, leaving me bereft.

*

It was a long night. I sat on the terrace, wrapped in a blanket, cradled by the crickets' song and watching the still, black profile of the mountains. A waning moon hung in the sky, moving slowly as the night went on. Sleep evaded me, of course. I kept thinking of Tommaso.

I cried tears of frustration and anger – because I understood a terrible truth: he knew he was being unfair, but he couldn't help himself. The Caporales had taken away his father's life, his wife and the boy he'd believed was his – everything he loved – and the slightest brush with them, even through me, hurt him terribly.

He was the first guy I'd opened up to in my twenty-one years of life, and now he despised me, for reasons completely out of my control. The injustice of it took my breath away.

I had to admit that Tommaso had been part of my decision to stay and accept Flora's offer of a job; but even without him, I would stay. I wanted to unravel my family's secrets, I wanted to be with Flora, as moody as she was; I wanted that job. I yearned to learn about naturopathy, and work in Passiflora. It fascinated me in a way I'd just never felt, for anything. Now that I'd come alive, I was beginning to realize how dead inside I'd been. Finally, life was mine for the taking. I would go ahead with my plans, no matter what Tommaso thought or did.

I checked my watch: it was the early hours of the morning here, afternoon in Texas. It was time. I went and perched myself on the windowsill where the signal was strong, and tried to phone Kirsten. I'd barely finished dialing, when she picked up as if she'd been waiting for me to call; I felt guilty, because I knew I'd been neglecting her. The long list of missed calls and messages I'd seen earlier that morning haunted me.

"Finally! I was worried! Is everything okay?" She was at the Windmill – I watched her picking up the call and rushing to the break room to speak. We weren't allowed to answer the phone when we were working, so I assumed she must have talked to Shanice about my silence and asked if she could reply if I called.

"I'm so sorry… things have been crazy."

"Tell me more!" She sat on one of the chairs in the break room – the familiarity of that scene tugged at my heart.

"Oh… it's… it's complicated." I'm not sure why I couldn't find it in myself to explain to her the tangled threads of all that had been happening. "I'm… staying a little longer."

"Oh. Oh." Her face fell. "Okay. Have you told Shanice?" she whispered, and briefly looked behind her. "Because she'll want to know." I could see Kirsten was trying to sound breezy, but she couldn't hide the hurt. And I felt terrible about it.

"Not yet."

"She'll freak." Another look behind her.

"Yes. But… I have to make some big decisions about my life, Kirsten."

"Your life is here!"

I stayed quiet.

"Callie, I'm worried for you."

"What? Why?" I asked, but of course I knew why. I was, after all, on the other side of the world, in a big house all by myself, chasing something that might turn out to be elusive.

"So far away… With those people…"

"Oh, is that Shanice there?" I saw my former manager coming in, and I didn't want to get into private business with her around.

"She is, yes… Shanice, Callie is on… Bye then, Callie," she said, and the coldness of her tone was unmistakable. Never before had a call between us come to a faster conclusion.

"Hey! Kirsten was carrying that phone everywhere, waiting for you," Shanice said, smiling. "I told her you were probably too busy sunning yourself and drinking vino to mind us!"

"Yeah. I've been doing that too. Shanice, look, I'm staying over here for a little longer."

"Oh."

I was disappointing everyone. Was I mad to undo all the work that I'd done to build myself a life?

"Ooo-kay," she continued. "What do you mean by that? Give me something a bit more precise."

"At least until the end of the summer."

The idea of summer in Montevino stretched before me: the sun, the lush garden of Firefly House, the long evenings laden with the scent of blooming flowers…

Shanice pulled me back to earth with a bang.

"Callie, honey, what do you mean by 'at least'? Because this girl I have now is leaving to go backpacking in China. If you're away until the end of the summer, I'll hire a student who'll go back to college in September, all fine. But if you tell me you're not coming back... I'm starting all over again. This place doesn't work like that. We're family. We work together. Servers who come and go just don't—"

"I know. I know." I had to interrupt her; I just couldn't hear anymore.

"You have a good thing here, Callie. That's all I'm saying," Shanice added.

"I have a good thing here too."

"Yeah. I'm sure. And I support you, girl. I'll tell you what. Take a week to decide, then let me know."

"Shanice... I *have* decided. I'm staying for the summer, like I said. If you can't keep my job open, I understand."

She sighed. "I will keep it open until Penny leaves for China. If you change your mind, let me know."

"I will," I said.

I won't, I thought.

I still wasn't ready to go to bed, so I made my way back to the terrace – I stopped still and smiled to myself. Little yellow lights were dancing on the grass. *Fireflies...* It was the first time I'd seen them in my garden.

I took it as a sign.

CHAPTER 12

I was walking down the hill towards Passiflora, when a burgundy car slowed down beside me. It was Michela, Flora's landlord. And the girl who, for some reason, I could not bring myself to warm to.

"Hello. Want a lift?"

"Ah, no, thanks. It's such a lovely morning."

"I was hoping to talk to you about the shop."

Me? Why would she not ask Flora? Maybe she had something to say that Flora couldn't hear; maybe it was about the rent; perhaps Flora had given me a sanitized version of her financial situation? If so, I had to help.

"Okay, then," I said with a smile. It was important to keep a good relationship with our landlord, and I was fond of Michela's sister, Paola; but there was something about Michela, something I couldn't quite put my finger on, that got on my nerves. It was skin deep.

"How are you finding life in Montevino?"

"Good. Great. What did you want to talk to me about?"

"Oh, nothing important. Just, Flora hasn't had a good track record of paying rent."

"I'm aware of that. She's not been very well…"

"Yeah…" she said, with fake compassion.

"She's on the mend now, so payments will be regular again, I can assure you."

"Mmmm. I hope so. She's been renting my place for a long time. But I need an income I can rely on."

"Yes, of course."

"We're going to have to see what happens next, if you know what I mean."

"No, I'm not sure what you mean."

"Just that I might be looking for another tenant."

My breath caught. Flora had it set up so well. That place was perfect. She'd put her heart and soul into it, despite her... her low moments. Michela couldn't possibly throw her out!

Right, Callie. Keep your cool.

"I understand. Like I said, she will be regular in her payments from now on."

"How do you know?"

Because I'll check, was the first answer that came to my mind – but that would be demeaning Flora in a way she would immediately disapprove of. "Because she's better, I told you," I said, trying to keep calm.

"We'll see. At this point, I'm even considering selling the shop. A couple of people have been asking."

"Oh, right. Well, I'll talk about it with Flora. Thanks for the lift, you can leave me here."

"It's no problem to take you all the way."

I was desperate to get out the car. "I'll walk." I stretched my mouth in a smile as she pulled over by a small shrine – a mound of gray stones with a plaque and some flowers – where I jumped out. The winding road from the castle was dotted with little shrines, but this one was different; it was empty. For some reason, I'd never looked at it properly before as I'd passed.

My eyes fell on the plaque, and I read the engraving.

In memory of
Lorenzo Pigna
14 years old
Here felled by Nazi invaders
During the Montevino slaughter
April 12 1945

Pietro's friend, the boy who'd walked all the way from Poland, whose mamma had lit so many candles in the church that they filled the floor. He'd come back only to be shot, in something called the "Montevino slaughter." Suddenly dangerously close to tears, I tried to compose myself. I now knew exactly what awaited me next in Elisa's diary.

What I didn't know was if she and her family had survived the massacre.

I swallowed back tears as grief overwhelmed me for the broken lives of these people now gone; for Lorenzo's short life and his mother's pain.

*

"Are you okay?" Flora asked as I arrived at the shop, making my way straight to the back room to leave my bag. My face probably said it all.

"Not really." The shrine and my conversation with Michela were playing on my mind. Should I tell Flora? I had to. It was her shop, and even if Michela, for some reason, had decided to speak to me and not to her, she needed to know.

"What's wrong?"

Wow! I suddenly saw how amazing she looked this morning, with a strappy top and a maxi skirt, her hair half-up and half down her back.

"I'm okay, yes. I just wanted to give you a heads-up. I just had a chat with Michela… She saw me walking down to the village and offered me a lift in her car. She said the rent here hasn't been paid on time for a while, but I said that we knew that, and that it's sorted now."

"Yes, it is."

"But apparently she's thinking of actually selling the place." I raised my shoulders, waiting for Flora's reaction; I was expecting defiance, instead she sounded dismayed.

"Oh, no," she said softly. My heart sank.

"What's her problem with you, Flora?" I said, half-jokingly.

"She has her eye on Marco Leone. Or on his money, more like," Flora said in that curt, direct way of hers.

"Oh, that explains it."

"I haven't been very regular in paying the rent, opening the shop, you know…"

"I know." I hated to see her so… ashamed.

"But I'm back on track now."

"Yes, totally! Michela won't have any reason to sell the place from under us."

"Yeah. Don't worry about that, Callie," she said, and I was touched. She was trying to reassure me. This was a different Flora from the one I'd met when I first arrived. "You look like you didn't sleep well."

"I didn't."

"I won't ask," she said, smiling. "But I'm guessing it starts with T and ends with Ommaso… I'll make you coffee!" she called, disappearing into the back.

"No," I replied.

"No coffee?"

"No Tommaso. No more, it seems."

"Why?"

"Because I am Paolo Caporale's daughter."

"*What?*"

I shrugged. "He can't accept who my father was."

"I'll give him a piece of my mind," she hissed, and began to make her way to the door.

I took her by the arm, half alarmed, half pleased that she was being so defensive of me. "Please don't, Flora. It'll only make things worse."

"Listen, Callie," she said, and her upset was palpable. "Paolo Caporale ruined your mother's life! And… and mine. Now he's dead, and he's still ruining our lives. We can't allow it! You have no idea…" For a moment, she looked as if her memories were simply unbearable. It broke my heart.

"Look, Flora. I told him what I thought. That it's horribly unfair he holds this against me. There's nothing else to do but hope he comes around."

"And if he doesn't?"

"Then he's not for me. If he can't get past who my father is…" I shrugged and shook my head.

"*Idiota*," Flora muttered. "If you change your mind… If you want me to go speak to him—"

"Speak? I don't think so!" I smiled. "You'd hit him over the head with a broom."

Her lips had curled into a little smile.

"Look, we'll prepare these orders together, and we'll talk about *your* love life, instead," I said, forcing myself to be cheerful, though the Tommaso situation weighed on my heart, heavy as a stone.

"Okay, if we're finished with terrible news, it's time for your first test," Flora said.

Now, that was a quick change of subject.

"What test?"

"I want to know what you learned from the books I gave you," she said, while her hands were working quickly, beautiful and skilled, lifting jars off the shelf, weighing herbs, slipping them into paper bags with lists stapled on them.

"Okay. Ready."

"Let's see… What can you use hibiscus for?"

"It's an antibacterial and it promotes menstrual flow."

"Careful if—"

"You have high blood pressure. A no-no if you're pregnant."

"Ten out of ten. Arthritis. What do you suggest?"

"Turmeric… cat's claw… aloe vera cream for painful joints, ginger to reduce inflammation."

"Okay, an easy one. Cellulite! Always a favorite."

"Dandelion, parsley, centella and fenugreek?"

"You forgot a crucial one…"

"Birch! *Betula pubescens*."

"Well, you've been studying! Keep going. Lollipop?" she asked and handed me one of the honey lollipops she kept on the counter for when children visited, making me smile.

"Thank you! So, the books you gave me are the ones you used on your course?" I asked.

"Some of them, yes. Please can you put the contents of these bags into Passiflora jars?" she asked, passing them to me.

Looming behind Flora were jars in several sizes: each had the Passiflora logo, a stylized Passiflora flower painted on top, and a removable label on which to write the herbs used. I began to decant the contents of the bags, now well blended, into the jars, then wrote the contents of each jar on a label, using a pen with black ink. We were a good team. We worked in harmony.

"I went to a college in Turin and I did three years there," Flora told me. "Then I specialized in herbal medicine, as part of the pharmacy course. People who think herbalism is all new-agey fluffy stuff have no idea what they're talking about. It's a science. And you know, there was a lot of math in the course. It's a miracle I passed, to be honest. I was terrible at math."

"Did you have to do math?"

"Oh yes. You must be able to calculate exact doses for things, exact proportions. Sometimes you have to calculate the dosage in relation to the weight of the patient. You can't take risks. If you make scented candles and bath bombs" – she gestured behind her – "you're safe. You can't overdose on a jasmine candle! But if you're preparing medicine, you must be careful. Licensed, and careful."

"The course you did sounds *amazing*. There was a leaflet tucked into one of the books."

"Oh, yes?" She smiled. "That was years ago. I was about your age... so that was what? Fifteen years ago."

She was thirty-seven. There were only sixteen years between us.

There was a question I'd wanted to ask for a while, but hadn't found the courage to. "Do you think... Well, do you think I would be suited to it? I mean, to study the same courses you did?"

But Flora didn't have time to reply, because a customer came in. I let go of the breath I'd been holding.

"*Ciao!* How are you?" Flora said to the woman who'd just entered. She seemed to know most of her customers – a lot of them came back again and again, and she followed them through weeks and months in whatever health journey they were making.

"I'm good... Well, actually, I'm having trouble sleeping these days," the woman said. She seemed to be in her early forties, and looked a bit despondent, with shadows under her eyes.

"Sure. Callie here will make you a blend. Callie?"

I formulated a "who, me?" in my mind, panicked, and rose to the challenge all in the space of a moment. "Oh. Yes. I can make you a blend," I said, throwing a glance to Flora, who gave me a small nod.

"Okay. So. Valerian, passionflower... our namesake... and chamomile." I scooped up the dried herbs from jars on the shelves behind us. "And lavender."

"Mmmm, I would say let's leave out the lavender," my aunt said gently. I wondered why. It was one of the best herbs for relaxation, but I didn't question.

"Sure. Would you like a sachet or one of our jars?"

"Oh, a Passiflora jar, please."

"You can bring it back when you're finished, and we'll refill it for you."

"Great. Thanks." The woman paid, and as was about to leave when Flora whispered to her: "Good luck."

"Thank you!"

And then, to me, after she'd gone: "You did well."

"Thank you. But this was easy."

"Not as easy as it looked. You know, the *signora* you just sold herbal tea to. She's trying for a baby. She's going to have treatment soon."

"Oh, wow! How do you know?"

"She's been here before. That's why I didn't want you to add lavender to the mixture."

"Oh, yes! I read it in one of the books: lavender is not good in the first three months of pregnancy. But how do you know she's trying for a baby? Are you aware of all your customers' private lives?"

"Those who come for healing, yes. 'Are you pregnant or trying for a baby?' is one of the key things you must ask. You get close to them, you know, it gets personal. That's the beauty of it. It's why I do it."

"Yes. I understand. Flora, you said the women in our family are mostly healers of some sort. What about my mother? What did she do?"

"She was a nurse. She worked with the elderly. So, yeah, she carried on the family tradition too. Though she died so young, of course."

I looked down for a moment. "My mom… I mean my adoptive mom… also worked in a retirement home. She was a nursing assistant there. She stopped when I was born."

"I see."

It suddenly occurred to me that that was how they might have met and arranged the adoption. I wanted to ask Flora, but something else, something that rose very quickly from the depths of me, came out instead.

"Flora… Why were you so horrible to me when I first arrived?"

She looked up from the oil bottles, and there was something in her expression that was almost… pained.

"It's okay, you can tell me. I'm tough, you know."

Am I?

"There are things you need to know. I'm trying to find a way to tell you all…" she began. But it wasn't to be, not then. The shop bell went, and another customer entered, followed by another and another until closing time. I knew by the end of the day that the moment had passed, that Flora wasn't ready to tell me just yet, just as I hadn't been ready to ask about how my adoptive parents and Malva met. I had to respect that.

After what felt like an endless day, every step dragged as I made my way up the hill in the light summer evening. I knew that at the end of the long climb I would be compelled to open Elisa's diary once more and to re-live the tragic news of Lorenzo's death all over again and find out who, if anyone, survived the massacre.

I passed Tommaso's cottage and saw that it was deserted, the door and the shutters closed. His garden and his small orchard seemed forlorn without him around, cheerfully going about his work. He must have taken Morella with him because there was no sign of her either.

A lonely figure was walking toward me: an elderly woman with a straw hat, a skirt and socks – the attire of local women when they worked the land, I'd noticed. "*Ciao*, Callie," she called. I wasn't sure who she was, then I realized how much she looked like Nonna Tina. She had to be Tina's sister. I didn't even ask myself how she knew who I was. The nonna-web, clearly.

"*Ciao*... Sorry, have you seen Tommaso today?" I gestured towards his cottage.

"Early this morning. He's gone to Milan. For business."

For business. Okay.

"*Grazie.*"

"*Prego*. Take care, child," she said sweetly, and stroked my face with cool, wrinkled hands, before walking on, slow and a bit rigid, the way old people do. She didn't even know me, except by name. For some reason, her affectionate touch had moved me.

It was lonely up here without Tommaso. Everything was turning out to be so complicated. But I would manage. I knew how to be alone and how to take care of myself. And things with Flora were improving. It wasn't all bad.

When I stepped inside, at least the house enveloped me with its warmth, as usual. There was something about Firefly House – it always seemed to welcome me, like it was happy I was back. Maybe it was just my imagination.

I changed into loungewear, and decided it was a night for comfort food. With glee, I made myself a PB&J sandwich. I'd been overjoyed when I saw peanut butter in the local grocery store. Of course I was into Italian food and those amazing flavors I was discovering, but every once in a while a girl wants a little taste of home.

I lit the fire in the sitting room – I was getting better at it – and performed what had become a sort of ritual, before reading Elisa's diary: I opened the window to let the breeze and the cricket song in, lit the candle Flora had given me, and curled up on one of the couches. I opened the small book onto the last page I'd read and turned the page. The next began with just three heartbreaking words: *Pietro is dead.*

I clasped my hand on my mouth and sat up.

My little brother, whom I fed and bathed as a baby, who used to play soldiers in the kitchen, running around with Mamma's wooden spoon, has been killed.
I feel like I am quite dead myself.

I steadied myself and kept on reading, blinking away the tears.

When I came back from work, I knew at once what had happened. I had a feeling in my bones. Too much bad news was coming from everywhere; it was almost sacrilegious to believe our family would be spared from the grief consuming the whole town. I could hear Zia Costanza's sobs all the way from the garden.

"He's gone," was all she said before holding me close and tight like she was drowning, until her sobs became silent and contained, like she always was. My eyes were dry with shock.

I found Mamma upstairs in Pietro's room, sitting by the window. She'd cried so much recently, and yet now that the worst had happened, she, too, was without tears. "They deceived him," she said softly. "They made him believe he was fighting for glory, for victory. For Italy. He was fighting for nothing. He died for nothing."

I ran to Mamma and laid my head in her lap. We comforted each other as best we could. She insisted on sleeping in Pietro's bed that night and I eventually convinced

*her to take some medicine that would help her sleep. Zia
Costanza sat by Mamma, praying until she did. Then I
went to see Papa, his hands bloody from where he'd pounded
them against the wall.*

I went out into the night, looking for Don Giuseppe...

"Callie! Come out at once! Callie!" A female voice, calling me from
the garden. I shook myself, dried my tears and ran downstairs.

"Don't you dare ignore me! Come out!" I recognized Sofia's
voice at once.

I took a breath and opened the door. "Stop screaming! What
are you doing here?"

She pushed past me and made her way inside. "You stay *away*
from my father."

"*What?*"

"You spoke to him. At the café."

"I said hello! He asked me how Flora was, I said she was good!
You're crazy!"

"Stop trying to get them back together! Flora almost destroyed
him. Everything was fine again, then you had to come along to
stir things up."

"What exactly did I stir?" I was trying to get my head around
what she was saying, but it wasn't easy. I was still lost in the diary,
and it was hard to come back to reality again. Especially a reality
where a virtual stranger had turned up at my door to shout at me.

"You're just like your aunt. And you know what your aunt
is? She's a whore."

Before I knew it, I'd slapped her. The sound of my palm on her
skin broke through the night. She held her cheek, burning red.

"Get out of my house now, or I swear..." I was panting with
fury. "How dare you speak about my aunt like that?"

"You don't know, do you?" she said, as she stepped through the doorway. There was a hint of pity in her voice.

"Stop playing games, Sofia."

"Flora had an affair with her sister's husband. *Malva's* husband. The man I assume was your father."

I was silent. Stunned. I couldn't believe what she'd just said. She was just a malicious village gossip.

"Don't come back, Sofia," I shouted, and slammed the door.

From the window, I watched her get into her car and drive away, my palm still burning from where I'd struck her.

And then they came. A steady stream of hot, bubbling tears. I didn't make any effort to stop them – nobody was there to hear me cry, and I just couldn't hold it all in anymore.

I cried myself to sleep that night, too upset and drained to even consider that Sofia's words might be true.

CHAPTER 13

I woke up on the sofa, still in the clothes I'd been wearing last night. The girl who looked back at me from the mirror was a complete mess. I had some eyes around my bags.

I did my best to make myself look presentable – a shower, fresh clothes and a bit of make-up did wonders - and downed a couple of cups of sugary espresso.

The diary beckoned me from the coffee table. Perhaps I could escape into Elisa's world for just a moment, but I just couldn't take any more emotion. I left it where it was, instead of slipping it into my bag to read at lunchtime, as I'd planned to do.

Apart from anything else, I could hardly go to Leone's for lunch, in case Sofia was there. I would go to Nonna Tina instead, and let her spoil me a little. I would tell her about what Sofia had said – she could further reassure me that it was all nonsense.

Why did I need reassurance at all? I mean, Flora and my father? She hated him! What sick imagination could make something like that up?

I opened the door, and I nearly tripped over something large that had been laid flat on the porch. It was a parcel wrapped in brown paper, flat and rectangular. I crouched down and picked it up gingerly, praying it wasn't some nasty trick left by Sofia the night before, then went back inside the house and took the parcel to the drawing room. I laid the object on the coffee table and unwrapped it.

It was a painting – the portrait of a woman with long black hair and clear eyes, surrounded by stormy skies that melted with her hair and with the hills behind her. It was a portrait of me. I turned it around, though there was no doubt to who'd painted it.

Rissi, June 2019,
Tommaso Carpentieri

I sat for a moment with the painting on my lap, looking at my own face translated onto canvas with such love, in a way that made me think yes, this is me. The woman in the painting had a vulnerable expression – there was something sweet about her, about me. Not the hardened girl I'd been before, so out of touch with her feelings, and maybe everyone else's too.

I lifted it up carefully and held it to me; it was then that I saw a note on the ground beneath, white against the red tiles. A tiny sketch of a slice of cake and a cup with steam seeping off it:

Lunch at Leone's today?
I'll come get you from Passiflora.
PS I'm an idiot.

*

I twirled into Passiflora. Well, not literally, but almost. I couldn't wait to see him, I couldn't wait to see his eyes full of tenderness, instead of the cold, distant look I never wanted to see again.

The second I saw Flora, though, my anxiety began to rise once more. I just couldn't forget what Sofia had said. The more I tried to put it out of my mind, the more it came back to me. I worked all morning barely uttering a word, but it didn't take long before I couldn't hold it in anymore.

"Flora. Sofia came to see me last night."

"She did?" Then, "Hey, Tommaso!" she called to all six foot of him behind me, his deep, moss-green eyes making my heart skip a beat, as usual.

"Hey! Hi, Flora. Rissi… I was wondering if you found my note? And if you wanted to have lunch with me at Leone's?"

"Yes. Yes, I'd love to. Well, maybe not at Leone's…" I shot a glance at Flora, who grimaced. Tommaso looked at us, from one to the other, trying to gauge the unspoken words between us.

"You go wherever you want, Callie. Don't let that girl have anything over you," Flora said. "And take the afternoon off, if you want to."

"Thanks so much."

Wait. What did she mean by not letting Sofia have anything over me? Did Sofia have something over my aunt?

Tommaso held out his hand, and I took it. He led me out of the shop, and into the clear sunshine; my heart was racing. And he was nervous, too, because for a while he avoided my eyes.

"Wow, Flora was almost *nice* there. What did you do to her?" he said, eventually.

"I have no idea. Things are so much better between us now, but she might change back at any moment. Tommaso… the portrait…"

"Yes. The portrait."

"It's… beautiful. Nobody ever did something like that for me before."

"I'm glad you like it."

"To say the least!"

He stopped and came close to me. The alley was deserted, no one to witness our sudden closeness. "It was… a message. A message for you."

"Yes."

"That I'm sorry, I've been…"

"An idiot. You said that in the note. But I don't think so, it was a gut reaction…"

"It was also a message about Federica." His face was so close to mine, I could almost feel his voice with my body. He smelled of woodsmoke and freshly cut grass. He smelled of Tommaso.

"What about her?" My voice was low and whispery, betraying how his closeness made me feel.

"That she's gone from my life, and from my heart. The portrait I made of you, that image… that's what my heart looks like now, Rissi."

And then he kissed me, his lips light on mine just as a group of apron-clad *nonnas*, carrying grocery bags, turned into the other end of the alley and began making their way toward us. We took a step away from each other, composing ourselves. One of the old ladies looked sour and disapproving, two were smiling, as they passed. "Oh, to be young!" I heard one of them saying longingly, and Tommaso and I laughed.

"So, Leone's?"

"Better not. Long story. I'll tell you about it somewhere more private."

"I'll tell you what, I'll get some picnic stuff and take you to this place I know."

"Sounds amazing," I said, and all my heart and soul opened into a smile.

We walked along the alley to the square, then, "Give me a moment," Tommaso said, as he left me standing in the half-shade of one of the majestic pines.

A few minutes later, he came back with a paper bag full of goodies and led me to his Jeep. We set off up the hill toward the castle. Once there, Tommaso parked the Jeep and I followed him along a narrow, paved path that led to the back of the castle. From here a flight of stone steps took us up to an exquisite internal courtyard.

"Oh, Tommaso, this is beautiful!"

A stone parapet enclosed the courtyard, and the whole of the perimeter was decorated by lemon trees in vases. A gentle breeze carried the scent of the lemons to us. In the far corner was a small round tower, covered in frescoes representing the weather, and the seasons, with the winds blowing from the four corners.

"That is called the Tower of Winds."

"It's amazing. Oh, let me see…" I walked to the parapet, and from there I could see the entire valley, with Montevino's red roofs beneath us, nestled among the vineyards. The sky was enormous and dotted with white clouds like watercolor brush strokes; the lemon-scented breeze was in my hair.

It was perfect.

"Come," Tommaso said, leading me toward another small set of steps in a corner of the courtyard. From here we descended to the castle grounds, where grassy fields, ancient trees and moss-covered stone statues eventually gave way to the woods.

"Look!" he whispered as we walked, and I caught a glimpse of two deer standing behind a tree. As soon as they saw us they bounded quickly away. This place was like a secret paradise.

At the edge of the woods was a stone gazebo, covered in exquisite stained glass that made everything look magical. We sat on circular stone benches in the gazebo; we ate focaccia bread and drank *chinotto* in small glass bottles, followed by tiny chocolate masterpieces that must have come from Leone's.

Full-bellied and happy, we lay down on the grass in the sunshine, my head in the crook of Tommaso's arm and our bodies glued to each other. I was grateful that he just cuddled me, without asking for more, despite the desire I felt. It would have been too soon for me.

"Oh, I could stay like this forever," I said lazily, after a while.

Tommaso shaded his eyes from the sun. "As could I. But we have to go."

"Do we?"

"Yeah. We have jobs to go back to, isn't that terrible?"

"But I'm happy here," I whined, nestling into him even tighter.

"The summer is still long, isn't it? There'll be plenty of time to…"

At that moment, it hit me. *Yes, the summer was ahead of us… but after?*

Tommaso didn't want to think about it either, it seemed, because he took me in his arms and in one fluid movement, he got us both up. He raised a hand toward my face and picked at my hair. "You've got grass in your hair. There. What would people think…"

I laughed, and then, on impulse, held him tight. A wave of affection swept me – different from the desire I'd felt and still felt, different from passionate love – a moment of pure affection. Like maybe the family I'd been looking for – that family didn't necessarily carry my same blood.

*

"Did you have fun?" Flora said when I returned, my nose and cheeks red from the sun, grass in my hair, and very sleepy.

"I might have," I said with a smile.

The working day went on, but my thoughts kept going back to what Sofia had said. I had to get it out of the way. I had to. I'd just finished wrapping some candles up for a customer, when

I introduced the subject. "I was trying to tell you earlier. Sofia came up to Firefly House…"

Flora rolled her eyes. "I can guess what she told you. She's paranoid. I've let Marco go."

"You guessed right, she said you have to stop pestering Marco. Clearly he hasn't let you go, otherwise Sofia wouldn't be so defensive of him."

"He should. Let me go, I mean.

"What happened with him?"

"Well, we loved each other, then I realized I didn't deserve him, that he's too good and I would just mess it all up."

I threw my hands in the air. "You don't deserve Firefly House. You don't deserve Marco. It sounds like you're punishing yourself! But for what, Zia?"

"Zia" meant "Aunt" in Italian. It was the first time I had ever called Flora that, but, if she noticed, she didn't say anything. I felt we were becoming closer by the day. I didn't want Sofia's horrible lies to come between us.

"He's a good person." She looked down.

"So are you."

"I love him."

I sucked my breath in. "From the way he was looking at you at the chocolate fair, I'd say he loves you too."

She looked at me for a moment, and I wasn't sure what was in her eyes.

Pain? Shame?

Guilt.

Flora had secrets. I could feel it.

"It's not because of Sofia, is it? Because she's crazy. I mean, she's full of crap. She started going on about you and my father. She said you saw my father behind Malva's back. She'll say anything to keep you two apart." I tried to laugh, but all that came out were coughs of air, and I immediately regretted telling her that. Why had I? I should have kept my mouth shut. Maybe I wanted reassurance.

Instead, I got silence.

"*Zia?*"

She looked at me again.

At that moment, I *knew*. "Oh my God."

"Callie…"

"You did it, didn't you? Sofia was telling the truth."

"I…"

"Tell me it's not true."

More silence.

"Please, tell me it's not true."

"I can't," she said. "Because it is."

CHAPTER 14

I ran all the way to Firefly House, breathless, tears blinding me. How could she have done that? How could she have betrayed my mother that way? *My father and Flora.*

I ran past Tommaso's cottage – I just wanted to hide myself in the little pink bedroom and cry.

"Rissi!"

I heard him calling me.

"Rissi!" His footsteps followed behind me. "What happened?"

Tommaso saw my face and the tears streaming down my cheeks, and his eyes widened. He was beside me in an instant. His arms enveloped me, tenderly, and he tucked me into him, folded me in. It took my breath away.

I froze for a moment, then I rested my hands on his, entwined over my waist. Even my tears must have been shocked, because they stopped falling, and I leaned back into him, letting go.

"I'm here for you," he whispered.

And suddenly, the hurt seemed to sting a little less, as I leaned against him and let him take my burdens for a moment, just for a moment before Morella jumped on us, and the spell was broken.

Tommaso turned me around and cupped my face in his hands. "Whatever it is, we'll sort it."

I nodded, unable to speak. Tommaso's face was smudged with dirt, and his hands had soil on them. I didn't mind.

"If anyone hurt you, I'll unleash Morella on them. They'll regret it."

Morella was sitting on her back legs, her mouth open and her tongue out, wagging her tail at the sound of her name.

"That's a terrible threat," I managed to joke.

"I know. Come. Don't be alone," he said, and he took my hand to lead me back to his cottage, followed by the murderous hound bouncing and wagging happily. He took me through the house and into the back garden, which I'd never seen before. We sat at a table under a canopy of jasmine in bloom, its scent beautiful, deep, and almost heady.

I unburdened myself. "Sofia was telling the truth. Flora pretty much admitted it."

"Okay. I see."

"How could she have done that, Tommaso! Her sister's husband!"

"Rissi, listen." A soft gust of breeze blew through the jasmine, and tiny flowers fell on the table between us. "You have no idea what the circumstances were. You have no idea what happened. Yes, Flora did a terrible thing. But she was sixteen, and Paolo Caporale was a lot older than her, and, I can quite assure you, was a complete bastard. God only knows why your mother married him. Paolo Caporale was a bad person, simple as. I'm sorry, I know that I'm talking about your father, but it's true."

I nodded. "Do you think he... brainwashed her or something? Flora did say that he ruined Malva's life."

"So how do you know that he didn't ruin Flora's life too?"

I didn't know how to answer that.

"Maybe he did, maybe he didn't," Tommaso continued. "And maybe Flora did do that deliberately. But it happened twenty years ago. People make mistakes, people change. You're trying to piece together events that happened a long time ago."

"Flora herself said it did happen, and it was her fault because she betrayed her sister. She said she never forgave herself."

"Anyone can see that something eats Flora inside. Whatever that is, she's refused anything good in her life from that time. She never had a family, for a start."

"I know that she's punishing herself. I told her."

"If she's punishing herself, maybe there's no need for you to punish her. And if she never forgave herself, maybe you could forgive her."

*

Tommaso's words still resounded in my mind as I urged him to go back to his work, while I returned to Firefly House. I had a shower, long and cool, and then I found refuge in my little round bedroom. I let myself fall on the bed with a sigh.

Elisa. I need Elisa's presence.

I ran to get her diary, abandoned on the coffee table downstairs, and performed a little evening ritual I'd started. With my hair still wet and in my nightie, even it was barely twilight, I curled up on the window seat. Everything was so silent, so peaceful. I sat and hugged my legs. The citronella candlelight was dancing and casting lovely shadows on the wall. I braced myself to read about the aftermath of Pietro's death. Sofia had interrupted me yesterday just as I was about to learn what Elisa did next, after the terrible news arrived.

> *… I went out into the night, looking for Don Giuseppe. Only he knew where Leo was. When I told him what had happened, he left quickly for Camosso, where he promised*

to ask a partisan collaborator to inform Leo. I don't know who this person is in Camosso.

I went home in the darkness, my heart heavy. It was a long wait, spent holding my mamma and Zia Costanza in my arms and crying with them; sitting with my papa, one hand on his shoulder, talking in whispers, or just sitting in silence, trying to swallow the enormity of our loss. Finally, as the sun was just beginning to rise after our terrible night, I heard Leo's secret call outside my window.

I packed a bag quickly: this diary, a blanket and some black bread. I could feel my parents' apprehension as I left, and I hated giving them more worry, but I had to do this. It was time to take sides.

Seeing Leo opened the floodgates in my heart, but I tried to be as silent as I could. Even in the darkness I could see he was so thin – I felt his bones as he hugged me quickly, before running to the High Woods. It was too dangerous for Leo to be seen at the house.

The night was so dark, with no moon in the sky. I kept tripping and Leo held me up. I could feel a build-up of sobs in my throat, sobs that would soon spill out, I knew it.

Oh, Pietro. The memory of a bouquet of wildflowers held tightly in your still-childish hands at my eighteenth birthday party assails me. Caught in-between, now you'll never grow up…

When we arrived at the cabin, Leo held me for a long time. I hid my face in his chest and didn't want to move ever again. If I did, I would have to face what had happened.

"If only he'd come with us," Leo whispered in my ear. "At least for now he'd still be safe."

"My brother believed in all that stuff, you know," I said. All the rage I felt was yearning to come out. I wanted to destroy everything around me, I wanted to scream and hit the trees until my hands bled. "The fascist cause. He thought he was doing good! He thought he was helping our country, defending it! And they killed him!" I began sobbing so hard, I couldn't speak anymore. My whole body trembled with anger, and now, as I'm writing these words, it still does.

"They deceived him," Leo murmured in my ear, and he echoed my mamma's words to the letter. I forced myself to take a step back from him and look at him in the face.

"I'm coming with you to the camp, Leo. You were right all along. I should have joined the Resistance when you did. I should have taken a side. You were right."

Leo shook his head, and for a horrible moment, I thought he wouldn't take me with him. "You must stay here with your parents."

"No! I want to fight too!"

"I know. I understand. But listen to me. I'm staying here with you. My comrades won't be at the camp for much longer. They'll be coming down from the mountain tomorrow night; everybody is returning to their villages."

"What? You'll be taken away!"

"We have to come back. News arrived from the south. The Nazis will be here in a matter of days. The Americans are taking back the south, the Germans are retreating and destroying as much as they can along the way. They have nothing to lose now, they just want to kill. Women and children too… We can't leave Montevino without anyone to defend it. There will be a battle, Elisa. Here, in our village. There are weapons hidden all over the place, including at your house."

"What? In our house?"

"Your father and Martino organized it all."

"Martino? Agnese's father?"

"Yes. He's the one who came to tell me about... about Pietro."

I closed my eyes for a moment. Weapons all over the place, including at our house. A battle coming. "What will you do now?"

"Stay here with you. At the cabin. I have some rifles buried here."

Rifles. Of course, I would have to handle a gun. I was thankful for the times I'd gone hunting with my father before his accident.

So here I am now, writing in the gloom, urgently, because if we're all to be killed, I want history to know what happened to us all.

Are these the last moments I'll spend with my husband? Because if they are, I want to be with him every second. Let's not waste a minute of this short life we have. I want to be in his arms until...

I suppose, until it's too late.

These words resounded with me in a way I could not quite describe.

I don't really know what possessed me, but I closed the diary and walked out of Firefly House and up to Tommaso's. He was in his garden, even though it was getting late, and I made my way to him, slowly. I could see his surprise as I went closer and closer to him, until my arms were around his waist and my head was against his chest. I held him for a moment, and his strong arms wrapped around me too; he squeezed me hard, like he wanted to savor my closeness. For someone who had been taken by surprise, he'd recovered his cool quickly.

"I've dreamed of this moment ever since I first met you," he whispered, and then he sealed my lips with his. As soon as my mouth was free again, I giggled.

"What's funny?"

"Nothing. I'm laughing because I'm happy."

"Come," he said, and his voice was suddenly low, with a touch of hoarseness to it. He took me by the hand, and began to lead me into the woods. It was like he'd read my mind. I wanted to go to the High Woods, to the stone cabin hidden away from the world. Me and Tommaso alone, like Elisa and Leo had been all those years before, celebrating their love with war and fear and chaos all around them.

He laid me on the soft grass just outside the cabin, swallows flying all around us. We were one, melting our bodies and souls into each other, and then it was all clear to me: everything that had happened in my life had taken me here, to this moment with Tommaso, the man from a faraway country who was meant to be my destiny, all along. Every moment of pain, of fear, of loneliness and confusion, every choice I'd had to make, every time I'd had to be strong and keep faith, and take risks with places and people I knew nothing about, everything was meant to lead me to here, and now.

CHAPTER 15

I awoke in his arms. "Good morning, *dormigliona*," he said. Sleepyhead.

For a moment I wondered where I was – and then I remembered – the woods, the cabin, Tommaso. A smile came from the depths of me, and I didn't regret a thing.

It had been my first time.

And the dreams I'd dreamed about that moment didn't even remotely match the reality of it.

I was in a haze as we walked back to Firefly House, separating as we went to shower and get dressed – even just that short separation was too much for both of us, because we came back together just to hug and say goodbye, before parting to go to work.

"Vineyards, today," he said.

"Okay." I kissed him again, and again. And then once more.

"I love you, Rissi."

Oh. "Seriously?"

He laughed. "Seriously. I do. You know, men from around here don't say such a thing easily..." I detected a little bit of fear, of insecurity.

"Texan girls don't say that easily either. I love you too," I said, and we kissed and we smiled and looked into each other's eyes without talking anymore, just taking each other in, until, reluctantly, we had to part.

I would not go to Passiflora. I was still smarting from Sofia's revelation. Yes, I knew I would forgive Flora, but not now, not yet.

I went to Leone's for breakfast instead, deciding I would just ignore Sofia, if she was there. Ten minutes later I was sitting in front of a slice of Century Cake and my decorated cappuccino. I opened the diary, immediately wishing that I hadn't.

April 12, 1945

Montevino is destroyed.

Leo and I were in the High Woods when we heard them, then saw them in the distance. Leo ran to call for help, to say that the soldiers had arrived earlier than we'd thought, that we needed men with rifles. He begged me to stay hidden, because running down with my little rifle now would mean certain death. I had to force all my muscles to stay still, not to move. It went against every instinct not to go and defend my parents and Zia Costanza.

I tossed and turned under the starlit sky, a cold, harsh moon watching us as we hid in the cabin in the High Woods. In the shadow of the mountain's gray granite boulders, I prayed the soldiers would not come all the way up here, or that they'd march past if they did, in too much of a rush to notice. Maybe these soldiers had already fulfilled their tribute of blood. With my kin, my people.

Below us Montevino was on fire. Shots resounded through the night – each bullet destined for a woman, a child, or a man too old or too sick to fight. That's all who remained now. All the young men had gone already.

I don't know how I fell asleep in such horror, hugging the rifle I barely knew how to use, my cheek against the barrel's cold metal, but I did. It was a sick, feverish sleep that brought with it a sort of delirium. A memory from a time so close and yet so far, when Leo and I were together, a time when everything that happened after was just unthinkable.

In my dream-memory, Leo and I lay together in a field not far from my home, with the sky so blue, dotted with soft white clouds. Sunlight played in the poplars and leaves rippled all around us like bunting at a village fair; and his hand, rough and used to manual work, was holding mine. Was it always meant to be, between Leo and me? Or would we dance around each other for years, with him offering his love and me forever running, forever having other plans?

I'd known him since I was a child, this man with eyes so perfectly black they reflected my soul, the man with a passion for vineyards, the motherless boy who'd spent evenings at our home basking in the warmth of our family. He had a strong mind and a kind heart. Leo Bordet was the man I was going to spend the rest of my life with, before the war came and tore everything apart.

He kissed me under the summer sky, and for a moment I couldn't breathe for happiness. In my dream, my family had gathered for us. I could hear them in the distance, not far away.

"Will you marry me?" Leo's words echoed in my mind just like I'd heard them a million times before. Like it was always meant to be, only it took me years of growing up before realizing it was so.

"Yes. Yes. Of course, I will. I will," I said, and let his eyes and mouth pull me to him. My family's voices raised to the sky as they surrounded us, their hands full of daisies and poppies and buttercups, teasing us, calling for another kiss. In the glare of the sun I thought I could see Papa rising out of his chair and standing tall, and Mamma was young and beautiful again, like she was before childbirth, before years of hard work, before grief. My Zia Costanza, her dark hair beautifully curled, a sweet, somehow otherworldly smile on her lips, her beloved rosary wrapped around her wrist. And Pietro! My little brother Pietro was there as well, wearing his soldier's uniform. Oh, Pietro!

Tears fell down my cheeks. Why was I crying when everyone was with me again, alive and well, and I was surrounded by love?

Because a part of me, even while asleep, knew it wasn't real.

It was then that my family began to fade, starting with my little brother. He waved his hand and slowly disappeared.

"Don't go. Don't go!" I cried as the light of the sunset in his eyes passed by and faded. And then Leo too began to dissolve right in front of me.

"Don't go."

He held me against him, one hand on the back of my head, the other around my waist, and whispered in my ear:

"I'll never leave your side."

*

I awoke calling his name, but Leo didn't answer – a rough hand grabbed my arm and pulled me up, shots and cries filling my ears. I knew I was about to be killed, but there was no point trying to run. If I couldn't escape, I reasoned,

I wanted to die on my feet, looking straight into the eyes of my murderer. I only had a minute to live, I wouldn't spend it running away. I wasn't a hero – I simply saw no way out, so I might as well be brave. How come I was so calm, coldly thinking about my own death? Maybe because I'd had the chance to contemplate this moment coming for a long time, maybe because Leo's silence told me he'd been killed already, therefore there was no point in me staying alive.

But it wasn't death that awaited me. The soldier who'd grabbed me stopped to look at my face. In the light of his torch, I saw his own hard, angular features. His eyes were the lightest blue I'd ever seen, like a frozen lake, so different from Leo's.

I can't say what happened next, because my mind and heart and soul left my body, and watched from some dark, secluded corner of my consciousness. The soldier's jagged, foreign words and grunts, the weight of his body on mine, are burned into my memory. But more than anything, those blue, blue eyes – almost white – will haunt me forever.

Leo, I called silently after the soldier was finished, awaiting the shot that would end my life. Yes, the end would be better than living in this hell.

The soldier looked young now, almost ashamed. Almost. I closed my eyes and waited.

But the shot didn't come, and an eternity later, dawn found me alive. There was no sign of my Leo, alive or dead. I staggered toward the smoking remains of Montevino. My mind flew into action, as it had been trained to do. The dead needed to be buried – but not everyone was dead. As soon as I saw the wounded, all those familiar faces covered in blood and ashes, women and children calling for help, I remembered: I wasn't just a broken, bleeding woman. I was a doctor, and I was needed.

Montevino, August 20, 1945

These days are so frantic; I am exhausted and sleepless, but I'm writing in this diary whenever I can because I want all this never to be forgotten. I want the generations who'll come after us to know what happened to Montevino, to remember the names of those who were killed.

Leo has vanished, maybe taken away, maybe buried in the woods. And it seems that the partisans in his division – Davide and the others – were all slain. Somebody had told the Germans where to find them.

Carlo Caporale came looking for me today at the parish house, where Dottor Quirico and I have organized a makeshift hospital. I wanted to hit him, yes, I wanted to kill him. But I kept doing my job.

"It was you, wasn't it? You told the soldiers where to find Leo's division," I said, folding the ripped-cloth bandages the women had made.

Good God, we have nothing. No medicine, not enough bandages, no supplies. Thank goodness for my mother's herbs and tinctures.

"Do you really think I would do this to you?"

"Who was it, then? Who?"

"I have no idea. But I'll find them."

I looked at him. "You're one of them. You hate the partisans. I don't believe you. You gave them away."

"I hated Leo because he took you. But I didn't give him away. I didn't give any of them away. I would never have harmed Leo because it would have harmed you."

I froze.

"You never took me seriously. To you, I was just a rich fool. I only existed to be made fun of, the man with the

fancy car and no brains. But I always loved you, Elisa. Whatever you may think of me. And if Leo is still alive, I promise I will do my best to find out where he is."

He strode out and left me gaping.

Some days later, Caporale came back to the hospital, this time with Davide Carpentieri. Davide had been shot and had a raging infection, but he was alive – the only one left out of Leo's division.

He wept as he told me what had happened. It was Agnese. She was the one who betrayed us all. Agnese, the sweet, blonde girl who'd hoped to be Leo's bride. She must have found out the whereabouts of the partisans from her father, who'd often come to our house to see my own papa. Did she realize that by denouncing them, she'd spelled the fate of her father too? How could she have done something so cruel, so foolish? Neither Davide nor Caporale know if Leo is dead or alive. Nobody has found his body. At least I have this to hold onto.

Agnese! The girl who'd been paired up with Leo by the village gossip? Leo had rejected her, and she'd denounced him. Because of her rage and jealousy, so many people had been destroyed. I couldn't believe it. And yet, I knew it was true: one person's fury or cruelty was enough to alter the course of many lives. Leo was gone, and Elisa… I couldn't even think the word.

Oh, Elisa, you have become so dear to me. Please, don't let the pain and humiliation destroy you. Please, Elisa, fight on. *Be strong*, remember?

And Caporale. Carlo Caporale had behaved like a decent man…

*

"Callie?" Marco Leone was standing beside my table, his apron on as usual, his eyes, shaded by heavy eyebrows, full of worry.

"Yes. Hello."

"Hello. You know I keep an eye on Flora… I just saw her down in the square. She's not in a good way. She looks like a ghost. She went home, and… Well, I think she needs someone there."

"She's…"

"No, not drunk. I think she's ill," he said bluntly.

Oh my God. I jumped onto my feet. "Thank you. I'm going at once."

"This is for her," Marco said, and handed me a beautifully wrapped package from Leone's.

I hurried down to Flora's apartment. I was expecting to find her intoxicated, despite what Marco had said, and my heart sank at the thought. She'd made so much progress, I hated the idea of her going backward instead of forward. But there was no alcohol involved. Flora was burning up, lying on the sofa as white as a sheet, but with feverish eyes.

"Callie?"

"Yes, it's me. Marco said you weren't well. So here I am."

"I'm okay. I don't need help."

"Of course, of course. I'll just make your bed and prepare some tea. Don't worry. I'll look after you."

"I don't need looking after."

"Everybody needs looking after," I said. "Here, some candies. From Marco."

"I don't need—"

"Be quiet, Flora," I said, putting the kettle on.

"Callie?"

"Mmmm?"

"You're here."

"Yeah."

"You don't hate me."

"No, most definitely not," I said, and held her hand. It was icy cold, though her forehead was burning.

"Flora... before I let you sleep, may I ask you a question?" She nodded.

"Are we related to a woman called Elisa?"

She nodded again. "Elisa gave birth to Alba, who gave birth to Rosa, who gave birth to me. And then, there was you."

I smiled. Elisa was my great-great grandmother.

"Now rest. Don't worry about anything. We'll sort it all out."

"But I did... I did what Sofia said." Her eyes were shiny, I wasn't sure if with fever or tears.

"Not anymore. It's over now. It's time for forgiveness. It's time for you to forgive yourself. If this is the reason why you're always saying you're not a good person, that you don't deserve Marco, Firefly House, or anything good... if this is why you punish yourself, it's time to stop now."

There was a moment of silence.

Then Flora let out a big sigh and fell asleep.

*

November 19, 1945

Caro *Diario,*

Mamma looked at me sitting at the window, just staring outside. Idle, like I never am. I'm tired to my bones. "Elisa. Come here, my love," she said. She laid a hand on my tummy and pressed gently.

"You're late, aren't you?"

It occurred to me for the first time. "I don't know."

"Elisa, you are with child."

Of course, she was right. She could tell before me, the doctor.

A little life is growing inside me.
The child of love, or the child of violence.
And I might never know which one.

May 23, 1946

Caro *Diario,*

I can now safely say that helping someone giving birth and giving birth yourself are two entirely different things. It was like being split in two, but I wasn't afraid, because Mamma was there, and she knew what she was doing. Yes, I've seen many situations where even the most straightforward of births went wrong; but even in excruciating pain, I felt calm. I was young, I was strong, the baby lay headfirst. It would be fine.

I still screamed. So loud that I thought even the Conte in his castle would hear me.

In my mind and my heart, two prayers:

Please God, let it be healthy.

Please God, let it be Leo's.

Mamma held my hand while Zia Costanza kept watch. Dottor Quirico, who we'd asked to be there, just in case, knew his place in a room full of women who'd had genera-tions of birthing wisdom passed on to them.

When the pain became unbearable, a thought hit me — still calm, still serene, as if I was looking at myself from somewhere far away — I'm dying. What a shame, I will never see my baby, I will never see Leo again. But at least I can say goodbye to Mamma.

The pain was so intense I lost consciousness – there, I'd died.

But it only lasted a moment, because seconds later I was awake, the agony was gone, and the cry of a newborn filled the room. Mamma had it in her arms, wrapped in a sheet she'd woven – I could see the baby's head, still encrusted with my blood, our blood.

Mamma was smiling as she gave me the child. "There. It's a girl."

Tears of joy ran down my cheeks and the feeling of inner calm was gone. I sobbed and shook, holding my daughter tight and studying her perfect little face, her scrunched-up fists. Oh, my love, may you be Leo's – but if you're not, still I love you, I love you, I love you.

Her name is Alba. Her eyes were dark blue when she was born, like all newborn babies; I prayed that they would turn black, like Leo's. But they didn't. They're ice blue, like nobody in both our families. They are the eyes of the soldier.

I see my parents and Zia Costanza looking at them, but they say nothing.

Elisa gave birth to Alba, who gave birth to Rosa, who gave birth to Flora and Malva, who gave birth to me – I repeated Flora's list in my mind. My female ancestors stretched behind me in an unbroken chain.

Almost subconsciously, I searched for my reflection in Flora's dressing table.

My eyes, light blue. The color of ice...

A low noise came from Flora's bedroom, and I put down the diary to go check on her. Images of little Alba and her ice-blue eyes danced in my mind. Flora's forehead burned beneath my hand still, and a sheen of sweat covered it. I gave her some paracetamol and a spoonful of the cold medicine she'd made herself, and then sat by her side.

"Forgive me…" she mumbled. Her hair was sticking onto her forehead, so I swept it back gently. Her light eyes, in my mind, mixed with Alba's – both were ice blue. And mine too.

"There's nothing to forgive. We've sorted it, remember?" I wasn't sure if she was referring to what happened between her and my father, or if she was somehow delirious because of the temperature.

"No, no. It's not okay. I have to tell you…" she began, but her words trailed away. Her cold medicine must have begun to work its magic, because her eyes closed and she drifted away to sleep, her whole body relaxing and letting go.

I made another cold compress, laid it on her forehead, and sat in wait, reading Elisa's diary. The tone of her writing had changed so much – from enthusiastic, to anxious but still full of life, to almost… robotic. Like she was living in suspended animation, somehow. Yes, she was suspended in hope, waiting for Leo to come back. Would he? It was unbearable to think that he'd been killed somewhere far away, never to see his home again. But still, it had happened to so many…

"Flora, I'm just going into the village for a bit. I'll get you some food. And I have to check something."

I walked up to the village square and to the monument. The names I'd tried to avoid reading for a long time… *Lorenzo Pigna*; my heart squeezed once again. *Pietro Scotti…* of course, the women take the name 'Stella', but the men keep their father's name. It wasn't an Italian tradition as far as I knew, just a quirk of the Stella family.

I held my breath, reading until the very last one...

No Leo Bordet. I checked and double-checked, going over the names of those poor young men and boys. There was no Leo Bordet.

Was there still hope?

CHAPTER 16

I texted Tommaso that I was staying at Flora's – thankfully her house had Wi-Fi. She had a rough night, and I resolved to call the doctor the next morning; but by dawn her fever had broken, and she was cool again. She looked strangely young and vulnerable, and so pale, with her hair so black against the pillow.

"Do you feel better?" I said, stroking her hair.

"Yes. Thanks for looking after me."

"I though you didn't need looking after?" I teased her.

"Maybe sometimes."

"Zia, there's something I never told you. Malva left me a diary. It was in the box my parents deposited for me at the lawyer's."

"A diary?"

"Elisa's diary."

"My great-grandmother... I never saw it. I never saw the diary... What's in it? I'd love to read it."

"Of course! You must! It's amazing. She talks about how she became a doctor, and she saved somebody's life – this girl who was dying from malaria! And everything that happened during the war, Alba's birth... The things Elisa went through. And the whole family. Us Stella women are so resilient," I said, and Flora smiled.

"Including you," she said and took a deep breath. "Callie, I need coffee."

"You need more sleep."

"That too. But first I need caffeine, because I need to be awake. I need some energy. I think the time has come to tell you all," she said.

I put the *caffettiera* on.

"You might hate me by the time I'm finished."

"I won't. I promise," I said, and squeezed her hand. She closed her eyes for a moment.

"I adored my sister Malva. I looked up to her. She was everything I wanted to be. Your grandmother, Rosa, didn't keep good health, so Malva was like a second mother to me. We'd known Paolo forever, Malva and I. And we knew what he was up to, what kind of person he was. Gambling, wheeling and dealing… some of his stuff is still up at Firefly House. I never had the stomach to go through it because I knew what he'd been up to. Malva never thought in a million years she would get involved with someone like that. And then our parents' health got worse. She was… vulnerable. And so was I.

"Paolo Caporale *hunted* her. And he got her. I can't begin to tell you the things he did to her."

My poor mother, my poor Malva!

"I tried all I could to separate them. I was so young. Fifteen, when they first got together. I couldn't face seeing my sister in that situation. They got married so fast… I thought I would prove to her what a bastard he was, and so I provoked him. This would show Malva that he was no good. But he wasn't stupid, you know? He was a clever man. Very, very clever. And I was so young. I set out to seduce him, but he seduced me. When I look back, I don't even know how it happened, how he did it. I thought *I* was in control, but he was. I fell for him… It wasn't love. No, not that. It was—"

"Brainwashing." I lowered my head. I had that man's blood in my veins. I was ashamed. But then, you are who you decide to be. I'd been brought up by good people. If my father was evil, well, it began and ended with him – it didn't continue with me.

"I can't say it was brainwashing. If I say that, it puts the whole responsibility onto him. And it was me who did it. It was me who betrayed Malva."

"He manipulated you. And, yes, you made a horrible, horrible mistake. But we already established it's high time you stop berating yourself."

Flora looked straight at me. "I got pregnant after she had married Paolo."

"You…"

"Yes."

I paused. Stumbling over the words. "That would make you…"

"Yes."

"My… you're my *mother*?"

A sob came out of me. My chest was heaving, and I thought I was dying, there and then. I thought my heart could not take it. "*You are my mother! And you hid it from me!*" I whispered. "Why lie? Why say it was Malva? Why did Malva write that letter? You both *lied* to me."

"Feel free to hate me," Flora said, and her face was drenched with tears. She was as white as her pillow. "But first let me finish. I was pregnant by my sister's husband. Malva hated me. Paolo said it had been me who had seduced him, and Malva believed him. They forced me to go to America with them so that people wouldn't see my tummy growing. I gave birth to you there, and Malva took you away. I was devastated, Callie! I wanted to keep you! I never wanted to give you away! But I felt I owed it to her."

"What? You didn't owe her, you owed me!"

"I know. But back then, I just felt I had no choice. I was so confused. Soon after, Malva got sick and died. It was so quick. Paolo disappeared. I thought I would have you then, but I found out that Malva had arranged to give you up, to an Italian couple in America."

"My mom and dad." By now, I was crying.

"My parents – your grandparents – knew nothing about all this. I guess Malva just didn't want you to have anything to do with me."

"So… it was Malva who kept us apart." That was the reason for Flora's outburst on the night of the chocolate festival. This news now compounded my gut feeling that there had been more to Malva's sweetness than met the eye.

"Yes. Malva was the sweetest, kindest person. But she never forgave me for what I did. And she kept us apart even after her death."

"You didn't look for me even then."

"I thought you'd be happy and settled in America with the Italian couple. I didn't want to destroy your life. And I thought I didn't deserve you… I hated myself for what I had done."

"Oh, Flora."

"I couldn't get married or have children. Not after you. Not after Paolo. When I fell for Marco… I pushed him away. I don't deserve anything, for what I did to Malva and for what I did to you."

"I'm here now. And we're together again."

She looked me straight in the eye.

"Callie. Can you forgive me?"

"Mamma," I allowed myself to whisper, and threw myself into her arms.

"My daughter. My daughter!" She teared up, and we were both crying, our tears mixing together.

Some time later, I sat on Flora's bed, holding her hand. "Who named me Callie?" I asked.

"Me. Malva wanted to change your name, but for some reason she allowed you to keep the name I'd given you."

"Why Callie? It doesn't sound very Italian."

"Calendula." Flora smiled. "Passiflora is the flower of passion, and it can be poisonous. But calendula is the healing flower. That's you, Callie."

CHAPTER 17

Tommaso and I lay together in the cabin, snuggled under a soft blanket, my head on his chest.

"So, she is your mother."

"Yes. She had me when she was only sixteen."

"Wow. I can't believe they managed to keep it a secret. It's almost impossible to keep secrets in Montevino."

"I know. And Paolo was my father. Nice. He went from Flora to Malva and back, and ended up destroying Malva and almost destroying... Flora." I struggled to call her "my mother." I'd gone from giving that title to my adoptive mother, to Malva, now to Flora. Confusing, to say the least. Now I knew the truth – but all that mattered was the present. I wanted to leave all ghosts to rest; everything that had been done to my family and to me – the injustice and the separation – all we had was now. "But it doesn't matter anymore, does it?"

"No. The past is past," he said. "But sometimes... well, some wounds don't heal." I knew he was talking about himself, not me. "The Caporale family cast a shadow on me too. But... this helps."

"What?"

"This, as in... you and me. This way I don't have to fight alone."

I smiled. "You'll never have to fight alone for anything, Tomma— Wait a minute." I sat upright.

"You okay, Rissi?"

"Yes. Yes, I'm fine. I need to check something back at the house."

I strode down through the woods, almost running, followed by Tommaso. Once inside Firefly House, I ran upstairs and barged into the master bedroom and opened every drawer in the cabinet, laying its contents on the wooden floor. Flora had said that Paolo's stuff was still up at the house, that she hadn't had the stomach to go through it. It was a mess of papers, folders, envelopes with old stamps and scribbled addresses. The color of the paper ranged from cream to yellow and brown, some crumbly and stiff, all smelling musty, old. The smell of memories.

I started going through each and every one of them – postcards, letters, old documents, tiny prayer books, cards for Christmases and birthdays past.

"What are you doing?" Tommaso asked.

"Looking for something. It's a long shot…"

"Okay. Want coffee?" People in Italy were addicted; perhaps I was now too.

"Yes, please. This will take me a while."

"Are you sure I can't help you?" he asked when he returned with a steaming espresso.

I shook my head. "No. Don't worry, just go home. This could be endless," I said.

"Nah, it's fine. I'll hang around."

"Okay." I didn't want to tell Tommaso what I was looking for, because if I didn't find it, which was likely, he'd be disappointed.

I suppose Tommaso came to regret the offer to stay, because over an hour later, I was still sitting among piles of documents, now with a crick in my back and the beginning of a headache.

"Listen, time is getting on," he said. "I need to dash and buy some groceries for my mamma. I'll get stuff for you as well if you want?"

"What?"

"Groceries? For you."

"Yeah. Yes, sure." I kept searching frantically, unwilling to stop.

An hour later, Tommaso was back, and I was deflated. There was no sign of any document. "You okay?" he asked. "My mum is desperate to meet you, by the way."

"Yeah."

"You don't seem very keen."

"Oh, no! Of course I am! I can't wait to meet Alice. It's just… Well, I thought I would find the document. *Your* document, the one that would get your vineyards back. But no sign of it."

"I see. So that's what you were looking for." He smiled.

"You don't seem disappointed," I said, surprised.

"Maybe it's time *I* stop looking back. Maybe it's time to look ahead. Like you're doing. Like Flora is doing. Because I saw her at Leone's, you know? She and Marco were holding hands under the table like two teenagers."

"Oh, that's great!"

"Which makes me think."

"Yes?"

"Are you hungry?"

I smiled mischievously. "For what?"

"Oh, well…" he said, and took my hand, leading me to the little pink bedroom. Was it possible, to be so happy? He began to kiss me, and we fell onto the bed. I closed my eyes as he covered my face in kisses, and then a thought hit me.

"Tommaso… Get off me!"

"Oh. Oh, sorry, did I… was I—"

"No. Not at all. Just… the box."

"What box?"

I shot up and opened the door of the closet. I picked up the box underneath the dresses – the one marked 'PC'... *Paolo Caporale.* I emptied the contents onto the floor and once again began searching.

"Rissi, what are you—"

"Oh my God."

"What?"

Without a word, I handed him the piece of paper.

"Let me see... *Oh, mio Dio. 'I, Antonio Caporale, commit myself to handing Carpentieri Vineyards and all its dependencies to Raffaele... Signed, Antonio Caporale.'* It's signed, Rissi. Signed and dated. That's what the lawyer said it should be."

"I know!"

"*Oh, mio Dio,*" he repeated.

"Don't faint!" I said, and took his hand. Both Tommaso's hands were shaking. I was half stricken, half touched to see that his eyes were full of tears.

"Want to know something strange? It was in this envelope," I said, and handed him the yellowed, rectangular envelope the document had been stored in.

"*Per garanzia...*"

"What does that mean?"

"It means something like an insurance... an insurance for what? Or against what? Clearly somebody needed this document, otherwise it would have been a lot easier just to get rid of it."

"*Per garanzia.* Yes. It makes sense."

"It does?" Tommaso was confused.

"I'll explain. Let me start from the beginning... Okay. When you told me about that document, I immediately thought to look for it in the house, but then I realized it made no sense for Antonio to keep it. He would have destroyed it, don't you think?"

"Yes."

"But he couldn't, because he didn't have it. Paolo did."

"How did you guess that?"

"Flora told me that Antonio's house was broken into, that everyone thought it'd been Paolo's doing. After that, my father seemed to come into money suddenly. It must have come from Antonio. It was blackmail. If he didn't pay up, Paolo would have unearthed this document and all the land would have been returned to your family."

"Paolo had this on his brother the whole time. No wonder Antonio had been paying him. I can't believe it's over. All these years... and now it is. I can't quite believe it." There were tears in his eyes, and I held him to me.

"You might say it has all just begun," I whispered.

EPILOGUE

"Welcome to Cascina Carpentieri!" Tommaso called, grinning wide, his right hand holding up a glass of red wine. We all joined in the toast, and clapped as soon as our hands were free. I was so happy for him. This was the moment he thought he'd never have, when his father's land would finally be his again... And then, Tommaso surprised me.

"This couldn't have been possible without you, Callie. Please, come up," he said, and extended his hand to me. I felt myself blushing, but I was happy to stand beside him in a room full of our families and friends.

Flora was there with Marco Leone, who kept finding an excuse to wrap an arm around her, or hold her hand, or rest a hand on her leg; and surprisingly, Flora was drinking in the tenderness like a thirsty flower.

Tommaso's mother, Alice, was there, her eyes brimming over with tears of long-awaited joy. This open outburst of emotion showed how intense her happiness and relief were, because she was a reserved, quiet woman. She'd welcomed me into Tommaso's and her life kindly but cautiously – I planned to win her over, of course, showing her that I was there to stay.

Yes, I was there to stay. Up at Firefly House, carefully piled on the bedside table in my little pink bedroom, was the paperwork to apply to the Turin School of Naturopathy, the same school Flora had attended.

I made my way around the table and stood beside Tommaso, surveying his guests' smiling faces – Nonna Tina and her sister; Adriana and the husband who refused to dance; Paola and her family; and even Signor Tava, who'd whispered to me earlier: "Giving the Carpentieris their home back has been one of the high points of my career. High point, for sure," and he'd downed another glass of wine, his expression softening even further after he'd done so. And there was Paola's brother, Alberto, deep in conversation with Sofia – yes, Sofia. She seemed to have thawed, somehow, though she maintained a certain aloofness.

In the middle of the table was a real banquet: Nonna Tina's homemade pasta with more sauces than I thought existed, courtesy of Alice, and on the side, a small table covered in desserts made by Leone. Just looking at it made my mouth water.

Tommaso clicked his glass against mine, and kissed me there and then, in front of everyone. I didn't hear cheering or clapping, though I knew they were happening; I was too lost in my bubble of joy, looking at Tommaso's face, so full of love, and looking at all those people who'd gathered for him, to wish him well. And then a huge, hairy body jumped up against mine, and among laughter and licks, we reassured Morella that she was very much part of the celebration.

"Are you happy, Rissi?" Tommaso whispered in my ear.

"Like a wolf with a pack," I replied.

We'd just finished the last bits of Century Cake, accompanied by a sweet wine called *passito*, which was like a dessert and wine in one, when Tommaso rose from his chair and called everyone together for a small tour of the property. We were all on the way out, when Flora caught me with a gentle touch on my arm.

"I didn't have the chance to tell you, but I have some stuff belonging to my great-grandparents, and I was having a look through when I found this. I thought you might be interested. I haven't read the letters yet."

It was a small parcel of letters in yellowed envelopes, kept together by a lavender ribbon. The addressee was *Suor Maria Costanza Scotti, Convento di Maria Immacolata*. Costanza? Could it be... I turned the parcel around and read the sender's name. Yes: 'Elisa Stella'.

I held them to my chest, almost reverently. "Thank you so much..."

"You're welcome. Quick, they're leaving," she said, holding my arm.

"I'll be there in a moment," I said, hoping I could get away with it. I was desperate to read those letters. Maybe I could disappear for just a moment...

"Rissi?" I heard Tommaso calling.

"Coming! I'll catch up with you!"

"She's annihilating the last bits of Century Cake," Flora laughed, making her way outside. As she opened the glass door onto the open fields and its harmonious patterns of vine, a breeze came in; and in it, for the first time, I could smell autumn. I stepped outside and stood in the fresh air, stealing a moment for Elisa and me to be together again.

*

Montevino, May 14, 1947

Dearest Zia Costanza,
    We miss you! But we are all so happy that you found peace in Santa Maria's Convent. Mamma saw it coming,

she said, but I didn't. It was a surprise to me when you announced you were taking the veil. Your presence still lingers here and sometimes I find myself looking for you, and then remembering you are away!

You have only been to the convent a few weeks and not much has changed. Alba brings us all so much joy, but you know what's in my heart, Zia Costanza!

Hope is so deceitful. Every day I hope from the moment I wake up to the moment I go to sleep, and every day my hope is disappointed. And yet, hope is something you can't go without. Like morphine when you're in pain.

I say to myself: This is the day I let Leo go; this is the day I stop waiting, and accept he will not come back.

This is the day I accept that Alba will have no father, and live through my days, as a mother and a doctor, the best I can.

I try that, and I almost make it…

And then news comes that someone, somewhere around here has made it back, and hope makes its way into my heart again.

A few days ago, a man from Camosso returned, Giovanni Fornero, remember him? He was a carpenter, before the war. Just like that: he turned up at his own front door, half the weight he was when he left, so much changed that his wife almost didn't recognize him. He'd spent two years in a camp in Poland, and then he was too sick to travel… but he's alive. And he's home.

Yes, hope is deceitful.
Yours always,
With all my love,
Elisa

Montevino, 12 August, 1947

Dear Zia Costanza!

Hope is deceitful. But sometimes it keeps its promises...

I was sitting under the chestnut tree, while Alba was down in the village with Mamma, and Papa was in the village with his friends. My heart was aching for Leo as it always does. And then I saw someone making their way through the garden. Someone thin, who limped slightly. Someone who needed a doctor, I thought. I got up slowly, summoning the energy to rise out of my sadness and embracing my duty.

"Buongiorno! Ha bisogno?" *I called.*

And then, as the man came closer, I almost fell to my knees.

Because the man, thin and limping as he was, with a beard and with his clothes hanging on him like rags on a scarecrow, was Leo. My Leo.

Oh, dearest Zia. I can't describe the happiness in seeing him again, but the pain in seeing him so thin and sickly; and then the joy again in knowing he's here and he'll never leave again! He's still Leo, he's still my love, my husband. Yes, he's malnourished, and traumatized, and there are signs of so much suffering in his face. But it's him!

He was so exhausted, he could barely talk. We held each other for a long time, crying and laughing together! I laid him onto my bed. Of course, as you know, we don't have a marital bed, we have nothing together! Because war stopped us from being a normal husband and wife, from being a family. But to see him there, in my childhood bed, was wonderful beyond words. He slept for hours, and I lay beside him, taking in his face like I'd seen it for the first time. I held his hand. I never, never want to let him go again.

When he awoke, he was a little more like his old self. His face, so weary and almost contorted with too much emotion, began to take its old, handsome shape, and he smiled. He looked at me and touched my face and held me, and we cried together once again.

"I'll never leave your side," he said. "Did I not promise that?"

And that was so strange, you know, because he'd said that to me, yes, but in a dream!

Oh, Zia, he needs food and sleep and medicine! He's not sick, as far as I can tell, but he's drained of all life, because of the deprivations they put them through. It's a miracle he didn't starve. I can feel his ribs when I hold him.

I gave him coffee and milk and bread, I helped him wash and change, and shave his beard. My Leo, the shadow of himself, but his eyes still shining, still strong.

"I'd like to sit outside, Elisa. I've been in a camp for so long. They rarely let us out…"

"Of course. Come," I said, and laid a blanket under the chestnut tree for him, so he would not catch any cold. He lay with his back against the tree, and I could almost see it, Zia Costanza, the burden of memories leaving his shoulders with a big sigh. I know it will take longer than this, before the terrible things he saw and went through become a thing of the past, but it's a beginning.

He closed his eyes… and then I heard Mamma came back with Alba.

"Mamma! Mamma, Leo is back!" I shouted.

"Oh, Gesù, Giuseppe e Maria!" she cried out, coming into the garden and giving Alba to me so that she could kneel beside Leo and hold him tight. "Jesus, Mary and Joseph, il nostro ragazzo! *Our boy! It's a miracle!"*

"Your daughter," I whispered, and Mamma stood up and stepped away a little, to give them some space. You know Alba, she's a placid child – she didn't cry, even in the arms of that strange man. She looked up at him that way she does, curious but calm. Thoughtful. And just to add to the river of tears we were all crying, tears fell down Leo's cheeks, quietly. For a moment I held my breath, but he broke into a smile and held her tight, but softly, as not to alarm her.

"My daughter," he said. "What did you call her?"

"Alba Leona," I said. "Leona… after her papa."

And that was their first encounter, Leo and Alba, both crying, with Leo too weak to hold her for long.

Now, as I write these words, Leo is asleep in my bed with Alba's cot beside him. Mamma and Papa are downstairs – you should have seen Papa's face when he saw Leo! Yes, adding to our river of tears!

I can't sleep. I can't even think. All I want to do is look at Leo's face and our daughter's face and take in the moment as long as I can.

Sorry if this letter was chaotic. I can't do any better today. Oh, my dear Zia, come back soon to see Leo, and all of us!

Yours always,

Elisa

Dear Zia Costanza,

What wonderful news that you're coming back for the Patron Saint's Day. We can't wait to see you. When you come, you'll find us well. It's been two weeks now since Leo returned. The poor man has to fend Mamma off constantly, because she's forever trying to feed him! The changes in him *are visible. He's filled in already. And he's beginning to do some work around the place, in spite of our protests! You know him! We decided we'll stay here, at Firefly House, to help Papa and Mamma out. Now that Pietro... our Pietro is gone.*

Papa gave us a wrought-iron bed that belonged to my grandparents. It's beautiful. Finally, we can live as man and wife. Leo doesn't sleep well. He has terrible nightmares and wakes up screaming. I hold him until he calms down. I know that it will be a long time before the wounds of the soul that war gave him will heal and he'll find some peace.

Since he came back, there's been something in the back of my mind, eating away at me. I knew he would see them: Alba's eyes. I knew he would see her milky skin and blonde hair standing out among us, dark-haired as we all are, with tanned skin.

I wrestled within my mind, whether to bring this up myself or wait, but thankfully, he took the decision from me.

We were in the High Woods, gathering kindling; he's still too weak to chop wood, but he needs something to do, he can't stay idle, so he does all these little jobs I would normally do, until he gains his strength again.

"Let's go to the cabin," he said. I hesitated.

I have memories linked to the cabin.

Memories I'd rather keep buried.

But he extended his hand to me, and looked at me in a way that stopped me from arguing. Alba was playing among the fallen leaves, and we stood in front of the cabin's wooden door.

"The night they took me away," he began, and a wave of panic swept over me. I didn't want to remember. I wanted to forget. It never happened, it never happened...

"Please, listen, amore mio. *I have to tell you this,"* Leo said, *and took both my hands. "The night they took me away. The last thing I heard were your screams."*

I felt so ashamed, when he said that. I know what happened wasn't my fault, but I still felt ashamed.

"Look at me, Elisa. There is no reason to lower your eyes," he said. "No reason at all."

"I..."

He shook his head, and laid a hand on my cheek. "I knew what was happening. They knocked me out, and took me away. I couldn't come to you. There was nothing I could do."

"You can't blame yourself..."

"And you can't blame yourself either."

"I know."

"I thought they'd killed you. But here you are. And there she is..." he continued, and turned to look at Alba, my milky white, blue-eyed little girl. "Our daughter. My daughter," he said.

He bent down to pick her up, and smiled as Alba touched his face, his eyes, his mouth. He scrunched his eyes and laughed. "Birichina!" he said. "You rascal!" Alba giggled too, that giggle she has that never fails to melt me. Leo held her with one arm, and wrapped the other around my waist. He enfolded us all in his embrace.

"My wife, my daughter. My family," he said. And the nightmare that happened there, in that place wasn't erased – no, that could never happen – but it was laid to rest.

In the evening we sat together in the garden, all of us, Mamma and Papa, too, and we missed you, but we know you're coming to visit soon. There is a hole in our heart,

*left by Pietro, our little Pietro. He is lost and a part of us
was lost with him, and always will be.*

*But, oh, Montevino was so beautiful, with its red roofs
below us, even with many of them destroyed and missing,
many are being built again… and the linden trees smelled
so good – you'll remember the scent of summer evenings in
Montevino – and Alba, who's usually so lively and unable
to sit still, stayed on Leo's lap, all placid, with her blonde
hair and light eyes– a forever reminder of the invaders,
and yet a forever reminder of our resilience, strength and
courage, and of the love that binds us all.*

All my love,
Elisa

I was startled when I felt a hand on my shoulder. "*Amore*, come,
I'm showing the… What happened? Rissi, what's wrong?" He'd
seen my tears, the hand clasped to my mouth. "Is that bad news?"

"No. No. Good news, actually."

"What?"

But it was too long to explain, so I just kissed him and thought
I could be Elisa, and he could be Leo, and the war might have
been raging inside us instead of outside of us, but now we were
together, and like Elisa said, tied by the love that binds us all.

A LETTER FROM DANIELA

My dear reader,

Thank you so much for taking the time to read *The Italian Villa*. I hope you enjoyed Callie's story as much as I loved writing it. If you'd like to stay up-to-date with what I'm writing next, then please sign up to my mailing list here

www.bookouture.com.au/daniela-sacerdoti

There are so many demands on our time these days. Our senses are overloaded and our minds are frazzled, and we're often way too busy to concentrate on something that moves deep and slow, like a good story, in the way it deserves.

In an era when everything is cheap and quick, the real currency is not money, but time. It's *your* time that I'm most grateful for. A book is slow by nature; the story unfolds at its own pace, and if the characters stay in your heart for longer than it took you to discover what happened to them, then I'll be even more grateful.

To have my story read and *felt*, by those of you who have followed me since Glen Avich times, to Seal Island, and now to the little Italian hamlet of Montevino, as well as by those of you who have only just discovered me, is a real privilege.

The Italian Villa is a new chapter for me, because while my previous books all took place in my adopted home, Scotland, where I lived for fifteen years, this is the first novel set in Northwest Italy, where I come from. The scenes set during the Second World War – Elisa's story – have been drawn heavily from my own grandmother's memories of that time; while the characters are imaginary, their adventures are very much inspired by reality. Montevino is based on the village of Caravino, a village of some 984 souls, where I now live. Here, everyone knows one other, the roads are dotted with shrines, and all is watched over by a castle. Oh, and the wine and chocolate are very real too!

I would love to know what you think of *The Italian Villa*, if you can take just a little more time to leave a review. I would also love you to reach out to me on Twitter or on Instagram. I always reply to my messages, because my readers' voices are a precious and important part of what I do.

I hope you'll follow Callie's journey and her quest for family and home and that maybe you'll walk part of her path beside her, if some of what she goes through resounds with you.

I hope that travelling back in time with Elisa, and observing her dedication to her work as a doctor inspires you as it inspired me.

Whether you've read this on a commute, on the beach, at the hairdresser's, or in bed before falling asleep; whether it's the first time you've explored a book of mine, or we've travelled together before, thank you for walking with me through the streets of Montevino.

Without you my world would be empty and my words silent.
Daniela

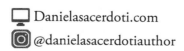

Danielasacerdoti.com

@danielasacerdotiauthor

ACKNOWLEDGMENTS

Thank you from the bottom of my heart to my editor, Jessie Botterill, and everyone at Bookouture.

My heartfelt thanks go to the people of Caravino; to Ivana Fornera (Mum!); to my beautiful, kind and clever girlfriends, Francesca, Irene and Simona; to Cinzia Tarditi for the gift of music, to Serena Pacquola and her wisdom and knowledge; to Sasha, for being the cutest and sweetest companion that ever was.

And, as always, to Ross, Sorley and Luca: my SG-1!